DUKE OF HONOR

Dukes of Distinction

Book 5

Alexa Aston

Text by Alexa Aston
Cover by Wicked Smart Designs

Dragonblade Publishing, Inc. is an imprint of Kathryn Le Veque Novels, Inc.
P.O. Box 7968
La Verne CA 91750
ceo@dragonbladepublishing.com

Produced in the United States of America

First Edition May 2021
Print Edition

ARE YOU SIGNED UP FOR DRAGONBLADE'S BLOG?

You'll get the latest news and information on exclusive giveaways, exclusive excerpts, coming releases, sales, free books, cover reveals and more.

Check out our complete list of authors, too!

No spam, no junk. That's a promise!

Sign Up Here

www.dragonbladepublishing.com

Dearest Reader;

Thank you for your support of a small press. At Dragonblade Publishing, we strive to bring you the highest quality Historical Romance from the some of the best authors in the business. Without your support, there is no 'us', so we sincerely hope you adore these stories and find some new favorite authors along the way.

Happy Reading!

CEO, Dragonblade Publishing

Additional Dragonblade books by Author Alexa Aston

Dukes of Distinction Series

Duke of Renown

Duke of Charm

Duke of Disrepute

Duke of Arrogance

Duke of Honor

The St. Clairs Series

Devoted to the Duke

Midnight with the Marquess

Embracing the Earl

Defending the Duke

Suddenly a St. Clair

Starlight Night

Soldiers & Soulmates Series

To Heal an Earl

To Tame a Rogue

To Trust a Duke

To Save a Love

To Win a Widow

The Lyon's Den Connected World

The Lyon's Lady Love

King's Cousins Series

The Pawn

The Heir

The Bastard

Medieval Runaway Wives

Song of the Heart

A Promise of Tomorrow

Destined for Love

Knights of Honor Series

Word of Honor

Marked by Honor

Code of Honor

Journey to Honor

Heart of Honor

Bold in Honor

Love and Honor

Gift of Honor

Path to Honor

Return to Honor

PROLOGUE

Hardwell Hall, Dorset—June 1806

SEBASTIAN COOPER, MARQUESS of Marbury, stood in front of the door to his mother's rooms. After hesitating a moment, he pushed the door open and entered.

For the first time in eleven years.

The Duchess of Hardwick had died in these rooms. Sebastian had just turned ten and, as usual, his mother was with child. She had spent the decade after his birth being impregnated by her volatile, cruel husband. Each time, she had either miscarried or given birth to a stillborn child—then the process started all over again.

Sebastian recalled the last argument he had overhead between his parents. His father had berated his mother for her lack of providing him with more sons, calling her stupid and worthless. His mother, the gentlest of creatures, had actually snapped back at her much older, powerful husband. Sebastian couldn't recall her exact words but what he did remember was the sound of the hard slap that quickly followed. As he ran into the room, he watched his mother's head snap back. Seen his father's palm print, a vivid red, imprinted on her pale cheek. Sebastian still felt the rage that rippled through him and remembered how he had run to the duke and attacked him, trying to protect his mother from further harm.

Hardwick had squashed his ten-year-old son like a bug. Slammed his fist into Sebastian's nose, breaking it, then lifting him and smashing him against the wall. He could still hear his mother's screams. Feel his arm crack. Taste the salt of tears and the tin of his blood that sprang forth as pain sizzled through him.

Hardwick immediately forbid his son to see his mother again after what he termed *the incident*. Those deadly words had rolled off the duke's tongue with ease. Mama, who had run to Sebastian and cradled him in comfort, eased him to the ground. She ran to her husband and fell to her knees before him, begging he relent.

Dukes did not capitulate to sobbing wives, especially ones they loathed. Good as his word, Sebastian had been kept away from his mother the next five months. She died in childbirth and he had always blamed Hardwick for her death. Part of him believed she died of a broken heart, not being able to see her only child. At least the babe had died along with her. No other child would have to suffer under the duke's heavy hand.

Sebastian had as little as possible to do with his father after her death. He had come to Mama's rooms, where her lady's maid had prepared her body, and kissed the cold, lifeless cheek. Then he had promised her he would be a good duke and a good father to his future children. The children he would have one day when he was duke and his father rotted in a grave, forgotten by everyone.

Especially his only son.

As the scene from his past faded, Sebastian walked through Mama's sitting room, remembering happier times. He paused and closed his eyes and imagined her still being here. In this room where she had read to him. Played with him. Taught him good manners and right from wrong. The Duchess of Hardwick had molded her son's character and made sure he knew how to practice kindness and humility. Mama had emphasized loyalty and patriotism and responsibility, telling him of the immense power he would one day possess as the Duke of Hardwick and how he must always use his position for good and take care of his people and others who were less fortunate.

He opened his eyes and continued into her large bedchamber, untouched since her death all those years ago. Opening the wardrobe where her gowns still hung, he buried his nose in the material, catching the faint scent of vanilla that still clung to the garment. A warmth rushed through him. Mama had been the reason he eagerly came home each school term. With her death, he found excuses to stay away from Hardwell Hall and often went home with friends during school holidays. On the rare occasions he came home, he avoided the duke like the plague.

Sighing, he steeled himself for the conversation he would now have with the man who had sired him. He would inform Hardwick of his plans to go away.

To war.

The duke would be livid. Sebastian was the heir apparent to a dukedom. The Marquess of Marbury. Men such as he didn't join the military, much less fight in an endless war that saw no end in sight.

Closing the wardrobe, he went to his mother's dressing table and opened a drawer. After searching a moment, he found the locket he had come for. Mama never took it off. He hadn't recalled seeing it around her neck on the day she had been buried and hoped it would be in her rooms. He intended to carry it with him as he left England and entered the madness of Bonaparte's war.

Slipping it into his pocket, he left the room and went downstairs. He found Radmore, the butler, who was new to the position but not the household.

"Where is His Grace?" he asked.

"In his study, my lord," the butler replied, his expression bland as suited the position.

"Thank you."

Sebastian walked down the corridor feeling like a man going to his execution. He took a calming breath, knowing anything he did always met with disapproval from the duke and he shouldn't be concerned about the upcoming tirade. Still, with trepidation, he rapped soundly on the door.

"Come."

He opened the door and stepped inside. The duke sat at his desk, which was littered in papers. As Sebastian approached, he took in his father's appearance for the first time in many years. At sixty-one, Hardwick was definitely showing signs of his age. His face was lined, deep crevices dug around his mouth. More lines sprang from the corners of his eyes. His hair, once dark, had gone iron gray. His body, once fit, now ran to fat.

The duke's graying brows rose. "What do you want?"

He almost laughed aloud. They hadn't spoken in years. "A brief audience, Your Grace."

Hardwick's mouth twitched in annoyance but he commanded, "Sit."

Sebastian took a seat in the chair in front of the desk.

"I have finished university," he began, trying to tamp down the nerves he felt in his man's presence.

"Have you?" Hardwick's tone almost mocked the accomplishment.

Sebastian had graduated with the highest of honors. He had been a model student, not carousing and drunk most of the time as many peers' sons were during the time away from their families. He had been thirsty for knowledge and enjoyed his studies. He had also made wonderful friends in Jon and the Eton Three, as he and Jon had dubbed Andrew, George, and Weston. The five men became inseparable during their days at Cambridge. Until now. He and Andrew had decided to embark on military careers, while the others would take their seats in the House of Lords. It was Sebastian's entry into the army that he would now reveal to the stranger who sat before him.

"Your Grace, I believe—"

"You do not need to believe anything," Hardwick interrupted

impatiently. "You are a marquess and my heir. You will believe what I want you to. I have let you play your little games all these years, Marbury. You have ignored me like a petulant child. Well, today you are a man and, by God, today you will—"

"As a man, I will form and cherish my own beliefs and make my own decisions," Sebastian said firmly, courage blossoming within him. He was determined to stand up to the duke as he had never done before. "I have come to inform you of one of them."

"Oh," Hardwick snarled. "And what might that be?"

"I feel a strong sense of duty and loyalty to my country."

"You should. This system will see you near the top of it one day. When I am gone and you are the new duke."

"I plan to enter the military."

The color drained from the duke's face. "You will not," he said, grounding out each word. "You are my heir. The heir to a dukedom. You won't go and get yourself killed on a battlefield by some crazed French bastard. I forbid it."

"It is not for you to say, Your Grace," Sebastian said coolly. "I have already purchased my commission. I leave today. I am merely extending the courtesy of telling you farewell." He stood, prepared to leave, not wanting to endure the barrage of curses to come.

"No!" Hardwick roared. "I won't let you."

"You didn't let a small boy see his mother as she lay dying. For that, I will never forgive you."

He frowned. "She was a disappointment to me. She was young and should have given me sons," the duke declared.

"*She* was my mother. You berated her. You were cruel to her. You were a mature man of forty and she but an eighteen-year-old girl when you wed. You could have been kind to her. Showed her some compassion."

The duke rose, his face darkening in anger. "Show her *sympathy* when she kept losing my babes? Wedding that woman was a waste.

She only had the one viable child—you—and you are just like her. Soft and weak. You look just like her. It's part of why I cannot stand the sight of you."

He had known it all along. "Then I am doing you a favor by leaving, Your Grace. I do feel a duty toward you, being your own flesh and blood. I will write to you merely because Mama would have wished for me to do so."

Hardwick slammed his fist onto the desk. "I won't read any letters from an insolent, disobedient cur."

Sebastian stiffened at the slur. "I will write them, nevertheless. And don't worry. I have seen to hiring the appropriate people to manage my estates and holdings while I am away."

A knowing light entered the duke's eyes. "My brother put you up to this, didn't he?"

"I did seek Uncle Sydney's advice. He helped—"

"Oh, I am certain he did more than help. Sydney has wanted to become the Duke of Hardwick from the moment he emerged from the womb. He is ten years my junior and always thought he knew better than I did. Can't you see, Marbury? Sydney *wants* you to be killed in action. That way, he would become my heir."

Sebastian had never understood the animosity between the two brothers. He only knew his uncle had treated him with kindness over the years, a far cry from the duke's behavior toward him.

"You actually believe your twisted lies." He shook his head sadly. "I feel sorry for you, Hardwick."

The duke glared at him. "You have no need to," he said viciously. "My good friend, the Earl of Pendell, has just passed. He's made me guardian to his thirteen-year-old child. Hadley is expected today. I will mold Hadley into my image. The Devil himself can take you, Marbury. Get out!"

"With pleasure."

Sebastian left, anger rolling off him in waves. The meeting went as he had expected. His father would never understand Sebastian's burning need to fight for England and a righteous cause. His mother would have. She had embedded the deep loyalty to country and his fellow man within her son. He paused and pulled the locket from his pocket. He would carry it into battle as his talisman. She would always be with him.

Going straight to the stables, he mounted his horse, which would be the only thing he took with him. Soon, he would be wearing his officer's uniform.

Without a backward glance at his childhood home, he tore down the lane leading to the main road, only pausing at the end because of an approaching carriage. The vehicle slowed and he assumed as it turned beside him that it contained the child his father had become guardian to. He tamped down pity for the boy and turned east. His new regiment—and life—awaited him.

LADY HADLEY HAMPTON tried very hard to hold her tears at bay. She might be thirteen but she still wanted her mother.

Even though she would never see Mama again.

She tried to push aside the image that lingered in her memory even after a month. Mama lying so still. Not breathing. Drained of color. She had been sick before but had always gotten better eventually. This time, though, the pneumonia claimed her.

It also took her father. He was old, though, and he had never spent much time with Hadley. In truth, he was so gruff that she had been more than a little bit frightened of him. She feared she would also be afraid of the Duke of Hardwick. He was Father's childhood friend so Hadley supposed he also would be old. Father had been married once before but when his wife had died, he had married her mama. Hadley was their only child. Part of her wished she had died with Mama. She didn't know what her life would be like now, with no living relatives, shipped off to the care of a stranger who lived hundreds of miles from everything she knew.

"We are almost at Hardwell Hall, Lady Hadley," Mr. Weld, her father's solicitor, said. "Just think—your new guardian is a duke. You are a most fortunate young lady."

She didn't feel fortunate at all. She felt lost and alone and wanted to scream at the top of her lungs until she had no voice left.

Then Mama's gentle voice came to her.

Hadley, you have an opportunity to forge a new life. Be strong. Be brave. Be a lady. Make something of yourself.

Mama always had such good advice. Could Hadley truly be brave and become happy in whatever this new life brought?

She had been bold as a small child, always ready to try new things, and had only grown tentative as she had gotten older. Perhaps this would be an opportunity to reinvent herself. She had grown shy over the last few years, losing herself in books since she didn't have any friends. Her father had preferred his country seat to town and so they never went to London. It wasn't appropriate for her to play with any of the servants. The neighboring baron had two boys close to her age but they never wanted her around. She had grown up using her imagination and entertaining herself.

It might be different here. *She* might be different.

Hadley sat up and blinked away her unshed tears. She glanced out the window and saw a man racing down a long lane on a magnificent horse of coal black. Their carriage slowed and turned just as he reached the juncture in the road and, for a brief moment, she studied him.

He sat a horse extremely well. He had dark blond hair and seemed tall and broad in the saddle. God-like. As their carriage turned, he wheeled his horse and headed to the east. Then he was gone.

Hadley wondered if the man had come from Hardwell Hall. Who he might be. She knew nothing of the place she was going to and had no idea if her new guardian was married. If he had children or grandchildren. Something in her stirred.

She wanted to know the man on that horse.

The coach rambled on another ten minutes and finally came to a stop. The door opened. Mr. Weld got out and Hadley followed. Her eyes swept over the large, imposing structure that dwarfed her former home. Grand didn't begin to do it justice. It seemed more like a palace fit for a king.

"Greetings. I am Radmore, His Grace's butler."

She turned and saw the servant who had just spoken. "I am Lady Hadley Hampton," she said bravely and with assurance. "This is Mr. Weld, my late father's solicitor."

"His Grace is expecting you, my lady. If you will follow me."

The butler led them inside and up a staircase. They arrived at the library. Hadley tried to take in all the opulent surroundings—the magnificent oil paintings, Aubusson carpets, and plush furniture. This was to be her new home. She looked to the walls, where bookcases were filled, thinking there must be thousands of books on them.

"Please remain here," the butler instructed. "His Grace will be with you shortly."

Hadley began wandering around, skimming the titles on the shelves. She saw books in Greek and Latin. The works of Chaucer and Shakespeare. Poets such as Byron, Shelley, and Wordsworth.

"I could live in here forever," she said under her breath, awed by the room and all the volumes she looked forward to reading.

"Come stand over here, my lady," Mr. Weld said. "Remember how we spoke of greeting His Grace?"

"I remember. I have an excellent memory."

Mr. Weld blinked and she realized her remark might sound too aggressive. Before she could apologize, however, the duke arrived.

Her eyes followed him as he crossed the room and their gazes met. This was a man who would miss nothing.

She dropped into a low curtsey, as Mr. Weld introduced her.

"I am pleased to meet you, Your Grace," she said, keeping her voice low and modulated, wanting to make Mama proud of her as she watched Hadley from heaven.

The duke harrumphed. "Finally, *someone* is pleased."

Whether he realized it or not, the duke's remark proved revealing. Hadley filed it away, knowing she wanted to learn everything about her new guardian.

Mr. Weld cleared his throat. "I have met with your solicitor, Your Grace, regarding everything involving Lady Hadley's property and dowry."

"I am sure it is all in order," the old man said gruffly. "That will be all."

Seeing that the duke had dismissed him, Mr. Weld thanked him and then said to Hadley, "My lady, it has been a pleasure handling your affairs and those of Lord Pendell's. I wish you well in your new home and circumstances."

"Thank you, Mr. Weld," she said graciously.

Then the solicitor was gone, leaving just the two of them. Hadley took the role of a hostess, wanting to put her new guardian at ease, and said, "Perhaps we could sit and learn a little about each other, Your Grace."

The duke snorted. "You are a forward one. And a girl. I was expecting a boy."

She thought he meant to bully her and, in truth, her legs were shaking. In order to earn his respect, though, she instinctively knew she must show no weakness.

"Hadley was my mother's maiden name," she said smoothly. "You are not the first to make that mistake."

He glared at her. "Dukes don't make mistakes."

"Forgive me, Your Grace. I meant to say assumption. Most everyone who hears my name assumes I am male."

"Are you one of those silly girls, emptyheaded and foolish?" he asked, studying her carefully.

"Not at all, Your Grace. My governess said I am the best pupil she has ever had the privilege of teaching. I love to read. I also enjoy riding and gardening. Just don't ask me to sew. It neither interests me nor do I excel at it. I do enjoy playing the pianoforte, however. Might you have one? I would like to play for you."

"Later," he said grumpily but continued to eye her with interest. "Do you play chess?'

"No, but I certainly would like to learn how to do so. Will you teach me?" she asked eagerly.

"I can. You might learn the rules but you will never beat me," he said boastfully.

"Not at first, Your Grace, for I will be a novice. The day *will* come when I do offer you a challenge, however."

He choked at what she thought he would deem her insolence but Hadley knew she was merely standing up for herself and that he would respect her for doing so.

"Impossible!" he proclaimed.

"I am a quick study. Shall we place a wager? Say I will win a game from you three months from now."

His eyes gleamed. "Then come have a seat now, Lady Hadley. I always did want to teach a young person how to play chess."

He led her to a small table where the pieces were already set up for play and indicated the chair she should take.

Hadley did so and asked, "Have you no children you might have taught the game to?"

A sour look crossed his face. "I have one son. Marbury." His mouth turned down. "He just left for the army. The fool will get himself killed."

So it was the son she had seen, one the duke obviously disapproved of for some reason.

"You are never to speak of him again," ordered the duke. "He is dead to me."

Hadley heard the strong emotion laced in the words and knew things must be very strained between the two for father to disavow his only son, who was obviously his heir. She would learn what she could of this Marbury from the servants. She had always gotten along well with those in her home and expected the same at Hardwell Hall.

As the duke went over each of the playing pieces with her, Hadley listened carefully. She determined to beat this old man at chess—and somehow reunite the duke with his son.

CHAPTER ONE

Nine years later . . .

HADLEY PLACED THE baby in Mrs. Soames' arms and watched as the mother cooed to the infant.

"I will be leaving now," she told the new mother.

"Already?" Worry immediately filled the woman's face.

"I will be back tomorrow to check on you and your son," she promised. "In the meantime, try to get some rest after you nurse him. Your neighbors will be a great help to you."

"I couldn't have done this without you, my lady. You are an angel," Mrs. Soames praised.

"I will send Mr. Soames in now. I am sure he is eager to meet his boy."

She went to the door of the lone bedchamber and opened it, gesturing to the new father. He rushed over from the group of men and women gathered around the fire.

"Your wife and son are ready to see you now, Mr. Soames. I plan to return tomorrow to make sure everything is fine with the both of them."

The farmer's face lit up. "A boy? We have a son? Thank you ever so much, my lady," the new father said, grinning from ear to ear.

"I look forward to hearing what you will name your child."

Hadley watched their tenant step inside and hurry to his wife's bed. For a moment, she drank in a bit of their happiness as the new family of three came together. Then she closed the door and addressed the group.

"Mrs. Soames gave birth to a healthy boy," she announced. "You all know the babe is her first so she will need your help over the next few weeks—and bits of advice—in small doses."

Everyone chuckled. Hadley had learned mothers were all too willing to overshare when it came to indoctrinating a new mother into their fold.

"I will visit them again tomorrow. In the meantime, please take good care of them."

She left the small cottage, tired but exhilarated after staying up all night with Mrs. Soames during her labor. First babies took their time coming and the Soames' son had been no exception. Mounting her horse, she swung her leg over, once again grateful that she wore breeches most of the time. Men certainly had the right idea in claiming them. It made movement and simple activities such as riding so much easier to accomplish. Being out and about on the estate most days, Hadley found wearing trousers more convenient. True, she had shocked many of the tenants and servants when she started wearing them a few years ago but she had found them practical and durable. The only subsequent problem was that she now hated donning gowns for when she went into the village for church services or shopping. Still, she knew she could only stretch the bounds of propriety so far.

Riding across the land, she inhaled the clean air of morning and drank in the green of England in the spring. She enjoyed the milder weather in the south, having come from near the Scottish border almost a decade ago when she became a ward to the duke. The years had seen her grow in confidence, the duke instilling a strong work ethic in her. She had gone from following him about the estate to actually managing it, due to his poor health and the retirement of his steward. For five years, ever since Hardwick's gout had flared up so badly that he had become almost bedridden, Hadley had been the duke's eyes and ears in all things. He had come to trust her implicitly in all matters.

She left her horse with a groom at the stables and headed to the house. Her heart skipped a beat when she spied Doctor Sloop's buggy, attended by one of their footmen. The duke's color hadn't looked good last night and his wheezing had increased. He had also had a cough he couldn't seem to shake. Worry filled her as she entered the house.

Radmore greeted her. "The birth went well, my lady?"

"Yes. Mrs. Soames has a healthy son. What about His Grace? I saw Dr. Sloop is here."

A shadow crossed the butler's face. "After you left to attend the birth, His Grace had a difficult night. His breathing has been quite labored this morning and Dixon suggested the doctor come to see to His Grace."

"I will go to him now."

"My lady," the butler cautioned, "you might wish to wash first. I will have hot water sent up at once. In fact, I anticipated your arrival and it has been simmering as we awaited your arrival."

Hadley glanced down and saw the blood covering her. The duke had an aversion to blood.

"Right as always, Radmore."

"Oh, and a letter came from the marquess, my lady. I will send it up with your water."

She quickly went to her room and peeled off her stained clothes. Millie, who served as her lady's maid at times, entered with two pails of water, one steaming. A folded piece of parchment was tucked under her arm. Hadley retrieved it and set it on a nearby table.

"I hear it's a boy for Mrs. Soames," the servant said. "You look a fright, my lady. Let's get you cleaned up so you can go and be with His Grace."

Millie dipped cloths into the hot water and wiped away the blood and grime from Hadley's long night of work. She washed her hands and donned fresh clothes.

"Don't worry about my hair, Millie. My braid will do. I need to see His Grace now."

Hadley claimed the letter from the marquess and hurried across the hall. She entered the duke's sitting room and found Dr. Sloop waiting. The physician rose.

"Good morning, my lady."

"Good morning, Doctor. How is His Grace?"

"His condition has grown serious rather quickly." He paused. "I fear it is the pneumonia."

A cold lump formed in the pit of her belly. Her parents had both died from the pneumonia. She had dreaded the sickness ever since.

"How serious?" she asked quickly.

"I will do what I can. The best thing is to make His Grace comfortable. Keep him warm. Have adequate pillows propping him up in order to aid his labored breathing."

Her throat grew thick at the news. "You are saying the end is near?"

"I fear it is, my lady. His Grace has been in ill health for some time, as you know. In his weakened condition, the pneumonia has gripped him. It could be a few days. With luck, a week or two."

Desolation filled her. The old man, who had been so crusty and difficult when she had first arrived, had eventually thawed in his demeanor and they had grown quite close over the years. She hadn't imagined life without him yet she knew now to prepare herself for that very time.

"Thank you for your honesty, Dr. Sloop. Not every physician would be so forthcoming with a woman."

He smiled. "You have never been one given to hysteria, my lady. You are as calm and competent as any man of my acquaintance. I will return early this evening to check on His Grace."

"Thank you."

She collapsed onto a chair, her head reeling. Then she glanced at the letter still in her hand.

From Sebastian.

Over the years, she had gotten to know the duke's son quite well through his correspondence. He wrote regularly, usually once a month, except for a gap of several months a few years ago. When the marquess' first letter arrived after she had come to Hardwell Hall and the duke ordered it burned, Hadley had boldly marched over to Radmore and taken it, proclaiming that the duke might not want to read it—but she certainly did.

She had instructed the butler to bring any future letters received from the marquess to her.

And thus began her one-sided friendship with Sebastian Cooper.

For over a year, she read the young lieutenant's letters to his father. In them, he described his fellow officers and the soldiers under him. The training. The drills. The terrible food. He had a way with words, painting pictures she easily created in her mind. She could see everything he wrote about. Gradually, she began dropping bits of information about Sebastian and what he wrote about in her conversations with the duke, piquing the old man's curiosity until he finally demanded she read all the previous letters that his son had written to him. Hadley had every one of them and had re-read them multiple times between new ones arriving.

After that, Radmore would bring her a new letter and she would share it with the duke. He would grunt rather than comment. She asked if he wished to write his son back but he refused. She then took it upon herself to find out the cause of their estrangement, knowing the old man would never share that with her. From the servants, Hadley learned the that duke had been a wild one, one of the biggest rakes in Polite Society. His mother had demanded upon her deathbed that her son wed and get himself an heir. Hardwick had been forty when he did so, marrying an eighteen-year-old golden-haired beauty, who had given birth to their only son, Sebastian.

After Sebastian came, the duchess suffered multiple miscarriages and stillbirths before dying alongside her last babe after a decade of marriage. According to various servants, things had never been the same between the duke and the marquess after the duchess' death. A deep gulf widened between boy and father and remained so for over ten years, when the son left for the Napoleonic wars.

Hadley knew it was rare for a marquess to purchase a commission. Usually, the military was reserved for second sons. Heirs—especially to dukedoms—did not march off to war. Knowing His Grace as she did, she knew the last conversation between the pair had been bitter and angry.

Yet Sebastian wrote to his father as any dutiful son would. Over the years, the officer moved from writing descriptions of everything he saw to the ugliness of war. He shared his fears regarding the battles fought alongside his men. His hopes for England's victory over the wily Corsican. He laid his soul bare. She felt she knew the marquess better than she had known anyone in her life. It was as if Sebastian were the person she was closest to, even closer than she was to Hardwick.

Yet he hadn't a clue she existed.

Sometimes, she wondered if she should have ever started reading his correspondence. His words had been meant for his father, not her. Yet if she hadn't intervened, the duke would never have read a word written to him by his son.

Hadley decided the time had come to write the marquess. Or Colonel Marbury, as he signed his letters. She knew it wasn't the done thing, a lady writing to a gentleman she had never met. The extenuating circumstances called for it, however. Sebastian needed to know of his father's serious illness and imminent death. She doubted he would abandon his men, though. Not with Bonaparte having escaped Elba and marching on Paris six weeks ago. Her gut told her the clash between the Anglo Alliance and French troops would be looming soon. She had learned long ago from Sebastian's letters that duty and honor meant the most to him. He would see this fight through until the end. Still, she would write and inform him of his father's condition. Once the duke passed, she would continue to see to his affairs until Sebastian came home for good and took up the duties of being the Duke of Hardwick.

She refolded the letter and placed it into her pocket before crossing the room to the bedchamber. Inside, she saw Dixon, the duke's valet, sitting at his bedside. The servant had dark circles under his eyes.

He rose as she approached. "His Grace has been asking for you, my lady, though he's asleep now."

"Thank you for staying with him, Dixon. I know you were awake all night seeing to his needs. Go and get some rest. I will stay with His Grace until you return."

The valet knew better than to argue with her. Hadley had a reputation for standing her ground. He rose and left the room. She took his place, the chair warm, and reached for the old man's hand, wrapping both of hers around his. She noted the blueness of his skin and how his body shook with chills and fever.

After a good hour of listening to his labored breathing, the duke opened his eyes. She saw relief in them when he recognized she had come.

"Hadley. You are here," he rasped.

"I am, Your Grace. Do you need anything?"

He sighed and then coughed, wincing as it racked his body. "No. Just your company, my dear."

They sat in companionable silence for some minutes and then he asked about the baby that she had gone to deliver the previous evening. She told him about the birth. How nervous Mrs. Soames had been, delivering a child for the first time. The duke had always been interested in the fine details no matter what the topic and she gave them to him, as always. Then she mentioned receiving a new letter from Sebastian.

"Read it to me," he urged before another coughing fit came hit.

She let it pass and pressed some lukewarm tea upon him. He drank it but refused to eat anything from the tray sitting beside the bed.

Hadley read the latest letter and then set it aside. "Sebastian sounds worried," she noted.

The duke nodded sagely. "He should be. Bonaparte is the wrong side of mad. And I am sure Marbury blames himself for what happened."

Hadley knew the duke referred to Sebastian leaving Elba Island, where the French emperor had been exiled after his abdication. Lord Castlereagh, Britain's Foreign Secretary, had assigned Colonel Neil Campbell as the British commissioner stationed on Elba. His purpose was to keep an eye on Bonaparte. Campbell had, at Wellington's suggestion, added Sebastian to his small staff. Sebastian had written to his father of Campbell's concerns regarding the emperor, worried Bonaparte would try and flee the island and make another run at seizing power. Campbell had sent Sebastian from the Mediterranean to London at the beginning of February to air his concerns about Bonaparte's intentions.

By the time Sebastian reached England, though, Colonel Campbell had also left Elba for Livorno on HMS *Partridge*. He carried a detailed dispatch for Lord Castlereagh, with new information Sebastian didn't possess. By the time Campbell returned to Elba after his brief sojourn, Bonaparte had vanished. Wellington, who had become plenipotentiary to the Congress of Vienna, returned immediately to military duty. Sebastian wrote to his father that he had rejoined his former commander, who was now in charge of the Anglo-Allied army set to go up against the French army once more.

"He shouldn't blame himself," Hadley defended. "Colonel Campbell sent Sebastian to London. It is not his fault the emperor escaped during Sebastian's absence."

"Campbell never should have left Elba," the duke said. "My son wouldn't have."

It warmed her heart to hear His Grace finally use the words *my son*. The duke never called Sebastian by name and only upon rare occasions referenced him as Marbury. She knew she should also think of him as Marbury or the colonel.

But he always seemed like Sebastian to her.

She still could picture him on the midnight black horse he rode, his fair hair blowing in the breeze, his posture perfect. A handsome, determined man setting out to give his best for his country. Hadley believed she knew him better than probably anyone, thanks to the dozens of letters she had read of his over the years. If he was as worried as he sounded, then things were dire. She knew the inevitable battle—or battles—would occur, pitting the coalition against the resurgent French army.

Hadley prayed that Sebastian would survive this war and come home.

To her.

It was foolish, she knew. But somewhere along the way, she had fallen in love with the man behind those letters. She prayed for his safe return every night, bargaining with God to protect him. And when he finally did arrive at Hardwell Hall?

She would be a total stranger to him.

The duke let out a long sigh and she saw he had fallen asleep. She would sit by his side until Dixon returned in a few hours. Then she would write Colonel Sebastian Cooper and let him know about the serious condition of his father. Hadley knew he wouldn't be able to leave. Even if he could, Sebastian was a man who would fight to the bitter end for God and country. His loyalty to Wellington alone would keep him by the duke's side until the threat of Bonaparte had ended—

or Sebastian lost his life.

When the valet returned, Hadley went straight to her study and wrote to the man she respected and harbored deep feelings for. She didn't mince words, knowing his time was always short. She informed him of his father's ill health and how Dr. Sloop anticipated the duke's demise in the next few weeks. She also added a few lines of encouragement, hoping Sebastian would take them to heart.

She decided to sign her correspondence as *H. Hampton*. A letter wasn't the place to explain who she was and why she was residing in the duke's household, much less why she was the one writing to him of His Grace's impending death.

Hadley found Radmore and asked that he post the letter to Colonel Cooper at once. The butler raised one eyebrow briefly, the only sign he was shocked that a missive was leaving Hardwell Hall, bound for the marquess after so many years of silence.

Wanting to feel closer to Sebastian, she went and changed into a gown and went out to the garden, where she cut a bouquet of flowers. She then drove a buggy to the village graveyard, where she went to the grave of the Duchess of Hardwick. She had taken to placing flowers on the duchess' grave several times a year.

Kneeling, she set the flowers on the earth in front of the tombstone and said, "I know you loved Sebastian, Your Grace, and you watch over him from heaven. I pray that he will remain safe and that this awful war will finally come to an end. I desperately want to meet your boy someday soon. I think we could become great friends."

Hadley rose. She had no friends beyond the duke. They had constantly traveled to his various estates during her first four years with him, helping her become familiar with Hardwick's vast holdings. These last five years, once the gout slowed him considerably, had them remaining at Hardwell Hall, where she had worked to keep the household running smoothly and dealt with the tenants both here and at the other holdings of the duke. She had made some acquaintances in the village and attended the few assemblies held each year, getting to dance a bit, which was something she enjoyed immensely. She kept busy but realized at times she was lonely. She longed for a family and foolishly had envisioned Sebastian as her husband and the father of her children in daydreams too numerous to count.

Hadley desperately wanted Sebastian to come home. The young girl who had caught a brief glimpse of a dashing, handsome marquess had fallen in love with the war hero he had become. She wanted to be his friend—and so much more. She told herself it would be next to impossible for this to occur and yet hope trickled through her at the thought of building a life with a man she had grown to admire.

She would be practical, though. Bonaparte must be defeated permanently. Only then would Sebastian resign his commission and come home to assume his role as the new duke. When he did, there might be a possibility of him getting to know her as she knew him. Even then, he might have corresponded with some sweetheart he knew before the war. She must prepare herself for that in case he came home with plans to wed another.

If he didn't, though, Hadley dreamed of the chance to make a life with Sebastian.

CHAPTER TWO

Waterloo, Belgium—June 1815

"COLONEL COOPER, PLEASE remain behind," the Duke of Wellington ordered.

The commander then dismissed the group of gathered officers. Besides British military personnel, officers from Germany, Belgium, and the Netherlands left the large tent, where Sebastian had presented a detailed account of the fighting at Ligny a day earlier. His report included the fact that Bonaparte had defeated the Prussians, under Field Marshal Gebhard Leberecht von Blucher's command.

After the last man left, Wellington sat and motioned for Sebastian to do the same. Though the duke existed on a diet of cold meat and bread, he was known for his taste in fine wines and now poured two glasses of a deep red for himself and Sebastian.

Accepting the glass, Sebastian waited until the slim, elegant Wellington, dressed in the perfectly cut civilian clothes he preferred to wear, took the first sip. Only then did Sebastian imbibe some himself. The wine, smooth and rich, slid down his parched throat.

"You have fine taste in wine, Your Grace," he said.

"Enough of wines," Wellington said dismissively. "What do you think of our chances? Speak frankly, Marbury. It is but the two of us present."

Sebastian had already gathered his thoughts, knowing his commander would ask for a truthful reply. His report to the officers an hour ago had informed the alliance's top officers of the particulars of the fighting at Ligny, spouting all the known facts he had gathered, including casualties and troop movements once the battle ended. Wellington would want much more. He would press Sebastian for his honest opinion. The duke was always interested in the smallest of details and had depended upon a handful of men whom he trusted, including Sebastian, to provide those over the last several years.

"I would say I possess guarded enthusiasm regarding victory, Your Grace," he began. "Our intelligence has shared that Bonaparte's new army practices the strategy of preemptive strikes, attempting to defeat our allied forces one by one before we can launch a united attack against him. The emperor believes the British and Prussian armies are the most capable—and therefore, the deadliest roadblock in his path to conquering Europe. That is why he attacked von Blucher's forces first and is on the move to strike ours next."

"But you said the French did not totally destroy the Prussian army," the duke said eagerly. "So, what do you think of our chances if von Blucher's remaining troops rush to join us? Our scouts know that the French madman is on the move and will surely engage us tomorrow, weather permitting."

"I agree that tomorrow is critical for the Seventh Coalition. All that stands between Bonaparte and success as it currently stands is His Majesty's army."

"If we only had time to mobilize all coalition forces, we would number close to eight hundred and fifty thousand men," Wellington pointed out. "From all reports, Bonaparte has only two hundred and fifty thousand soldiers at his disposal." He took a long pull on his wine.

"True, but for the Seventh to amass would take another two weeks. That is why Bonaparte is attacking now, before we can accomplish that and outnumber him. The British and Prussians are the greatest threats that stand in his way and he has already dealt a severe blow to von Blucher's troops."

The duke sighed. "I have no more than sixty-eight thousand men under my command now. Intelligence reports say Bonaparte will have between seventy and one hundred thousand when he faces us. In all likelihood, that will be tomorrow. *If* this blasted rain will ever come to an end."

Sebastian knew from experience how horrible fighting in the rain could be. "Von Blucher himself promised me he would lead his remaining troops in our direction. If we can hold our position until they arrive, I believe our combined numbers will allow us to defeat the French tomorrow and finally end this nightmare."

Wellington nodded curtly. "I hope so, Marbury. I hope so." He remained lost in thought a moment and then said, "Thank you for being my eyes and ears at Ligny and taking my dispatches to von Blucher. I know what that has cost you in the past."

He stilled. Memories of pain and darkness and despair shot through him. He clamped down and shoved them into a far corner.

"I am happy to serve in whatever capacity you need, Your Grace."

"*Your Grace*," Wellington echoed. "Just a year ago, I was made a duke for my actions that led to Bonaparte's abdication. I thought this was all behind us. Little did I realize what a cesspool the politics of Europe are, Marbury. Trying to make headway with diplomats is worse than being a private, slogging through the mud and blood, attacking the enemy. Who knew we would be forced to return to the battlefield and have to defeat the Little General again?"

Sebastian remained silent, realizing Wellington's musings were his way of trying to cope with the turmoil that had occurred after Bonaparte fled Elba Island and marched triumphantly back into Paris. Sebastian had longed to return to England after that last battle but had accepted the position of Colonel Campbell's second-in-command after Wellington recommended him for the position. Sebastian had thought he would have no need to return to Elba once he discussed Campbell's concerns with Lord Castlereagh. It had been his intention to sell his commission and return to his estates at that point.

Yet here he was, ready to once more go into battle. His gut told him tomorrow would make or break the future of the Continent. He only hoped the British army could hold on until the Prussians could arrive. Without them, victory would be impossible. Even with victory, what would be done with Bonaparte would be the question that remained. Previously awarding him his own island and allowing him to retain his title of emperor had been extremely foolish. Bonaparte had invaded and claimed Elba from Tuscany over a dozen years ago. The Italians weren't happy that the Mediterranean island wasn't returned to them after the war and that Bonaparte had free reign over the place. More trouble had surfaced when the new Bourbon king reneged on paying Bonaparte the agreed upon annual sum of two million francs. The situation had become a powder keg, which had exploded, leading to tomorrow's fight.

"You truly believe the Prussians will get here in time?" Wellington asked, doubt in his eyes.

"If we maintain our position, then I believe we will claim victory, Your Grace."

Wellington nodded. "You are dismissed, Marbury."

He stood and saluted the commander, whom he had the greatest admiration for. Wellington was a canny strategist and had kept Bonaparte guessing and off-balance for many years, preventing Europe from falling into the emperor's hands. The duke had also sent in troops to find and rescue Sebastian when he had been captured behind enemy lines. He owed his very life to Wellington.

Returning to his tent, he was stopped by a soldier. "Letters for you, Colonel Cooper."

Sebastian accepted them. "Thank you."

It still amazed him how his friends could get correspondence through to him in a time of war. When he wrote to them, he never revealed his position. He supposed a duke—actually, four dukes—had the power and seized the right opportunities, allowing their correspondence to be placed in dispatches that came from London.

Over the long years, his friends' letters had been his lifeline to England and the life he had once known there. George, Weston, and Jon had left university and taken their place as dukes, managing vast fortunes and estates and partaking of the Season in London each year. They wrote of mundane things but he relished each word of every letter they sent. Andrew had finally left the military, thanks to the death of his father and older brother, and he, too, had assumed the title of duke. Andrew had wed a widow and he and Phoebe now had a son.

Two of the others had also wed within the last year. George had married Samantha, the tomboy sister of Weston. Sebastian had always liked Samantha and knew she would be a good influence on George. Weston, who had gone even wilder than George once his wedding had been called off, had recently wed a widow who had a young daughter his friend seemed crazy about. Sebastian liked reading about how normal their lives seemed, so different from the years he had spent at war.

He took the letters to his tent and began with the first one, from Andrew. In it, he wrote of how becoming a father had changed him and what a wonderful mother Phoebe was to their infant son. Andrew extended an invitation for Sebastian to come to Windowmere once the war finally ended, saying he and Phoebe would give a house party for all their friends to attend and have time to spend with Sebastian, catching up with what had happened over the years since they had last been in one another's company. They would ride and boat. Fish and hunt. Play parlor games and have picnics. It sounded so idyllic and hard to comprehend that life had gone on for most of the *ton* while he had spent his entire twenties on the Continent on the battlefields.

Folding the letter, he set it aside and glanced at the next one, recognizing Jon's handwriting. His friend hadn't written to him in several months and he wondered if Jon's sister, Lady Elizabeth, had finally made a match. Sebastian had liked the outspoken little girl, whom he hadn't seen in a dozen years. Jon wrote last year of Elizabeth's come-out Season and how she had taken the *ton* by storm. In the end, Lady Elizabeth had not chosen a husband. Jon said his sister wanted to find love.

Sebastian doubted it existed. Not after seeing the ravages of war. Not having grown up in a household where his overbearing father railed against his gentle mother. Yet he knew three of his friends had found love. It didn't surprise him that Andrew had. Andrew was loyal and honorable and it seemed only natural he would attract a wonderful woman and they would share a deep, abiding affection for one another.

George and Weston, though, surprised him. They had become two of Polite Society's best known rakes after being abandoned by their betrotheds. From their correspondence over the years, neither of the so-called Bad Dukes believed in love and had worked their way through the beauties of the *ton*, discarding them left and right. Yet each had found good women, both young widows, and George and Weston no longer were scoundrels—they were the good men he had always known, blanketed by love and returning it in kind to their wives.

He wondered if Fortune would ever smile on him in such a way as to find a happily ever after once the hell of war ceased.

Breaking the seal, he began reading. A smile came to his face.

Jon . . . had found a wife. Jon, his cynical friend, loved and was loved.

A woman named Arabella had tamed the arrogant beast. Sebastian laughed aloud at some of Jon's descriptions of their odd courtship and delighted in hearing of the school Arabella planned to establish for bright, young, impoverished lads.

"Good for you, Arabella," he murmured softly. "And good for you,

Jon. You found your perfect mate." A warm glow filled him, knowing Jon, who had suffered the loss of his twin and taken up the mantle of Duke of Blackmore, a title he had never wanted or expected, now had found complete happiness.

Sebastian folded the letter and set it aside, taking up the last one. The handwriting was unfamiliar. He turned it and froze.

The seal of the Duke of Hardwick.

In all his years away from England, his father had never written to him. Sebastian had sent regular letters home out of a sense of duty, except for that one dark time that he tried to forget.

Why would Hardwick write now after all this time?

With trepidation, he broke the seal.

Dear Colonel Cooper –

I am writing on behalf of your father, the Duke of Hardwick, who has been in ill health for the past five years. Gout has bedridden him and in his weakened state, the duke has contracted the pneumonia. Dr. Sloop, the local doctor, has said to prepare for His Grace's imminent death, most likely within the next week or so. His Grace's affairs are in order and all estates are being well managed, as is his household. This is merely to inform you of His Grace's circumstances and prepare you for his demise.

Though your father has not corresponded with you, I can assure you that he has read every letter you have sent over the years. He is proud of your service to our country and the leadership which you have shown on the battlefield with your men. You are a true hero and England owes everything to men such as you. The newspapers write of the upcoming clash between the allied forces and those of Bonaparte's, most likely in Belgium. I pray that you will come through this horrific time unscathed.

Sincerely,
H. Hampton

The old man was finally dying. Sebastian had thought Hardwick too mean to actually succumb to death. He realized the duke would be seventy by now. The last time Sebastian had seen him, he already had run to fat. It surprised him Hardwick had actually lived this long. He had always had a heavy hand in managing all of his various properties so at least that had been taken care of. Sebastian knew that if he survived this engagement at Waterloo tomorrow and the Anglo Alliance prevailed, he might actually be going home soon. It was good to know the estate hadn't been bankrupted during his long time abroad.

But who on earth was this Hampton? It wasn't the name of the steward of Hardwick lands, unless the previous one had retired and a new one had been hired in his stead during Sebastian's absence. Hampton wasn't the family solicitor, either.

Wait. Buried in the depths of his memory, Sebastian heard the name being spoken aloud. He turned it over in his mind, trying to recall where and when he had heard it uttered.

The ward. Lord Pendell's boy. The one who was supposed to arrive the day Sebastian left to join his regiment. Was he still at Hardwick after all of these years? Had Hampton taken on management of the estate?

It didn't matter. What was important was to concentrate on tomorrow's fight. His focus needed to be on his men and attacking their enemy.

If successful, only then would he worry about the impending death of the Duke of Hardwick.

And how it impacted his future.

Chapter Three

Weymouth, England—End of July 1815

SEBASTIAN DISEMBARKED FROM the ship and walked along the docks, still sensing the motion of the sea rolling beneath him. He carried nothing with him save for a small satchel with a fresh shirt, a bar of soap, his razor, and a few letters. Pitiful, when he thought about it, to have so little to show for his years away.

As he continued walking, enjoying stretching his legs, he thought of how grateful he was to be back on English soil. After so long at war, events of the last month wrapped up surprisingly quickly. Bonaparte abdicated—again—and, this time, where the powers that be decided to banish the broken emperor wouldn't be Sebastian's concern. Wellington had pulled Sebastian aside and told him it was time for the both of them to return to England. He had shared with the duke how a letter had arrived on the eve of the battle at Waterloo that informed him his father was on his deathbed. Wellington had gripped Sebastian's shoulder and told him that he had new duties to see to now since the Duke of Hardwick had vast holdings throughout England. Now, Sebastian would manage tenants and properties instead of regiments of soldiers.

He had landed about five miles from Hardwell Hall, which lay to the southeast of Abbotsbury. Weymouth was the closest port to his destination and he had been lucky to gain a spot on the civilian ship that had brought him here. Most soldiers were taking military ships back to England and would land in Portsmouth, dispersing from there.

His years in the army had left him in excellent shape and so he determined to walk to Hardwell Hall. He would be able to do so in a little more than an hour with his wide stride. First, though, he would visit his tailor. Nothing left at his former home would fit him and would be terribly out of date, though he cared little for fashion. Since he was already here and Weymouth was larger than Abbotsbury, he would see to a new wardrobe now. He chuckled, thinking Weston or George would prefer being with him, giving him advice on what to choose. Most likely, they would demand that he go to London and be fitted by one of their tailors. He would need to travel to town at some point, especially since Hampton's letter said the duke hadn't ventured from his bed in five years. Sebastian wanted to check on the Cooper London townhouse to see what shape it might be in after so long a time of neglect, as well as meet with his solicitors while there.

For now, he would have a few clothes made up in Weymouth. He also would write to his friends and inform them that he had finally returned from the Continent. Once he saw that Hardwell Hall and his other properties were in working order, he looked forward to the house party Andrew had offered to hold so they could all reunite for a time. Sebastian had missed his friends dreadfully. At first, he had tried making new ones from among his fellow officers but oftentimes they were transferred about—or killed in action. He couldn't fraternize with his own men, many whom also met their demise in war. To protect himself, he had withdrawn inside himself. If he wasn't close to anyone, their deaths couldn't hurt him as much.

Or so he thought.

He looked forward to being in his closest companions' company again and meeting the four women who were now a part of their circle. And Andrew's son, of course. He smiled, thinking the next generation had begun. With George, Weston, and Jon having all we
in the last year, he knew they, too, would be starting families of

own.

It would be something he also needed to address. Being the Duke of Hardwick meant he must provide an heir to the dukedom. That meant marriage and children. Perhaps one of his friends' wives had a sister or cousin that he could consider making his duchess. Sebastian didn't really care whom he wed, as long as she produced the requisite heir. He did plan to treat his wife with kindness, though, something that had not existed in his father's vocabulary. Hardwick had been a hard man, bullying and intimidating his own family and everyone who surrounded him. He thought again of Lord Pendell's son and wondered if Hampton had cowered before the duke or stood up to him better than Sebastian ever had.

He traveled several blocks inland until he came to the familiar tailor shop of Mr. Wilson. The man had made up all of Sebastian's clothes during his youth through university days. He opened the shop door and stepped inside.

A young man no more than twenty eagerly stepped forward to greet him. He favored Wilson and might actually be the tailor's son or another close relative.

"Good morning, sir." The man glanced at the stripes on Sebastian's coat. "Is it Colonel?"

"It was," he said. "I have recently sold out. I am Lord Marbury."

At least he was if the duke still lived. He wouldn't know until he reached Hardwell Hall.

"Lord Marbury?" a voice called out and he saw Mr. Wilson hurrying from behind a curtain, a huge smile crossing his face. "My lord, it is most wonderful to see you again."

He offered his hand, which the tailor pumped enthusiastically.

"My, it's been what—almost a decade?"

"Yes, Mr. Wilson. You last outfitted me before my final year at Cambridge. I have been wearing uniforms ever since that time."

"I cannot thank you enough for your service to England, my lord."

Wilson paused. "I should say . . . oh, you might not know . . ." The tailor's voice faded away.

"That I am now His Grace?" Sebastian ventured. "It is possible. I received word about six weeks ago that Hardwick was near death."

Sorrow crossed Wilson's face. "He did pass on, Your Grace. I think it has been more than a month, hasn't it, John?"

"Yes, Father," the young man who had greeted Sebastian replied.

"This is my boy, John," the tailor said. "He works with me now and will one day take over the shop."

He offered his hand. "I am happy to make your acquaintance, John. I seem to remember you as small, mischievous boy."

John grinned. "I was certainly that, Your Grace. I have settled down, though, and apprenticed with Father for several years."

"Then I will ask the two of you to make up a wardrobe for me," he declared, deciding he really didn't care about putting coin into some smart London tailor's hand when Wilson had done such a fine job all these years.

"What do you have in mind, Your Grace?" the older man asked.

"I will need everything, Mr. Wilson. Shirts, coats, trousers, waistcoats. A greatcoat for when the weather grows colder."

"Yes, Your Grace," said the younger Wilson with enthusiasm. He snatched up a pad and removed the pencil which had been tucked behind his ear. "How many of each? And of course, we have materials for you to look at."

Sebastian bit back a smile at the young man's eagerness and turned to the father. "You know my taste, Mr. Wilson, as well as what men are wearing nowadays. I haven't worn civilian clothing since I left England nine years ago. I haven't a clue what I will need except that I will need everything. Spare no cost. I want the best of everything you have in your shop."

As the Duke of Hardwick, he knew he had a role to play and would need to look his best at all times. It would be a far cry from his usual attire of the past decade. While he and his batman had striven to keep his uniforms clean and presentable, it was beyond difficult to maintain a pristine appearance in a time of war.

"I am humbled, Your Grace," the tailor said. "I will be careful in what I make up for you and will wish for your approval before I supply you with everything you desire. I do know your taste in apparel but I will need to measure you. Your frame has filled out since you last came to visit me."

Dread filled him. He remembered Mr. Wilson was meticulous in his measurements, part of what made him such an excellent tailor. Sebastian only hoped he would be able to leave on some of his clothes. A flash of pain rippled through him and he winced.

"Are you all right, Your Grace?" Mr. Wilson asked worriedly.

"Yes. Quite fine," he said curtly. "Shall we commence?"

"Come to the dressing rooms, Your Grace," John said.

"No, John, I will measure His Grace. You watch the shop for me."

Disappointment filled the son's face. "Yes, Father."

Sebastian accompanied Wilson to the rear of the shop and they went through a set of curtains, turning left and entering a small room. He went and stood on the raised platform as Wilson closed the door.

Shrugging out of his scarlet jacket, he handed it to the tailor, who hung it carefully and said, "That is all you need to remove, Your Grace."

Somehow, Sebastian knew that Wilson suspected something was wrong and that his client would be loath to remove anything beyond his coat.

The tailor took his tape and carefully measured everything on Sebastian, from the width of his chest to his inseams. Wilson jotted the numbers down in his neat hand.

"I will make up three coats and waistcoats, Your Grace, along with five shirts. Two pair of buff breeches and three dark trousers. Once you have seen those and only if you are pleased, we will go from there."

"What about evening wear?" he asked, thinking of the house party he longed to attend to reacquaint himself with his friends.

"I can make up a set, as well as your cravats."

"And a banyan," Sebastian added. "In silk." He longed for the luxurious material against his skin, the one item of pampering he had missed during his war years.

"Certainly, Your Grace. Will you be visiting the hatmaker and bootmaker?"

"Yes, I will do that once I leave your shop. Then I will head to Hardwell Hall."

"How will you get there, Your Grace?"

He chuckled. "I suppose I will walk. I have literally just gotten off the ship that brought me to England and knew I should see about clothing before I returned home."

"Stop back here and I will have John take you in our wagon."

"I wouldn't want to trouble you."

"Oh, it is no trouble at all, Your Grace. The boy will be eager to hear about the war."

That was the last thing Sebastian wanted to discuss but he realized it would be a popular topic of conversation wherever he went and he might as well get used to it.

"Thank you for your thoughtfulness, Mr. Wilson."

He stepped down and the tailor helped him into his coat.

"It is good to have you back, Your Grace," Mr. Wilson said. "You didn't have to go to war but you chose to do so. You have earned the respect of those far and wide."

Once, he would have longed for the respect of men. His time at war had changed that, though. He merely wanted to be a good lord to his people and left alone by others. Wilson might not have asked but Sebastian knew those he ran into would want tales of the glory of war.

He had nothing to give them. War was dark and ugly and purged a man's soul from his body. Sebastian never wanted to think of the war again. Unfortunately, he would see the reminders of it every day when he dressed.

After stops to have several new hats made up and a pair of boots and leather-laced shoes, Sebastian returned to the tailor's shop. John escorted him to the rear, where he had already harnessed a horse, and they climbed into the waiting cart. Wilson must have cautioned his son about peppering Sebastian with questions because John asked not a single one. Instead, the younger Wilson told him a bit about what had happened in the area during the last few years.

The weather was warm but not unbearable and the conversation friendly as they traveled west. When they reached the village closest to Hardwell Hall, he asked John to stop.

"But it's still another mile or more to our destination," John protested.

"I wish to visit my mother's grave," he said quietly.

"Very well, Your Grace."

John drove to the church yard's gate and brought the horse to a halt.

"I can wait for you if you wish."

He wanted privacy more than company and said, "No. I don't know how long I will be. Besides, I am not far from home now. Thank you for bringing me this far."

John beamed. "It was my pleasure, Your Grace. Count on Father and me. You will be pleased at what we make up for you."

"I know I will."

He climbed from the cart and waved. John turned the wagon and continued back toward Weymouth while Sebastian crossed the road and entered the graveyard. He made his way through the markers, catching a name or two of someone he hadn't known was now deceased.

Finally, he arrived at his mother's grave. Surprise filled him. A fresh bouquet of flowers graced the plot, tied with a pastel ribbon. He recognized pink dahlias, tall irises, and the purple stocks that his mother had loved most of all.

Kneeling, he said, "I am home, Mama. Finally home."

His hand went to his chest and rested against the familiar locket he had worn under his regimental colors since he had taken it from her dressing table.

"I know you watched over me, Mama. Even in those darkest of times. Know that I appreciated that and could feel you with me always."

Sebastian remained at the grave a long time before rising. He kissed his fingers and placed them to her headstone before retreating. Then he looked around the area, seeking and finding the newest addition to the Cooper section.

The Duke of Hardwick.

He went to the grave. Hovering above it at the head was a tall monument. The duke's dates of birth and death were inscribed into the stone. Ironically, Hardwick died on the day of the fighting at Waterloo.

"I am home, Your Grace. I plan to be the duke you never were. Slow to anger. Generous with my tenants. Kind to the wife I take. Loving to my children."

He spit on the grave and strode away.

Chapter Four

SEBASTIAN CUT THROUGH the cemetery instead of returning to the main road. The shortcut would get him to Hardwell Hall more quickly and allow him to cross a bit of the land so he could see the condition it was in. He would ride the property tomorrow after speaking with the steward and see what immediate needs should be met. He wanted to see the state of the tenants' cottages and view the crops and livestock. The autumn harvest would be upon them soon and he had many decisions to make, not only about Hardwell, but his many other properties, as well.

He came across a fence and hopped over it, deciding to follow it. As he walked, he saw someone ahead near the fence, hammering. Drawing closer, he looked upon the extremely short coat in distaste. If this was the new fashion, he should immediately turn around and return to Weymouth to instruct Mr. Wilson he wanted no part of it.

Then his eyes dipped lower and he halted. The most deliciously rounded derriere was below the jacket, shown off by tight, fawn breeches. Long, slim legs were encased in tall boots. He realized it was a woman—dressed as a man—a gentlemen's hat perched on her head. Angry, Sebastian strode toward the figure bending over.

"What the devil are you doing?" he shouted.

The woman started as the hammer came down, striking her hand instead of the nail's head. She swore, dropping the hammer and ripping off her left glove. She pushed her thumb into her mouth. A frisson of desire rippled through him.

He wanted to suck on that thumb.

She pushed to her feet and wheeled, anger sparking in eyes of cornflower blue, color high on her cheeks.

"Who do you think you . . . oh . . . Sebastian!"

She knew him?

He had never seen her before. He would certainly remember if he had for she was a beauty. Flawless porcelain skin. High cheekbones and plump, pink lips. Her hat sat back on her head and he caught a glimpse of rich, auburn hair. He stared, no words coming.

Color now flooded her face and she said, "I apologize, Your Grace."

She attempted to curtsey but had no skirts to clutch and the curtsey became more of a bow. As she leaned forward, dipping her head, the wind caught the hat and it toppled from her head. Immediately, the auburn tresses spilled about her shoulders and down to her waist, the sun lighting them on fire.

"Oh, I am very sorry," she repeated, capturing and twisting the abundant waves with her fingers. She somehow tamed the mass and placed it atop her head. Bending low, she retrieved the hat, which had seen better days, and jammed it on her head again, shoving a few errant strands back under it until her tresses were mostly hidden.

"Usually, I braid it. I had no time today. I needed to—"

"Who *are* you?" he asked in wonder.

She licked her lips nervously and desire ran through him again. It had been a long time since he'd had a woman, not wanting to take a chance with the field doxies that followed the army.

"I am Lady Hadley Hampton," she stated boldly, confidence now brimming through her. "I was—"

"You are a woman?" he asked, confusion filling him. "You aren't a boy at all."

She certainly wasn't. Lady Hadley was all woman. Tall and slender, but with a sweet curve to her hips and high, firm breasts. And that plump bottom, which his fingers longed to squeeze.

Chuckling, she said, "I didn't think you knew about me."

"Hardwick mentioned you moments before I left to join my regiment." Then Sebastian laughed aloud. "What I would have given to have seen his face when you showed up instead of the young boy he expected."

She smiled and it was as if the sun radiated from her. "His Grace was a bit flummoxed at first. Then angry. I suppose becoming guardian to a gawky thirteen-year-old girl wasn't in his plans."

"Frankly, I am surprised he didn't toss you from Hardwell Hall and wash his hands of you altogether."

She sniffed. "If he had tried, I wouldn't have let him. As it was, he readily accepted me and taught me quite a bit."

Her words drew him aback. "He . . . taught you?"

"Oh, yes," she said breezily. "His Grace started the first day I arrived at Hardwell Hall. We began with him teaching me the game of chess. I told him I would defeat him in three months' time—and I did."

Sebastian understood the words Lady Hadley spoke but their meaning seemed garbled.

"My . . . His Grace . . . *he* taught you how to play chess."

"Yes. I didn't know how and was eager to learn. It was the first of many lessons at the duke's hands."

He frowned. "What other lessons did you partake in?" He could think of nothing Hardwick would care to teach a female. He couldn't imagine the duke spending any time with a child, especially one who was a girl.

"I learned about horses. His Grace was quite fond of them and very knowledgeable. I soon knew what lines to look for. How to evaluate a horse's balance and look for equal lengths in its shoulders, back, and hips. Checking that both its head and neck are in correct proportion and if the back is shorter than its underline. Observing its muscles and structure. His Grace taught me how to ride and to watch for a long, straight, even gait. That its coat should be glossy. And also to spend enough time with the animal to learn its temperament before purchasing it."

Sebastian was amazed. These were all things he had learned over years of experience—and none of them had come from the duke sharing his knowledge with his son.

"What else did your guardian teach you, my lady?" he asked, curious about the relationship between this exquisite creature and the man he loathed.

"How to run an estate, for the most part," she replied, surprising him even further. "I know how to keep accurate ledgers and make sure they are balanced. I learned about various breeding methods and the livestock at Hardwell. How to examine the cottages and see what repairs are necessary. When and where to rotate crops for maximum output. I have even begun a program to—"

"Wait," he commanded, his head dizzy from all the information that flowed from those plump lips. "The *duke* taught you all of this?"

"Yes. We traveled throughout England during my first few years with him. I have visited every estate among the holdings. When I was seventeen, however, His Grace's gout made it impossible to do so and we remained at Hardwell. When his steward retired, I took over."

"You . . . you *run* the estate now, my lady?"

"Yes, Your Grace." She rewarded him with a brilliant smile. "And without sounding as if I am bragging, I do an excellent job at it." She frowned a moment and held up her thumb, which was now swollen and discolored. "Except when I bash my hand with a hammer. In my defense, you did startle me."

Sebastian shook his head. "Lady Hadley, I am at a loss for words."

Sympathy filled her face. "I know it must be hard to return home and know your father is dead." She drew in a quick breath. "Oh, dear. Did you know that? Did you receive my letter? I wasn't sure with the action occurring at Waterloo if you did or not." She bit her lip, her uncertainty touching.

"I did receive your letter. From H. Hampton."

A blush stained her cheeks. "I didn't think it appropriate for a lady to be writing a gentleman to whom she had not been properly introduced. I am sorry, Your Grace, that I hid my identity from you. I did want you to know about your father's condition, though. Why don't we go back to the house as soon as I finish repairing this fence? I can speak to you in more detail regarding your father's passing."

He bent and retrieved the hammer. "I will fix the fence, my lady. You may return to the house and change into something more appropriate for our conversation."

She glanced down and then her cool gaze met his. "I don't believe I need to change at all, Your Grace. I will wash up, however, and meet you in the library."

Lady Hadley marched off, obviously angered by his suggestion. Sebastian watched the sweet sway of her hips in the tight breeches and tamped down the desire running through him.

She was an impertinent chit. Obviously, the duke had been besotted with her and in his feeble state of mind and health had turned over the running of his lands to the woman. It was inconceivable and yet it had happened.

He thought back to what she spoke of regarding the first day she arrived. How Hardwick had volunteered to teach her how to play chess, something he had never offered to his only son and heir. Of course, Sebastian rarely was in the same room with the man who had sired him. When they were, as during the occasional meal together, they never spoke. To think that Lady Hadley had the insolence to declare she would beat the duke at the game he loved best.

And she had.

To have learned such a complicated game of intricate strategies in such a short amount of time to the level of defeating a man known for his skill at the game was a remarkable feat. The knowledge she easily spouted about horses also surprised him, as did the fact she was now managing the Hardwick estates.

Could a woman truly be capable of doing all of this?

Sebastian gripped the hammer and picked up where Lady Hadley had left off. Within minutes, the fence stood firm again. Why had she been the one seeing to its maintenance? And why was she dressed as a man? She hadn't taken kindly to his suggestion to change her clothing. He wondered if she often dressed in such a manner.

His mind wandered to her rounded bottom in those tight breeches. How his hands longed to grip it. Knead it. His body flushed with heat at the thought of her in his arms, his hands roaming places they shouldn't. Shaking his head, he tried to dispel the notion. Lady Hadley was not the kind of woman he would ever want as his wife. She was much too opinionated. Obviously, rather stubborn. She had been given free rein at Hardwick for far too long.

That would end today. He was home now. He was the Duke of Hardwick. All decisions would be made by him.

The first?

Asking Lady Hadley Hampton to leave.

HADLEY STORMED INTO the house. She couldn't remember the last time she had been so angry. Probably never. She passed a footman and demanded, "Hot water. Now."

He looked startled and she realized none of the servants had ever seen her behave in such a manner. It was not fair to take out her anger at Sebastian on one of them.

Tamping down her rage, she said, "I am sorry. Please let someone know I wish for hot water for a bath."

The footman, who hadn't moved, blinked and said, "Yes, my lady," and quickly hurried off.

She marched up the stairs to her room and sat in her favorite chair to strip off her boots. The Hessians had been made for her in Weymouth and she wore them most days. They were covered in mud now since she had been tramping through the field, examining the fence. She paused and lifted her sore, bruised thumb. It ached something terrible, having taken the full brunt of the hammer's swing that had been meant for the nail's head. She saw it was actually bloody and hoped she hadn't damaged the nail.

Millie appeared, looking frazzled. "You are already back, my lady?"

"Yes. I have called for a bath."

"Water is being brought up now. Shall I set out something for you to wear?"

He wanted her in a gown. Something befitting a lady. Hadley could already tell Colonel Cooper was a rigid man, probably made so by his years spent in the military. Well, she didn't care what the blasted man wanted. She would wear whatever she wished to wear. Let him be scandalized or disapproving. It didn't matter to her.

But it did.

All these years, she had built up Sebastian in her mind as the perfect man. Handsome. Courageous. Patriotic. Heroic. Reality had proven in the few minutes they had spent together that he was still handsome. And he probably was courageous and all those wonderful things an officer needed to be. But he seemed stubborn and judgmental. Not at all what she was expecting.

"Yes, Millie," she finally replied. "Place out my usual." She shrugged out of her short coat and tossed her hat aside. "This coat will need to be brushed. And my boots cleaned and polished."

"Yes, my lady."

The maid came and helped tug off the boots and then Hadley stripped off the waistcoat and then pulled the lawn shirt over her head. She stood and wriggled from the breeches, leaving all the clothing in a heap. She didn't want to take the time to wash her hair and went to her dressing table. Quickly, she secured her hair atop her head with several pins to keep it out of the water.

Padding to her dressing room, she found the tub filled, with jugs of water to cleanse herself sitting next to it. Easing into the warm water, she sank up to her neck, resting it on the edge. A long sigh came from her as she luxuriated in the water. Her day had been physical and her muscles needed this respite.

She reached for the cake of soap and lathered herself, her thoughts returning to the man she had wished to meet for years. She should have known he wouldn't be all she dreamed of. She had to remember, though, that he had known nothing of her existence, other than he believed a young boy was coming to Hardwell Hall after his departure. Hadley had to admit that her life had become unconventional, with her managing both the household and the estate. To a man who had been around nothing but men for a decade, it would be hard to grasp a female being capable enough to handle the affairs of a duke. Her temper calmed with these thoughts.

She must give Sebastian a chance. He was the new duke and everything was now different from when he had left all those years ago. Putting herself into his shoes, she realized how odd it would have seemed to come home after an extended absence only to find a total stranger in charge of her household. Also, he would be adjusting to civilian life after living abroad and engaged in fighting for numerous years. Sebastian deserved the benefit of the doubt.

Reaching for the bath sheet Millie had left out for her, Hadley stood and toweled off. She returned to her bedchamber and dressed in the fresh clothes lying on the bed. She unpinned her hair and took the time to brush it before deciding to sweep it into a chignon instead of placing it into her usual braid. Part of that was vanity. She wanted to look good for Sebastian. This was his chance to begin to know her. Perhaps they would find that they had some things in common. If by some miracle he thought they suited, he might offer her marriage and then she would never have to leave the place which had become home to her.

Everything depended upon this next meeting between them. Hadley promised herself to be demure instead of confrontational. To go slowly and not throw too much at him at once. She would listen more than she spoke and they would become better acquainted. They had gotten off on the wrong foot. This meeting was a chance to right things between them.

Brimming with optimism, Hadley left her bedchamber and made her way to the library.

Chapter Five

SEBASTIAN SWUNG THE hammer in one hand and his satchel in the other as he approached Hardwell Hall. Anger had built within him the closer he came to the main house. As he reached it, he stopped and studied the imposing structure.

This was his. The Duke of Hardwick was finally gone. All the pain and disappointment and frustration at being the son of that man seemed to float away. Serenity filled him. He could walk in and go wherever he liked. No more skulking around, avoiding contact with the man he resented and loathed. Hardwell Hall was his home. His sanctuary. It would be where he lived out the rest of his life. Raised a family. Grew old.

He would remember the promises made to his mother and keep them. He would treat all women with respect. Guilt rose within him. Asking Lady Hadley to vacate the premises wasn't respectful. It was an aggressive, rude move on his part. This had been her home for as long as he had been away. It didn't seem right to toss her from the place as if she were rubbish. He would need to check into his finances and hers, as well, since the duke would have had access to manage whatever monies she had been left by her father. Pendell would have earmarked certain funds to be her dowry. Sebastian would review everything and then meet with her, coming to a decision on how and when she would leave Dorset.

Poor woman. She hadn't even had a London Season. From what

she had said, she had been bound to this property for the last five years. Years she should have made her come-out. Married. Started a family of her own. Instead, she had stayed and managed things for the duke. Her sacrifice should be rewarded. Perhaps he should give her one of the unentailed estates in compensation for wasting her youth. It might quickly help attract a husband for her and then he would be absolved of any responsibility for her.

He entered the house, startling a footman who passed by. The servant looked to be no more than twenty and scared as a rabbit. Before Sebastian could explain who he was, the footman took off at a run, shouting, "Mr. Radmore! Mr. Radmore!"

He might as well wait here and greet Radmore. It was good to know the butler was still in charge. Radmore had moved up in the household to the position of butler only weeks before Sebastian left, placing him in charge of all of the servants in the household. Unless Mrs. Sewell was still the housekeeper. She ruled with an iron fist, though she had always had a tender spot for Sebastian.

Suddenly, Radmore appeared. He looked at Sebastian as if he had seen a ghost, which told him Lady Hadley hadn't bothered to let the butler know that the new Duke of Hardwick had come home.

"Lord Marbury! I mean . . . Your Grace. We were not expecting you." The butler rushed to him. "This is a wonderful surprise." A shadow crossed his face. "Did you receive Lady Hadley's letter? About your father?"

"I did. I knew by the time I arrived home that His Grace would have passed on."

"He did, Your Grace. On the very day you fought at Waterloo. Oh, England is so grateful that you ended Bonaparte's domination."

He chuckled. "Well, I didn't do it singlehandedly, Radmore. I had help, you know. Starting with the Duke of Wellington."

The butler nodded. "We are still grateful for your sacrifices, Your Grace. Are you home for good?"

"Yes, I have sold out. I have no plans of returning to the military. I look forward to a quiet life in the country after enduring years of turmoil."

Radmore brightened. "Everything is in exceptional order, Your Grace, thanks to Lady Hadley."

"It is?" The butler's words piqued his curiosity. "How so?"

"Lady Hadley worked wonders with His Grace. I am speaking out of turn but I am sure you know how . . . difficult . . . His Grace could be."

"Yes, he was," agreed Sebastian.

"From the moment she arrived—and she was quite young—Lady Hadley managed His Grace with aplomb. She wouldn't tolerate his temper tantrums. She insisted he treat his staff with courtesy. She took over running the household."

"How did Mrs. Sewell take to that?"

Radmore chuckled. "They butted heads a bit but now Mrs. Sewell is her ladyship's greatest supporter."

"What of the estate?" he asked, wondering if the lady had exaggerated her role in its management.

The butler smiled broadly. "No fears there, Your Grace. After the steward retired, Lady Hadley has seamlessly managed everything. She soaked up everything His Grace could teach her and went far beyond that. She knows the intricacies of the harvest. She has excellent taste in horseflesh. Hardwell has never been run better than under her steady hand."

He still found it hard to believe yet knew Radmore had no reason to lie to him regarding the woman's skills.

"I see the doubt on your face, Your Grace. Suffice it to say that Lady Hadley is nothing short of a miracle worker. She taught His Grace as much as he taught her. She was a godsend."

"I see. Well, she is to meet me in the library now."

"She is?" asked Radmore, obviously puzzled.

"Yes. I stumbled across her as I made my way here. She was mending a fence."

The butler laughed. "That is Lady Hadley. Always taking a personal interest in everything, leaving no stone unturned." He paused. "Would you like to wash before you meet with her?"

Although he desperately wanted to get the dust of the road off him, he said, "No. I will see her first and then go to my room."

"Lady Hadley had His Grace's things cleared out, anticipating your arrival once Bonaparte was stopped in Belgium. The personal items you left behind have all been transferred to the duke's rooms."

"She did? It seems the lady thinks of everything."

The butler chuckled. "Frankly, she does. She may be young in years but she is the wisest person I know," Radmore said, his admiration for the woman obvious.

Sebastian handed his satchel over. "Please take this to my chambers. You may send hot water for a bath in an hour. I am sure my meeting with Lady Hadley will have concluded by then."

"Very good, Your Grace."

He headed upstairs to the library and entered it. The room had always been his favorite at Hardwell Hall and he had spent many hours poring over books and especially the atlas, wanting to go to far-off lands such as Egypt and India. Instead, his destination had been closer to home, where the ravages of war had sucked his soul dry. He moved about the room, fingers brushing against the leather-bound volumes, eyes wandering over the magnificent furniture and landscapes adorning the walls. The richness of the room overwhelmed him. After living in tents for almost ten years, being alone in such splendor caused his senses to reel. His quarters on Elba had been spartan after his time in the field. Returning to Hardwell Hall seemed like living in a palace. It astounded him that he had grown up in such surroundings—and taken them for granted.

Sebastian wondered if he would even be able to sleep in the duke's quarters. Wellington had confided to him once they had been reunited in Belgium that he had yet to sleep in a regular bed, opting for a camp bed after all his nights spent in one. Sebastian wouldn't mind a regular bed but the thought of sleeping where Hardwick once had left him with a bad taste in his mouth. Of course, as a wealthy duke, he could simply have the bed removed and burned and replace it with one of his choosing.

He moved to one of the large windows that overlooked the gardens. They were something he had missed. He had yearned to see the beauty of a fragile flower and inhale its sweet scent. He and the army had certainly trampled upon enough of them. Sebastian took a calming breath, one meant to center him.

"Your Grace?"

He turned and saw Lady Hadley had arrived, wearing the attire he knew she would. Her rich, auburn hair had been swept into a low chignon. With her manly attire, she shouldn't look so desirable but what she wore made her seem even more feminine than most women in the fanciest of gowns. She came toward him, wearing an easy smile and air of confidence.

"I have asked Radmore for tea to be brought," she said. "I thought we could spend some time discussing your father and the estate."

"I have no need to hear anything more regarding Hardwick," he said dismissively and took a seat.

She sat in a chair to his right. "Whether you wish to hear of him or not, you are going to. Quit acting like a petulant child."

Her words echoed those of the duke's on that last day before Sebastian left. He wondered if Hardwick had used the same phrase to describe his rebellious son.

The teacart arrived and Lady Hadley busied herself with pouring out. She did so gracefully, with an ease that spoke of generations of good breeding. He placed two sandwiches and a few sweets on his plate, his mouth salivating at seeing such delicious items. The food in the army was notoriously bad and at Elba it had been even worse, barely edible.

Lady Hadley handed him a cup and saucer. "I hope tea was a good choice. I didn't know if you preferred coffee at this hour. You mentioned coffee several times in your letters."

"You read my letters? They were not addressed to you." He thought of all the times he had bared his soul—or what was left of it—in those letters. "You had no right to do so," he said angrily.

Her face flamed. "Forgive me, Your Grace. I did so to try and get your father to read them."

"Why would he bother to do so?"

"Why would you bother to write to him if you didn't believe he would?" she fired back.

Sebastian took a sip of the hot brew, not trusting himself to speak. The flavor exploded in his mouth. Oh, how he had missed English tea and everything about his homeland.

"I apologize, Your Grace." Lady Hadley looked at him earnestly. "But why did you write, knowing the pages wouldn't be read?"

"Because I knew Hardwick. He was a cold, hard, unforgiving bastard."

"He was . . . when I first arrived. The duke changed over time. Mellowed with the years, I daresay. He was quite proud of you and eagerly awaited news from you." She sighed. "I tried to get him to respond but he refused."

"Tigers don't change their stripes, Lady Hadley."

"I know you were estranged. I wasn't apprised of the details."

He snorted. "I would say more than estranged, my lady. We went for several years without a word between us."

Shock filled her face. "I see. My father was . . . difficult, as well. I was close to Mama but he frightened me to no end. He was so old and impatient anytime I was around him, which thankfully wasn't very frequent."

"Pendell was a contemporary of the duke's. Didn't Hardwick seem old to you?"

"Yes, but he actually spoke to me. With me. My father never did so. You never answered me, Your Grace. Why did you write to your father?"

"Because it was what my mother would have wanted." He could feel the locket against the skin of his chest, where it always rested. "And because it helped me survive."

Curiosity filled those large, purple-blue eyes. "How so?"

"I poured my heart out in those letters," he admitted. "Said things that I couldn't say to my commanders and would never say to my men. The thoughts I expressed were private ones. I suppose writing them was like talking aloud to myself. Committing to paper my deepest fears. Somehow by writing of them, I could let them go. Those letters helped me keep my sanity. Find my courage."

"They were wonderful," she said, admiration obvious in her voice. "So detailed. I could see everything you wrote of. Your men. The battles. The tedious drills and sleepless nights. I breathed the air rife with the scent of cannon fire. Heard the moans of the dying."

Lady Hadley shook her head. "You were so very brave, Sebastian." She started. "I mean, Your Grace. Oh, I am sorry for sounding so familiar. I am a stranger to you. You know nothing of me and I seem to know everything about you. More than I ought to. I came to know you over the years, you see. Your letters showed me a different world. I felt as though . . . oh, I know this sounds foolish." She swallowed. "I felt as if you were my friend. Someone I had always known and learned to grow close to over the years."

His fingers tightened around the delicate cup's handle and he set the saucer down, lest he break it.

"You see, I always wanted to reunite you and the duke. I saved the first letter you sent from being destroyed. I read it and kept it. Radmore continued bringing them to me at my request and I would mention things you wrote about to the duke. Finally, His Grace couldn't stand it any longer and demanded to read the letters himself."

"You saved them?" he asked hoarsely.

"Of course. I read them over and over again. I was a young girl, barely ten and three, and you were this great adventurer, showing me the world. His Grace read all of them and then as new ones came, he had me read them aloud to him. Several times until the next one arrived. We were quite worried when they stopped coming for a while since they arrived so regularly but we decided that in war, a few letters will go astray every now and then."

He gripped his knees, his knuckles turning white. She talked of a time he had done his best to lock away.

And failed, miserably.

"I understand I should not have read them. I ask for your forgiveness."

Sebastian saw her pained expression. "It is nothing to worry about, my lady."

"I will return them to you."

"No. Burn them. I have no intention of being drawn back into that time ever again."

He took one of the sandwiches and bit ferociously into it, unnerved by their conversation. She ate daintily as he wolfed down everything on his plate and then set it aside.

"Would you like to talk of the estate now, Your Grace?"

"No. Instead, we should talk of your future."

"My future?" she asked, seeming dazed. "Oh, of course. You will want me gone. I understand." Her gaze fell to her lap.

Something in her tone seemed so bereft. He didn't want to hurt this woman.

"You have done a great service to the Cooper family, Lady Hadley. I merely thought you would wish to get on with your life now that Hardwick is gone."

"Yes, that is true."

"How old are you now?"

"Two and twenty."

"You should have had a London Season long ago," he told her. "If you hadn't been caring for my father and seeing to his responsibilities, you would be wed by now. You would have children." He paused. "You do want those things, don't you?"

"Yes. I was an only child and have no family left. I very much long to have a family of my own."

"I plan to go to London tomorrow. I want to meet with my solicitor there and since no one has been at the London townhouse, I should check on it."

"There is a staff in place," she said, her eyes still lowered. "I thought the property should be maintained, whether it was being used or not. In fact, I rented it out. A place is better when lived in and not left standing lonely and idle."

It was clever of her to have done so, generating income that way.

"I will check on what Lord Pendell left you and –"

"No need to do so, Your Grace. I have been in touch with your father's solicitors and know my income. I was also left a dowry. If I am not wed by the time I reach twenty-five, that will be mine to do with as I choose."

"Surely, you will wed before then, Lady Hadley."

Finally, she raised her head, her steady gaze meeting his. "Perhaps."

"I intend to gift you with one of the estate's unentailed properties. Since you are familiar with them, you may choose the one you wish to own."

Astonishment filled her face. "That is not necessary, Your Grace."

"I believe it is, my lady. You put your life on hold to care for a sick, old man. You should be rewarded for your good deed."

She pushed to her feet, anger sparking in her eyes. "I did what I did out of kindness, not expecting any type of reward. I am sorry, Your Grace, but I will accept no gifts from you."

He stood. "I will leave for London in the morning and discuss my financial situation while I am there. I will ask that a solicitor accompany me home to meet with you regarding your affairs. At that time, you may bring me up to date on everything at Hardwell Hall."

Her jaw tightened. "Very well. Once I do so, I will then leave and you may have your home all to yourself."

"I don't wish to rush you, my lady."

She assessed him. "But you do want me gone. That is clear. I understand, Your Grace. Good day."

Sebastian watched her walk away, the temptation of her lovely rump swaying back and forth doing odd things to his insides. It would be better for her to be gone. She was headstrong and knew far too much about him for comfort. The sooner she left Hardwell Hall, the better. She could go to London and place herself on the Marriage Mart and find some willing lord to make her his responsibility. He could be the one to tell her to dress appropriately and make her behave properly. Kiss those plump, rosy lips and give her half a dozen children.

The thought should appease Sebastian yet, for some reason, the idea of Lady Hadley kissing anyone bothered him a great deal.

Chapter Six

SEBASTIAN SAW NO reason to wait and decided to leave for London immediately. His feelings were mixed about Lady Hadley and he felt he needed to get away. He went to what was now his chambers where the bath awaited him, a luxury he had been looking forward to for longer than he could remember. It felt heavenly to sink into the hot water. He scrubbed away the grime, wishing he could wash away all the ugliness, both within and without. He refused to look at his marred limbs, staring off in the distance as he ran the soap over them. He was aware, though, as his fingers skimmed his chest of all of the multitude of scars from that time of torture. He squeezed his eyes shut, hearing his screams, finding his heart racing uncontrollably.

"Get a grip, man," he ordered himself.

Miraculously, the vision receded until only blackness was left. His heartbeat slowed. The memories had been pushed away, once more under lock and key. For how long, Sebastian never knew.

He finished bathing and rinsed, standing quickly to towel off. Locating his satchel, he removed the razor and shaved before dressing in his fresh shirt and placing the rest of his uniform back on. Going downstairs, he found Radmore.

"I am leaving for London and cannot say when I shall return. I want to take the carriage. Please have it readied for me immediately."

"At once, Your Grace," the butler said, his face a blank, reserving judgment.

Sebastian went outside, wishing to avoid seeing Lady Hadley again and waited in front of Hardwell Hall until the carriage was brought around. The driver was new to him, and he introduced himself. He made a split decision that before traveling to London, he would journey to see Jon. Blackstone Manor was only ten miles away, slightly out of his way, but he hoped he would find Jon there. He explained to Thomas where to head and then climbed inside the vehicle.

There was a possibility Jon and his bride were still in London. The Season wouldn't be over for a week or two by his estimate but he needed to see his friend desperately. Jon might be a rake but he was a loyal, steadfast friend. Sebastian badly needed to see a friend now.

He watched the passing scenery, almost numb to it, wondering if he would ever fit in again in England and the life he had left behind. War had scarred his body. His mind. His soul. He might never escape from the nightmares of it.

The carriage came to a halt and Sebastian threw the door open. He saw Roy, Jon's butler, hurrying to greet him.

"My goodness! Your Grace, it is so very good to see you again after so long a time."

"Hello, Roy. Might the duke and duchess be home?"

"They certainly are, Your Grace. Lady Elizabeth, too."

Suddenly, a voice cried out, "Sebastian!" and he saw his old friend racing toward him, wearing a huge grin on his face.

Jon threw his arms around Sebastian and pounded his back heartily "My God, when did you get home?" Jon asked.

"Today, actually," Sebastian said. "I took a chance to see if you might be home."

"I am. We are." Jon turned and Sebastian saw two women approaching them.

He recognized Elizabeth, though the skinny, awkward girl had turned into quite the beauty. She, too, embraced him.

"Your Grace, it is so very good to have you back on English soil.

You do remember me? I am Elizabeth, Jon's sister."

"How could I forget the tomboy who could skim rocks across the pond so well? Do you still like to do that, my lady?"

She grinned. "Very much so, Your Grace. In fact, if you stay, I will challenge you to a contest and we will see who can skim stones the best. But you must meet my new sister-in-law."

Elizabeth turned and the blond angel that had accompanied her stepped forward.

Jon quickly said, "This is Arabella, my duchess."

Sebastian heard the emotion behind the words Jon spoke. He bowed over the new duchess' hand and said, "It is a pleasure to meet you, Your Grace."

She smiled warmly. "It is an honor to meet a war hero of your stature, Your Grace. But please, call me Arabella. I know you are dear to my husband and I hope that we will see much of you since our estates are so close together."

"I hope for the same, Arabella," he said. "Please, call me Sebastian."

"Won't you come inside?" she asked.

"I would like that very much."

He went into the familiar residence. Very little had changed, giving him a feeling of comfort. They went to the drawing room and Arabella asked Sebastian if he would like tea.

"No, thank you. I only want to stay a few minutes. I am actually on my way to London now."

"London? But you just got home," Jon complained.

"I want to meet with my solicitors and get a clear picture of my finances," he said.

"Well, I have heard your estate is thriving. It's said to be in excellent order," Jon said.

"Oh. So you know about Lady Hadley," Sebastian noted.

"I know of her but have yet to meet her."

"Truly? But you live so close."

His friend frowned. "I know what Hardwick did to you, Sebastian. I wasn't going to be overly friendly to him once you left and I assumed my responsibilities here. Frankly, I have spent most of my year in London, only returning to Dorset for brief periods of time. That will change now."

Jon reached and clasped his wife's fingers. "Arabella and I want to spend more of our time in the country."

As the pair gazed lovingly upon one another, Sebastian felt the very air in the room change.

Elizabeth chuckled. "Sometimes, they are in their own world. They are so in love they don't know anyone else exists around them."

Reluctantly, Jon tore his gaze from Arabella's and said to Sebastian, "I highly recommend love and marriage, my friend. Are you thinking about it?" he asked pointedly.

Sebastian sighed. "I do know I will need an heir. I suppose I will have to wait until next Season and check out the Marriage Mart then."

"Oh, we can do better for you," Arabella said brightly. "We returned early from the Season because we are holding a house party in ten days' time for friends and our surrounding neighbors."

"You are?" he asked. "Andrew and I had corresponded and he had told me that he and Phoebe would hold one in my honor so that all of our old friends could get together and I could meet their wives."

"The plan had been for Weston and Elise, George and Samantha, and the three of us to go to Windowmere after the Season ended," Jon revealed. "You do know they have a son now. Robby."

"Yes, I had received news of that from Andrew. Imagine Andrew as a father now."

"Arabella decided everyone should come here instead," Jon continued. "That it might be too much for a new mother to plan for all of those guests to descend upon them."

"Phoebe is a little restless after so long at Windowmere during her confinement and beyond," Arabella interjected. "She would like to get out. They will bring the baby with them."

"The point is," Jon said, "everyone is already coming here for a house party. It will include our circle of friends, as well as some of Elizabeth's and several eligible men for the young ladies to get to know better."

Sebastian looked to Elizabeth. "I am surprised you have not wed yet, my lady. You have grown into quite the beauty."

She sighed. "I am enjoying myself. I know I have gone through two Seasons but think of all the men who go through five or ten before they ever settle down and choose a mate."

"You don't want to wait that long," her brother chided.

"You may wait as long as you wish," Arabella said. "Elizabeth is waiting for love, Sebastian."

He looked at the younger woman. "Then I hope you find it."

She smiled. "I hope you do, as well, Your Grace. You may like some of my friends. Who knows? You might find a wife among them."

He had thought to see if one of his friends' new wives had a friend or relative that he could make his duchess. He also made a quick decision to wrangle an invitation for Lady Hadley. If eligible men would be in attendance and one was drawn to her beauty and intelligence, she could quickly marry and no longer be a problem to him.

"What is that look in your eyes?" Jon asked. "It's the same one you used to have when you had an idea that would lead us into trouble of some sort."

Sebastian chuckled. "I would ask that you issue an invitation for Lady Hadley to attend your house party. She has never made a formal come-out, thanks to her remaining at Hardwell Hall all these years to look after the duke and the estate. She needs to mix in society now that he is gone."

Arabella nodded with approval. "A house party would be an ideal way to introduce Lady Hadley to society. Certainly it would be much better than being thrown into the *ton* as I was."

He wondered about her remark but had the good manners not to inquire about what she meant.

"Jon and I have heard she has managed your father's holdings for several years. It is one of the first things we heard upon our return a few days ago."

"Yes," he confirmed. "It seems she has not only run the household but assumed everything that was the duke's responsibility."

"She must be a remarkable woman," Arabella said. "I cannot wait to meet her. I believe we will become good friends."

"I think so, too," Elizabeth said brightly. "She is close to my age and has done so much. I am sure that I could learn a great deal from her."

They chatted for a few more minutes and then Sebastian said that he needed to get on his way.

"Are you sure you wouldn't wish to spend the night here and then have a fresh start for London in the morning?" Arabella asked.

"I suppose I could," he said, grateful for her extending an invitation for him to remain.

"Then that settles it," Jon said. "We will have dinner and talk about old times."

HADLEY HAD ALMOST finished going through the post at breakfast when a footman appeared with a silver tray bearing a note.

He approached her and said, "It is from the Duke and Duchess of Blackmore. Their messenger has been instructed to wait for a reply."

"Thank you."

She took the parchment and saw the seal of the Duke of Blackmore. She had known the name since the estate was but ten miles from Hardwell Hall, just a few miles on the other side of the local village, but she had never had any interactions with the duke or his family. Hardwick had mentioned once that the new duke was a former schoolmate of Sebastian's. From what she had learned through gossip over the years, Blackmore rarely came to his country seat, preferring to work his way through the ladies of London. She had recently heard, though, that the duke had taken a bride. Perhaps it was the duchess who now reached out to her.

The thought saddened Hadley. Over the years, she had longed for some feminine companionship. Unfortunately, she would be leaving Hardwell Hall all too soon and most likely never see the duchess again, much less gain her friendship. She wondered how far Sebastian had gotten on his journey to London, having learned of it when she came down to dinner last night. She had even made an effort and changed into one of the three gowns she owned. All were quite dated but she had thought to try and reconcile with him over the course of dinner. Radmore had informed her the duke had already left for London, making her feel small and embarrassed for the effort she had put into her appearance. She had told the butler she didn't have much of an appetite and requested a tray with the meal be sent to her room. She had picked at it, which was why she had gobbled down her breakfast so quickly this morning.

Breaking the seal, she opened the note and read it quickly.

My dear Lady Hadley –

I must first introduce myself. I am the Duchess of Blackmore, newly wed to the duke, and I wish to invite you to our upcoming house party, the dates of which are listed below. Several of my husband's friends, including the Duke of Hardwick, will be in attendance, along with some of our closest neighbors. Hardwick suggested that this would be a wonderful opportunity for you to enter society and both my husband and I agree. I have heard so much about you and I and my sister-in-law, Lady Elizabeth Sutton, look forward to making your acquaintance.

I do hope you will accept our invitation, my lady. I am eager to hear of all that you have accomplished at Hardwell Hall and am optimistic that we will become close friends.

Arabella, Duchess of Blackmore

A house party. Hadley remembered hearing of these long ago from her mother. Mama had said they were an excellent opportunity for a small segment of society to get to know one another on a deeper level and that, oftentimes, more than one betrothal would be announced at the end of them. Mama had talked of parlor games, musical evenings, riding, and tea parties. It had all seemed heavenly to Hadley. They never went anywhere and her father never invited company to be entertained. She had fallen asleep many an evening thinking about how fun such a social occasion might be.

It surprised her that the duchess had mentioned Sebastian. She supposed he must have stopped by to call on the Blackmores on his way to London. In a few of his letters, Sebastian had mentioned how he missed his friends from university and would certainly visit with them at length once he returned from war. She hadn't known the Duke of Blackmore was one of the men he was close to. She couldn't help but wonder what Sebastian had told the duke about her. Had they plotted together for a way for him to be rid of her?

She knew her time at Hardwell was coming to an end. Sebastian himself had told her once he returned from London, he wanted to receive a report of the estate. Hadley had planned to work on this during his absence. Then it would be time for her to find a new home. Perhaps she might make a friend or two if she attended this house party. Better yet, the possibility of a romantic connection might occur. She desperately needed something to take her mind off her absurd daydreams of Sebastian falling in love with her and begging her to remain at Hardwell Hall as his duchess. Those had been the fantasies of a foolish young girl who had been taken with the dashing war hero she had barely glimpsed. Though she believed she knew Sebastian almost as well as he knew himself from having read a hundred letters written by him, he had held her at arm's length from the moment he had arrived. She was but a stranger and it was obvious he didn't like or trust her much.

Why not end things on a high note and attend this party?

Hadley rose and told the waiting footman, "I shall write to the duchess now. Please come to the study and retrieve my reply in ten minutes."

She went to the desk where she spent a good deal of her time and composed her brief response, telling the duchess she would be delighted to attend the house party and how she looked forward to meeting both the Blackmores and Lady Elizabeth. Sealing it, she waited until the footman arrived to collect it for the messenger.

Once he left, worry set in. With only the three worn and outdated gowns to her name, she would have to do something regarding her lack of wardrobe. Sewing was a task she despised and had no talent for. She would have to go into Weymouth and see how many gowns could be made up in such a short time.

Since she had decided to go into town, she went and changed from her usual attire into one of the gowns. It had seen better days though she wore it infrequently. She wondered now what Sebastian would have thought of her in it last night. He probably would have laughed. Suddenly, she needed him to see her in feminine attire. She wanted to look beautiful. He may wish her gone but she wanted him to regret it long after she had vacated Hardwell Hall.

Going to the stables, she asked for her horse to be saddled. As the chestnut mare was brought to her, Hadley hoped that Sebastian would allow her to take the horse with her. She had picked out Hestia, naming and training the horse herself. The animal had been her closest companion after the duke. If she had to leave Hestia behind, both their hearts might break. Surely Sebastian wouldn't be so cruel as to deny her the horse. He had offered her an estate of her own. If he was willing to part with a house and land, surely he would allow her the mount.

Hadley rode to Weymouth and went straight to the dressmaker's shop. Mrs. Porter greeted her warmly.

"My, Lady Hadley, it's been forever and a day since I have seen you," the woman exclaimed. "I am sorry for your loss. I know you and the duke were quite close."

"Thank you, Mrs. Porter. The reason I am here today is that I need several new gowns."

The older woman sniffed. "You are stating the obvious, my lady. This gown is practically threadbare."

"I will be leaving Hardwell Hall soon. Before I go, I have been invited to a house party being given by the Duke and Duchess of Blackmore."

"Oh, my! That is good news. You will need an entire new wardrobe. Day dresses. Evening ones, too. When is the event?"

"In nine days."

"Oh! My stars!" the seamstress exclaimed, distress filling her plump face.

"I know that is not much time."

Mrs. Porter nodded. "I will sew night and day to see to your gowns, Lady Hadley. My sister and her two girls can help me. Come and let me measure you. We'll look at fabrics and—"

"The measuring is fine. As for fabrics, I will leave that in your capable hands, Mrs. Porter. Clothing has never interested me much and I have no idea what the current fashions might entail. I will let you make up what you see fit."

"Very well, my lady."

The seamstress measured Hadley and told her to return in three days' time for a fitting for the first batch of gowns.

As Hadley mounted Hestia and rode back to Hardwell Hall, she found it hard to contain her excitement. She would be meeting new people and turning the page to a new chapter in her life. Though it saddened her that it wouldn't include Sebastian, she brimmed with enthusiasm. She almost felt like a butterfly, shedding her cocoon and spreading her wings.

Passing the church, she decided to stop at the graveyard and went to the Duchess of Hardwick's grave. The flowers she had placed upon it still looked fresh.

Kneeling, she said, "Your son is home, Your Grace. He is a handsome man. A hero for helping bring Bonaparte to his knees. You know that I had told you my hopes of one day being his bride. That was only wishful thinking on my part. I will be going soon. I will miss having you to talk to. I feel as though we have been friends. I must look to my future, however."

Hadley touched the headstone. "I will come and tell you goodbye when my time here comes to a close."

She rose and mounted Hestia again and headed for home. No, not home. Hardwell Hall. She must start preparing herself for the day she would soon leave. In the meantime, she would begin preparing the reports Sebastian had requested, compiling everything she had done since she had taken the reins from the Duke of Hardwick. She wanted it to be letter-perfect. It would be her last gesture before departing for the unknown.

Chapter Seven

SEBASTIAN HAD BRAVELY met the enemy in Spain. Portugal. Belgium. So why was he sitting inside a Weymouth inn when he lived but a handful of miles away?

The answer was a pert, auburn-haired beauty with curves in all the right places and a smile that stole his breath.

He had arrived in Weymouth late last night and told himself it was easier to stay over and see his tailor first thing in the morning rather than return to Hardwell Hall and then come back to Weymouth to meet with Wilson. He had brought with him several items of clothing he'd had made up in London during his time in town. After three, lengthy meetings with his solicitors, he felt he had a firm grasp on his financial situation, which was very good, indeed, in no small part thanks to Lady Hadley. The London team was quite familiar with her, having met her years ago when she first came under Hardwick's guardianship. At least one of the members of the firm had gone to Dorset twice a year to visit with her and the duke and elaborate on the state of the Cooper family finances. From everything he had learned, the lady was thoroughly involved in the duke's financial affairs, offering him advice and helping manage his investments.

Though Lady Hadley had come of age and her money was no longer managed by his family, the same firm of solicitors had taken over for her and she'd had a direct hand in her own affairs. She had chosen wisely and had doubled the income her father had left her for her wardrobe and incidentals during her come-out. The dowry, twenty thousand pounds, remained untouched until she wed or would be hers outright if she had not entered a state of matrimony by the time she turned twenty-five.

He might have managed troops and contributed to military strategies but Sebastian had little idea how to manage an estate, much less so astutely. He found himself intimidated by the woman, more so than any opponent he had met on the battlefield. It might actually do him some good to invite her to remain at Hardwell Hall for several weeks and help him learn about the estate. Eventually, he would hire a manager for it but he wanted to have a hand in matters as the previous duke did. At some point, he would also need to journey to his other properties throughout England and see how those were being administered.

For now, though, he would collect his wardrobe from Wilson and then return home. From there, he would need to leave for Jon's estate and the house party. Sebastian wondered if Lady Hadley had accepted the invitation issued to her. If she had, they would need to ride in the carriage together to Blackstone Manor. The thought of being alone with her seemed daunting. She was a stranger to him—yet she knew incredibly intimate details about him. He didn't like that he had been laid bare to her. She was a clever woman. Stubborn, too, from the little he knew about her. It would be uncomfortable riding with just the two of them.

What he didn't want to admit was his attraction to her. She had more than beauty. She had an unusual intelligence rarely found in a man, much less a woman. For several years, she had been responsible for a vast estate and handled duties only that a man would normally manage. The combination of her brains and beauty might prove lethal to him. In so many ways he was undeserving of a creature like her. Though most citizens of Great Britain would deem him a hero, Sebastian knew exactly what he had done during the war and that he was anything but heroic.

Ultimately, he was unworthy of a woman with Lady Hadley's talents and attributes. Because of that, he didn't want to like her. He certainly didn't want to wed her. He needed a quiet, pliable creature who would be a good hostess and provide him with an heir. Someone who wouldn't trouble him too much and let him live within himself. His duchess needed to give him room to breathe.

Lady Hadley seemed to suck the very air from him.

Worse, he was itching to run his fingers through her auburn tresses. Kiss those plump, pink lips. Explore the sweet curves of her rounded bottom.

No, Hadley Hampton could never be the woman for him. She would push him. Question him. Want to know him. Sebastian didn't want any woman to do so, much less the one he chose for his wife. He would find a promising, polite, sweet-natured young miss, one who wouldn't be demanding. Lady Hadley seemed nothing but demanding. He feared it would be hard to hide his fears and inadequacies from her as it was.

What he needed were his friends. A little light entertainment at this house party. Mindless, pleasant activities to ease him back into society. From what Arabella had said, a few young ladies would be in attendance. Elizabeth had thought Sebastian might actually suit with one of her friends. It would be convenient if he did find his future spouse at this gathering. If he didn't, he dreaded going to London for the Season and having to attend dozens of events. He didn't like crowds of people anymore. He had never been very social before the war and was considered more on the quiet side to his friends.

Determination filled him. He would reunite with his closest friends and find a bride during the duration of the party. Hopefully, Lady Hadley could do the same and no longer be his responsibility. Not that she ever had been legally but she had given a great deal to the estate during her years with Hardwick. She deserved to start her own life now and find a bit of happiness.

He ventured downstairs to the inn's common room and soon had breakfast in front of him. He ate heartily and asked for a second cup of coffee, sipping it as his thoughts turned to his circle of friends. He had served with Andrew for a while and had last seen him three years ago before Andrew returned to England. It had been much longer since he'd been in George's and Weston's company, having bid them farewell when they had left university almost a decade ago. The same had been true for Jon until their quick reunion last week. He wondered how much the four men had changed since their younger days. They had all been kind and written him over the years, letters he had cherished since none came from home.

Things would be different now. He was different. Not the idealistic young man full of patriotism who marched off to war. He returned older, savaged by his time at war, with experiences the others would never be able to relate to. They also all had wed and their priorities would be their families, along with their responsibilities as dukes of England. Would he still fit in with them? Or had he changed so much that the friendships between them might never be as they once were?

Sebastian drained the remainder of the coffee and found Thomas in the stables.

"I will head to Mr. Wilson's tailor shop now. Bring the carriage around in an hour and then, hopefully, we can make for Hardwell Hall. After a brief respite, we will leave for Blackstone Manor."

"Yes, Your Grace."

He liked the driver, mostly because Thomas didn't speak much. He acted as a good soldier, never questioning orders, always doing what he was told.

Hadley Hampton would have made a terrible soldier. She would have challenged the wisdom of every order. Demanded to know why they marched in a certain direction or how they would engage the enemy. On the other hand, the lady would have made for an excellent general. She seemed perfectly capable of issuing orders and not liking to be questioned about them.

Sebastian shook his head. He had to stop thinking about the chit. She would soon be out of his life. All he wanted was peace and quiet. He doubted that would occur while Lady Hadley remained in residence at Hardwell Hall.

Arriving at the tailor shop, he stepped inside and greeted John.

"Good morning, Your Grace. I think you are going to be pleased with what Father and I have managed to come up with for you. We still have several items to finish but we have made good headway on your wardrobe."

Sebastian had called upon the two tailors as he left for London, telling them they would have more than a week to work on his order before he returned. He had deliberately worn his officer's uniform today, not wishing to hurt their feelings by showing he had also shopped in London for additional items.

"Ah, Your Grace," Mr. Wilson said as he came through the curtains. "It is very good to see you. Come, I want to have you try on a few things. I believe you will be able to leave today with most everything we've finished so far."

"I will be attending a house party at the Duke of Blackmore's for the next week or so. Because of that, there is no rush, Mr. Wilson. I can visit you again once I am back at Hardwell Hall."

The tailor had everything laid out for Sebastian. "Try on the shirts first, Your Grace. I will be back in a few minutes."

Grateful for the man's absence, he removed his uniform, including the shirt, and slipped the first one over his head, deliberately ignoring his scarred torso and arms. The garment fit well. So did the second. He left it on and told the tailor upon his return that since the first two fit, he was certain the others would, as well.

Wilson helped Sebastian into various items, not commenting on the array of marks on his legs. The shirt hid the worst of them.

"Everything seems to be in perfect order," he told the older man. "Your meticulous measurements made sure of that. I cannot see even a single trouser leg that needed a readjustment."

"I am glad you are pleased, Your Grace. John had a heavy hand in creating your ensembles."

"Then I will heap praise upon him. You plan for him to take over soon?"

Wilson chuckled. "Not nearly as soon as he would like. No, you will be stuck with me for another good ten years or more, Your Grace."

Sebastian made a point of thanking John for his hard work and declaring how the fit was better than anything in London. John flushed, glowing with the compliments.

"I will load everything into the wagon and deliver your wardrobe immediately, Your Grace," the younger Wilson told him.

"Please do so. I need to leave shortly after I arrive home for Blackstone Manor and will need to pack much of what you bring."

He returned to his waiting carriage and was glad the young tailor was bringing his purchases separately because the interior was full of boxes from his London tailors. He would need several footmen to bring them up to his chambers. Possibly Radmore could help him sort through these and what John would bring and help him pack for the house party. He hadn't asked about the duke's valet, a man Sebastian had loathed almost as much as the duke himself. If Sebastian had inherited the servant, he would ship him off to one of his other houses because he certainly didn't want the former valet hovering about, much less trusting him to put a razor to Sebastian's throat and shave him.

The trip to Hardwell Hall took little time with his carriage horses. He climbed from the vehicle and Radmore greeted him.

"Welcome home again, Your Grace."

"Good morning, Radmore. I have numerous boxes in the carriage that need to be brought up to my suite. Young John Wilson will also be arriving soon with things he and his father made up for me during my time in London. Those, too, should be brought straight up."

"I will see to it now, Your Grace. Your valet will be able to sort through everything and help you pack for His Grace's house party."

"About that, Radmore," Sebastian began.

"Never fear, Your Grace. Mr. Bardham arrived three days ago. He went to town with Lady Hadley this morning but they should be back any moment now. He is certainly looking forward to seeing you. Lady Hadley has had Mr. Bardham helping in the stables while you were away because she knew he wanted to be useful."

Surprise filled him. "Bardham . . . is here?"

"Yes, Your Grace. He is already a favorite with all the servants. A very friendly man. And he refused to allow Lady Hadley to drive into Weymouth this morning unaccompanied."

"I see."

"Why, here they come now," the butler proclaimed.

Sebastian turned and saw Bardham with the reins in hand. Literally, his one hand—since Bardham had lost his right arm during the war. He had been one of Sebastian's best soldiers and had refused to ship out for home after losing the limb, begging Sebastian to make him his batman instead. When Bonaparte had been defeated at Waterloo and Sebastian knew the war drew to an end, he had told Bardham if he ever wanted for a position, he should come to Dorset. It seemed his batman had done just that.

He glanced to Lady Hadley and saw her in a gown for the first time. It looked as if it had seen better days, being faded and worn. She must wear one when going to town. The back of the cart she rode in was filled with boxes similar to the ones he had brought with him. It hit him that she would have had to have a wardrobe made up herself if she had accepted the Blackmores' invitation.

Bardham pulled up. "Colonel Cooper! You are back."

The batman jumped from the cart and then reached his hand to help Lady Hadley down.

"I will see to carrying in your things, my lady, but first I want to say hello to the colonel. His Grace, I mean," Bardham corrected.

"Thank you for accompanying me to town, Mr. Bardham. I so enjoy your company." She turned and the smile she had worn when addressing the servant faded as she glanced at Sebastian. "Your Grace," she said stiffly. "I hope you had a safe journey from London."

"I did, my lady. Might you be attending the house party given by the Duke and Duchess of Blackmore?"

"Yes, I received their invitation and agreed to come."

"We will need to leave in an hour's time."

"I will be ready, Your Grace."

She went into the house and Bardham beamed at him. "Lady Hadley is wonderful, isn't she? A nicer lady than I have ever met. But how are you, Your Grace? How is being a duke?"

He chuckled. "I feel exactly the same, Bardham. Nothing has changed on my part, just having to remember to reply when I am addressed in a different manner."

"Let me get Lady Hadley's things taken up to her and then I will come for yours. I hear it's a house party we are going to. I hope you have something to wear other than your uniform."

Sebastian enjoyed the frankness of Bardham. He doubted anyone would ever speak so plainly to him now that he was a duke.

"I am glad you took up my offer to come to Dorset."

"I got to thinking about it and decided we were peas in a pod, Your Grace. Wouldn't be right to be separated. I know Lady Hadley—and Mr. Radmore—had their doubts when I arrived but you know me. I showed them what I could do." He grinned. "It's not every man who can say they lost an arm and yet gained more skills than he had before."

"I hear you have been working in the stables."

"Yes, I always did love horses. I have seen your estate. Lady Hadley took me around it on horseback."

He shook his head. "Then you have done more than I have since I have been home."

By now, an army of footmen had arrived and emptied his carriage of boxes. Sebastian saw John Wilson coming up the drive and once he stopped, introduced him to his new valet. More footmen arrived and emptied the tailor's wagon and others did the same for the cart Bardham had driven.

Bidding the young tailor goodbye, Sebastian motioned for Bardham to accompany him inside.

"So what did Lady Hadley need in town?" he inquired.

"We went to a dress shop. Mrs. Porter's, to be exact. Lady Hadley needed some gowns. She said she has never socialized much. Just gone to church and to town for a few assemblies. She needed things to wear for this fancy house party we are going to."

It tickled Sebastian how Bardham assumed he would attend the house party but Sebastian supposed every man invited would bring a valet. He might as well do the same.

"Will Lady Hadley be bringing a lady's maid?" he asked, thinking Bardham was already on good terms with Lady Hadley and might know.

"Yes, Your Grace. Millie helps Lady Hadley every now and then. She's not a real lady's maid but is good in a pinch."

It pained him to know Lady Hadley had gone without the help of her own maid. Sebastian still owed the woman debt of gratitude. Perhaps he could find her a true lady's maid before she left Hardwell Hall.

"Let's go upstairs, Bardham. We have much to sift through and pack in a short time."

"Never fear, Your Grace. Lady Hadley told me all about house parties and what to expect. I will have everything ready for you in no time."

As Sebastian accompanied his new valet upstairs, he wondered how a woman who had never made her come-out knew what occurred at a house party.

Chapter Eight

HADLEY HURRIED FROM the stables back to the main house, cutting through the kitchens and racing to the foyer where Millie paced.

"His Grace is already in the carriage!" her maid said urgently. "Threatening to leave at any moment."

"Do you have my—"

"I have everything, my lady. Come!" Millie urged.

They walked out the front door. Two carriages awaited. The large, grand ducal one would be for her and Sebastian. The second one would take their trunks, along with Millie and Bardham.

A nervous footman caught sight of her and quit pacing. He said, "She's here, Your Grace," and he offered Hadley his hand.

She ascended into the carriage and was dismayed that Sebastian sat on her preferred side, sprawled across the cushion, his mouth tight in disapproval. She took the seat opposite him as the footman shut the door. Immediately, the carriage swept into motion.

"I was about to leave you behind."

"I am sorry for my tardiness, Your Grace. I know you are used to the military and everything running precisely on a schedule but sometimes unavoidable delays can crop up and must be dealt with."

"What?" he asked brusquely.

"It's nothing," she assured him.

"If it delayed you, I should know."

"Suffice it to say it involved females." She left it at that, hoping he wouldn't press the point. Of course, the females had been mares and not people but he didn't need to know that.

"I see."

They traveled in silence for a few minutes and her heart should have slowed but she could still feel it racing inside her. They were alone. His very presence, so masculine in nature, had her pulse fluttering. Her belly, though, was roiling for a different reason.

"You look quite presentable," he said begrudgingly. "Much better than when I last saw you."

Hadley glanced down at the muslin gown, the palest of green, with darker green sprigging along its hem and neckline. She was a bit uncomfortable with the neckline, having never showed a smidgeon of her bosom before. Mrs. Porter assured her that this gown's cut would be considered demure. It was—when compared with other gowns the seamstress and her army had created for Hadley in a short time. She felt a blush tinge her cheeks, embarrassed to recall some of the afternoon and evening gowns that she had tried on and just how much cleavage they revealed.

"Thank you. I only had three dresses to my name and wear them infrequently. I had to go into Weymouth to have a small wardrobe fashioned." She paused. "You look very nice, as well, Your Grace. I assume we won't see you in your uniform anymore?"

"I told Bardham to burn it," he said, his jaw tightening.

The words told her everything she had suspected. Sebastian was uncomfortable with her because of everything he had put to parchment in his letters. Words he never said aloud to anyone. Words he had never thought would be read. He had arrived home to learn of her and discovered that she knew his innermost, most private thoughts. His every secret. She held a power over him that he worried she would let loose.

"Your Grace, I . . ." She stopped speaking and swallowed quickly, saliva springing in her mouth. "I . . . oh, please . . . stop the carriage. I fear I am going to be sick."

Quickly, he rapped twice and the vehicle slowed. Before a footman could open the door, Sebastian threw it back and leaped to the ground, reaching for her. Hadley stepped forward. His hands captured her waist and lowered her to the ground. He turned her away from him but still held on to her as she bent and retched. Embarrassment flooded her. Turning her again, he kept one hand steadying her and removed his handkerchief.

Grateful he had offered it, she said, "Thank you," and wiped her mouth, tears now filling her eyes.

"You should have told me you were ill," he said, his tone kind. "I will have Thomas return to Hardwell Hall."

"No, I am not ill."

His eyebrows rose.

"At least, not in the usual way. I merely . . . well . . . I cannot ride backward in a carriage," she blurted out. "It causes my stomach to roil something fierce."

His other hand had returned to her waist, lightly clasping it. "Then why did you not tell me when you entered?"

"I did not want to inconvenience you, Your Grace."

"Inconvenience me? You would rather be sick?" he demanded.

She winced. "I thought I could manage the distance."

Anger flushed his face. "I do not want to be treated in such a manner."

Hadley couldn't help but chuckle. "Well, you *are* a duke. Whether you like it or not, you will be treated thus until you go to your grave."

"It shouldn't matter," he said. "I am the same person I have been all my life. I have only been in England a short time and, already, I tire of hearing me constantly referred to as *Your Grace*."

"Better get used to it. You are one of the most powerful men in all of England now. You will have a seat in the House of Lords. Your rank means men will bow to you, not only because they possess a lesser rank but because many will behave in an obsequious manner."

"I don't wish to be fawned over."

"It's inevitable." She dabbed her mouth with his handkerchief, catching a whiff of sandalwood from it.

Or was it because she stood so close to him?

"We should continue on," she suggested.

"You are well enough to do so?" he asked, concern in his voice.

Hadley laughed. "I have lost all of my breakfast. There's nothing else left to come up."

Sebastian released her and they returned to the carriage. He clasped her waist again and placed her inside.

"Sit where I did before. That is an order, my lady."

Hadley took the seat and he sat opposite her. She was still ashamed of being sick in front of him but at least nothing had gotten on her gown.

He rapped twice and Thomas started the carriage in motion again. "Better?"

"Yes. Much."

They didn't speak for several minutes and then she asked, "Might you tell me something about the guests coming to Blackstone Manor? Part of my belly's grumblings could be blamed upon where I sat earlier but I will admit that I am very nervous to meet so many new people. Mama said twenty to thirty people attend house parties."

He studied her a moment. "Is that how you know about them? From your mother?"

"Yes." Hadley smiled. "Mama loved a house party. She told me about all of the activities and how fun they were to participate in. I have never attended any type of social event at all and while I am looking forward to it, my nerves are getting the better of me. I do know there will be things such as picnics and riding. Possibly rowing if there is a nearby lake. Lawn games during the day and parlor games in the evening."

"Yes, all of that and much more." He paused and then said, "I can tell you a bit about my friends that will be there. First, are the Eton Three—the Dukes of Windham, Colebourne, and Treadwell. They met at school when they were boys and were a tight circle of three, generously opening their ranks to Blackmore and me when we all arrived at Cambridge.

"Windham served in the Peninsular Wars with me."

"A duke went to war?" she asked, astonished by that bit of information. "I thought it quite unusual that you, as a marquess, joined the military."

Sebastian smiled and Hadley warmed at the first genuine smile from him. It made him even more handsome than usual.

"Windham wasn't a duke when we graduated. He was a second son destined for the army. Circumstances saw his father and his elder brother pass. That's when he returned to England and assumed the title. He wed a widow who had lost her husband and child in a carriage accident. The duchess recently gave birth to their first child, a son they named Robby. My understanding is the baby will accompany them to Blackstone Manor."

He raked a hand through his thick waves of dark blond hair. "Colebourne and Treadwell grew up on neighboring estates. Both men had broken betrothals and ran wild through society for a good number of years until they each wed within the last year. Colebourne married Treadwell's sister, a widow." He paused. "I had always thought they would be a good match. They weren't childhood sweethearts but I don't think I imagined the spark between them. I suppose it is a good thing they discovered it after all these years."

"What of Treadwell and his bride?" Hadley asked.

"He found his duchess when her carriage broke down in front of his country estate in Devon. She, too, is a widow and has a young girl. Treadwell seems as much in love with little Claire as he is with her mother."

"So, they are a love match? That is rare."

He shrugged. "Not as rare as I had thought. All four of my friends seemed to have found love while I was abroad."

His words surprised her. Her mother had prepared Hadley, telling her that people of their class did not wed for love. Her parents' marriage was the perfect example of that. She had wanted more and dreamed of love with Sebastian as she had come to know him through his letters over the years. After meeting him and seeing how war had hardened him, though, she knew it would take a miracle to tear down the walls he had built around himself.

Especially his heart.

"And what of our hosts?" she asked.

"Blackmore and I were closest when at university, being the two outsiders of the five of us. Don't misunderstand me. All four of my friends are loyal to a fault and good men but I seemed to always spend more time with him. Blackmore was very carefree. Everything came to him with ease. He only wed a few months ago. He wrote that his duchess is the daughter of a former Oxford don who became an earl. I had the privilege of meeting his duchess on my way to London. She is quite remarkable."

"I so look forward to meeting all of them. And the others who are invited. I would like . . . I would like to find a friend among them," she said quietly. "I have never had one before."

"Not a one?" he asked, his surprise obvious.

"No. Mama and I never left our country estate. The only two children of my class and similar age were two boys who were brothers. They refused to have anything to do with me simply because I was a girl. Then I came to your father and we did not socialize at all. Besides His Grace and my horse, Hestia, I have never truly had a friend."

Sebastian leaned over and took one of her hands in his. A delicious warmth spread through her at the contact.

"I hope you make several friends at this house party, Lady Hadley." He gently squeezed her fingers and then released her hand, sitting back and contemplating her. "Lady Elizabeth is close to your age."

"Who is she?"

"She is Blackmore's sister and has been out for two Seasons. I believe she is the reason the house party is being given in the first place."

"Oh, so she is a wallflower who has yet to find a husband?"

He laughed, a deep, rich laugh, which made her wish he did so more often. "Elizabeth is no wallflower. She is very strong-willed and I am sure most gentlemen don't want to take on such a handful. She was an interesting child. A true tomboy though she has grown into a beautiful woman."

Hadley heard the admiration in his voice for this woman and the little hope she had for them ever being together died. It was obvious Sebastian was interested in his friend's sister. After all, he had known her before he went to war. She was the daughter of one duke and the sister to another. From his words, Lady Elizabeth seemed spirited. The very kind of woman who should become a duchess.

"You will like Lady Elizabeth. She—and her sister-in-law—are very excited to meet you. They have heard of how easily you have handled all of the heavy responsibilities placed upon you."

"That won't be any longer, Your Grace. When we return home, I will go over my reports with you."

"Reports?"

"Yes. I prepared detailed ones for each of your estates and will let you read over them so I may answer any questions you might have. After that, I will be on my way. Who knows? I may find a husband at Blackstone."

"What?" he barked.

Hadley shrugged. "Mama told me house parties were often where those of the *ton* found their mates. I know I am a burden to you, Your

Grace. As long as I am around, some of your people will inevitably turn to me. Even if their loyalties should lie with you. The sooner I am gone, the more quickly you will settle into your role as Duke of Hardwick. I won't pay any attention to a gentlemen Lady Elizabeth might be interested in but if I find a man whom I believe would suit me, it would be best for all of us if I accept his offer and start a new life away from Hardwell Hall."

Chapter Nine

Lady Hadley's words troubled him even though he had hoped she would find a match at the house party. True, he wanted her gone. She made an excellent point regarding his servants and tenants. They had looked to her for so long that they might feel disloyal to her by turning to him. A case in point was why she caused them to be late in leaving for Blackstone Manor. Sebastian knew there was more to her story regarding females and problems but he hadn't wanted to press her. All he had wanted to do was look at her—and gobble her up.

The confident woman who wore her tight buckskin breeches and jaunty hats had morphed into even more of a beauty when tamed and placed into the proper attire. The gown she wore made her appear as a springtime flower and he longed to nibble the long column of her exposed throat. The swell of her rounded breasts had him salivating. She was the most beautiful woman he had ever seen. Not a conventional beauty but one all of her own making.

And he didn't want any other man to touch her, much less possess her.

Sebastian couldn't stop her from meeting the gentlemen attending Jon's house party. What he could do is let those men know *he* was interested in her. As a duke, they would back away and allow him the freedom to pursue her.

Is that what he wanted?

He hadn't thought so. She knew too much of his past for him to be truly comfortable. At least he had never put words on paper regarding that dark time. That was for him and him alone. No one would ever learn of what had been done to him behind enemy lines.

No, he should look for another woman that interested him. One who knew little to nothing about him. One who would be sweet and pliant and undemanding. Lady Hadley was none of those things. Yet his every thought continued to be about her. He wanted to kiss her. Taste her. Possess her. It had been difficult to keep his touch gentle as he held her while she had been sick and shaking. If Thomas and the footman hadn't been there, Sebastian would have been more than tempted to lower his head to hers and kiss the life out of her.

He firmed his resolve, knowing she wasn't the woman he should commit to. He would see if some more suitable candidate for his duchess would be in attendance at the house party. If so, he would court her and convince her to wed quickly, allowing him to avoid the Marriage Mart next Season. If no other woman caught his eye, he would bide his time until a more pliable candidate could be considered. Anyone other than the very tempting Lady Hadley Hampton.

The carriage began to slow and he glanced out the window. "We are almost there," he announced.

He watched as Lady Hadley turned to look out the window. She had a beautiful profile, with a straight nose and full, rosy lips. She leaned forward and sunlight caught the hair not hidden under her bonnet. It was as if it caught fire. She was fire to his ice. Sebastian knew in that moment that he would have to kiss her at least once. Perhaps if he did so, he could get these deepening urges out of his system and pursue a more appropriate candidate for his wife.

"Oh, it's very nice. Almost as nice as Hardwell Hall," she noted, pride evident in her voice.

He thought so, too. He had forgotten how grand his childhood home was until he had arrived there after so long an absence. Despite not wanting to be a duke, he certainly didn't mind residing in such a magnificent residence.

As the carriage halted, he told her, "That is the Duke and Duchess of Blackmore coming to greet us. Windham and his wife are behind them."

The door opened and the footman placed the stairs before her. Before she could move, Sebastian had already left the carriage and held a hand out to her. She took it and he seemed to draw strength and comfort from her small hand in his. She looked at him, perplexed, as he guided her down the steps.

Turning, he smiled widely, his body relaxing at the sight of his friends. "Greetings!" he called. "May I introduce Lady Hadley Hampton to you all?"

Jon and Arabella immediately moved toward her as Sebastian captured Andrew in a bear hug.

"It's been a few years, old friend," he said.

"It has, Sebastian. You look as if you came out unscathed."

For a moment, his heart seemed to stop and then he gave Andrew a ready smile. Glancing to the woman nearby, he said, "I assume this is the Duchess of Windham?" He took her hand and kissed it as he bowed. "I am truly delighted to meet you, Your Grace. But where is your son?"

She laughed, her azure eyes drawing him in. "Robby is napping at the moment. He is four and a half months old and besides smiling, he has discovered his voice. You should have heard his squeals during the carriage ride from Windowmere to Blackstone Manor. In fact, I am certain you did."

Sebastian liked her very much, as he had liked Arabella upon meeting her. Andrew and Jon had done well for themselves.

"Lady Hadley, I am so pleased to meet you," Andrew said. "Jon and Arabella have been telling us of how you have run Hardwick's estates for a good number of years. My Phoebe has decided I should bear our next child while she sees to managing Windowmere."

Everyone laughed heartily and Lady Hadley spoke to both the Windhams before Arabella encouraged everyone to come inside.

"Elizabeth is in the drawing room. Both the Colebournes and Treadwells arrived not a quarter-hour ago. We are all to rendezvous in the drawing room for tea," Arabella said. She slipped her arm through Lady Hadley's. "I hope you like lemon cake, my lady. Our cook's is light and moist."

They made their way inside and up the stairs to the drawing room, finding Elizabeth supervising where the several teacarts should stand. Immediately, she rushed over.

"Oh, you must be Lady Hadley. I am Lady Elizabeth Sutton and so very glad to meet you."

"Sebastian's here?" a voice roared.

He turned and saw Weston hurrying toward him. They greeted one another and then George was there.

"You are a sight for sore eyes," George proclaimed. "I never thought that blasted war would end. How are you, Sebastian?"

"As good as can be expected," he replied. "I arrived home and then quickly set out for London in order to meet with the family solicitors."

"At least you had time to get to a tailor," Weston said. "I am sure after wearing a uniform for years it feels wonderful to be dressed in civilian clothes."

"Yes, it does. I stopped in Weymouth first and then had additional clothes made up in London. I never want to be seen in red again," he joked.

Hearing voices, he turned and saw two women entering the drawing room. There was no mistaking Samantha, with her raven hair and aquamarine eyes mirroring those of Weston, her brother. Samantha had been a very young woman the last time he had seen her. Now, her beauty had matured and she glowed, in part because she was with child.

"Sebastian!" she cried, flinging her arms about him. "You seem even taller and broader than before."

"I would have known you anywhere, Your Grace."

"Oh, please, I am Samantha to you. Surely, that hasn't changed."

George came and slipped his arm about his wife's waist. "You can see I am the happiest of men, Sebastian. I have the best wife in the world and cannot wait for our child to be born this coming December."

Weston snorted as he led his new wife to Sebastian. She had rich brown hair and the most arresting violet eyes. "Meet Elise, my duchess and my world."

"I feel I already know you, Your Grace. Weston has spoken of you often and very fondly." Her eyes glimmered with mischief. "Perhaps we can talk later and you can tell me about some of your escapades at Cambridge. He has been reluctant to divulge any of them."

He chuckled. "I can—but all of us would be guilty as charged. What one of us did, the other four followed with gusto." He paused. "Have you met Lady Hadley?"

Sebastian didn't want her to be left out. He knew from her earlier words that she had never been in large or small social groups. He was at an advantage because he knew or had been introduced to almost everyone here. She, on the other hand, would most likely be overwhelmed meeting so many people at once.

He motioned them over and introduced the newcomers to her. He couldn't help but observe how gracious her greetings were and that she moved with a natural grace. A deep longing rose within him, which he quickly tamped down.

"Do you have feelings for her?" Jon asked quietly.

"No," he denied. "I merely feel responsible for her. Hardwick isolated her for many years. She has yet to be out in society. This must be overwhelming to her."

Jon snorted. "She seems quite in her element to me."

Sebastian looked and saw Lady Hadley speaking with several of the women with ease.

"Perhaps I shouldn't have worried. She seems to be holding her own."

"Shall we all sit for tea?" Arabella asked.

They seated themselves and the men and women naturally broke into two groups. He enjoyed catching up with his friends and hearing in detail about how they had all come to meet their spouses. Each man seemed besotted with his wife, causing a pang of jealousy to rise within him.

"When do your other guests arrive?" he asked.

"Not until tomorrow," Jon said. "We wanted our small group to come together first and celebrate having you back in our fold before the others descended upon us."

"Do you think Elizabeth will find a mate?" he asked.

Jon grew thoughtful. "It's possible. Several eligible gentlemen will be in attendance, as will be young ladies of marriageable age."

"Are you looking for a duchess?" Andrew asked.

Sebastian chose his words carefully. "I am aware now that I have returned to England that I have many responsibilities as a duke. One is getting an heir. I would like to wed quickly and quietly. If a woman attending this house party strikes my fancy, I am not opposed to a wedding sooner rather than later."

George glanced to the ladies and back. "Have you considered Lady Hadley? She has an unusual beauty and, from all reports, is highly intelligent. I know you, Sebastian. You will need a woman to challenge you."

"Lady Hadley certainly would do so," he agreed, "but I prefer a more docile, quiet wife. Lady Hadley seems to have strong opinions about everything."

"What is wrong with that?" Weston asked. "She has had to do a man's job for years. Your job. You couldn't choose a more eligible woman. She is intimately familiar with Hardwell Hall and your entire estate and properties."

"Too familiar," he said succinctly, hoping to move the conversation in another direction.

Unfortunately, his friends wanted to remain fixed on the topic of Lady Hadley.

"I, for one, think that Lady Hadley's familiarity with both the estate and your tenants would be beneficial," Andrew pointed out. "Let me tell you, becoming an instant duke with no training and no idea of what the title involved was hard on us all. Fortunately, Phoebe had run a household before we wed and was able to manage it and the servants with ease. What I didn't expect was how clever she would be with dispensing advice regarding the estate."

"Arabella may not have run an estate or a household but she is good with people and put my tenants at ease with her candor and charm," Jon said. "From what I know, Lady Hadley has the trust and ear of your people. That would go far, Sebastian, in helping you adjust to your new role in civilian life."

"My little bluestocking has proven her worth as a duchess many times over," commented Weston. "Elise is smarter than I am and keeps me on my toes as far as estate business is concerned. And our servants and tenants adore her."

"Sam comes up with many creative solutions when I am struggling regarding estate matters," admitted George. "My tenants love her almost as much as I do." He chuckled. "Sometimes, I believe she should be the duke since she has a more level head than I do and makes better decisions. I bow to her judgment more often than not."

George studied Sebastian, who grew uncomfortable under his friend's scrutiny. "If Lady Hadley has managed your father's affairs for as long as she has and done such an excellent job, she would be an ideal duchess." He paused, looking over at the women who were cackling like hens. "You would be a fool, Sebastian, if you passed over her in favor of another."

He didn't reply, feeling as if his friends' loyalty had shifted from him to Lady Hadley, a woman they merely knew by reputation.

"If you aren't interested in her, she will certainly be spoken for before the house party ends," predicted Jon, breaking the uncomfortable silence. "That is, if she is interested in marriage."

"She is," Sebastian confirmed. "She shared with me that she is ready to leave Hardwell Hall and start a new chapter in her life."

At that moment, he heard Elizabeth say, "To new chapters!"

Turning, he saw all the ladies with raised teacups, smiles on their faces as they toasted one another. Lady Hadley looked as if she were among friends she'd had for life, her face flushed, a wide smile on those tempting lips.

He tamped down the urge to march over and yank her to her feet and kiss her in front of the entire gathering.

Jon leaned over. "Are you certain you have no interest in her, Sebastian?" he pressed.

"None whatsoever," he lied smoothly.

Chapter Ten

Sebastian was considering slamming his fist into Lord Dean's pretty little nose. Or soundly thrashing Lord Banfield. Perhaps challenging Lord Stanhope to a duel. And he hadn't ruled out murdering Lord Hayward.

The house party's other guests had arrived yesterday and Arabella had scheduled activities for the afternoon and last night. Today would also see a full slate of things to participate in. Sebastian had kept his distance from Lady Hadley but his eyes were never off her for long. She had proven to be popular with both the men and women in attendance.

Thus, his reasons for contemplating vile deeds against the four gentlemen who had paid her the most attention.

He watched now as Lord Hayward, a rakehell if he ever saw one, demonstrated how Lady Hadley should knock her lawn croquet ball to achieve the most success. If he touched her, Sebastian would beat him to a pulp.

"Do you agree, Your Grace?"

He turned his attention back to his companions, three of the loveliest ladies at the house party and all friends of Elizabeth's. Lady Callamina was blond, petite, and very shy. Lady Veronica had dark hair and a curvy figure and was a terrible flirt. Lady Pamela had dark brown hair and a boyish frame and seemed a bit mischievous.

"I would rather hear your opinion, Lady Veronica," he said

smoothly.

As she spoke, he glanced back at Lord Hayward, who winced as his pupil's ball went astray.

"That's not quite right, my lady," the earl told Hadley.

Sebastian rose. "If you will excuse me. Hayward seems to be mucking things up."

He sauntered to where the earl stood. "I think you have done all you can, my lord. Let me see if I can help instruct Lady Hadley in the fine art of croquet."

Glaring at the man, Hayward finally received Sebastian's message. "Of course, Your Grace," he said. "I will leave it to you."

"It is not Lord Hayward's fault. I just don't seem to understand how to strike the ball in order to make it go in the direction I choose." Lady Hadley sighed. "I have never played games before. I was hoping I would be better at them."

She worried her bottom lip, causing a sear of flames to lick him.

"You were excellent at lawn tennis yesterday. And you and Lord Dean won at charades last night."

She smiled. "That is because Lord Dean is very clever. I merely attached myself to him and that is why I met with success."

"You are being modest," he chided. "You are every bit as smart as the viscount." He cleared his throat. "On to improving your croquet game."

"I suppose any improvement will be welcomed," she said, a teasing light in her eyes. "At this point, no one will want to partner with me. I appreciate you taking the time to work with me, Your Grace."

"You should call me Sebastian," he told her.

She frowned, an adorable crease in her brow causing his heart to sing. "That would not be appropriate, Your Grace."

"Not in front of everyone. Just when we are alone," he suggested.

Color rose on her cheeks. "I don't see when that would ever happen. It is not advisable for a young lady to be alone in a gentleman's company."

"The rules of Polite Society aren't enforced quite as strictly as house parties," he assured her.

"I would rather not," she said dismissively.

Ignoring her remarks, he addressed the game. "The first thing you should always do is stalk your ball. That means walking the line to where you wish to place your shot. Even if it is a short distance. You want to see if there are any impediments along the route."

She slowly nodded. "I see. That makes sense. Lord Hayward never mentioned I should do that."

He was certain Hayward had been too busy peering down the front of Lady Hadley's gown, which revealed the hint of creamy breasts.

"Hayward is an idiot."

"I beg your pardon? I have found the earl to be quite amiable."

Ignoring her defense of the man, Sebastian continued. "Next, you will return to where you will make your shot and grip your mallet firmly, keeping your hands steady. Move to your ball and make sure your toe is level with the handle of your mallet where you plan to strike."

She said, "Let me try."

Her face serious, she walked along the path her ball would travel and returned. Gripping her mallet, she stepped to the ball. Sebastian moved directly behind her, his arms coming around her, his body pressed against hers. The scent of vanilla wafted from her, teasing him.

"Your hands are not close enough," he said, adjusting her grip.

He sensed the hitch in her breath as he continued to lean against her, his hands over hers, their bare skin touching.

"It's good to always take a few practice swings to calm yourself."

He guided her back a few steps and then helped her swing the mallet.

"Before, you were raising your mallet too high as it came back.

Have it go no further than this."

He demonstrated again and then let her power the swing, his hands still resting along hers. Neither wore gloves, due to the informality of the house party and the heat of the summer sun. Her skin was as soft as silk and he longed to skim his fingers up her arms.

"Keep your shoulders still. Concentrate on the exact place you wish to hit your ball."

"I am looking at it," she said, her voice small and low.

"Good. Now, we'll swing the mallet back slowly. The further you wish the ball to go, the longer your backswing."

"Oh. I didn't know that."

He brought her arms back, his upper arm lightly brushing against her full, round breast. "Keep looking at the point of impact. Guide your mallet, pulling it forward. Keep your wrists firm. Not locked. A bit of flexibility helps. Then follow through directly along the line of your aim."

Sebastian guided her through several practice swings and then moved her closer to the ball. He fought the urge to brush his lips along her neck. He knew he should step away soon before he became too aroused but he was thoroughly enjoying the feel of her in his arms and the heady scent of vanilla swimming about him.

"Are you ready?" he asked.

"Yes." The word came out as a whisper.

"We'll do this together."

He helped her strike the ball, using just the right amount of pressure. It ran along the lawn and came to a halt.

"I did it!" she exclaimed. "Oh, that made so much sense."

Reluctantly, he released her. "It could be beginner's luck. Try again."

This time, he stepped away from her as she walked through all of the steps he had taught her. Her second ball stayed true to the course.

"You should not want for a partner now, Lady Hadley."

Her radiant smile threatened to tear through the walls he had built around himself.

"Thank you, Sebastian," she said softly.

Hearing his name on those kissable lips caused desire to flicker within him.

"You are welcome, Hadley," he replied.

Suddenly, Lord Hayward appeared. "It seems our hostess is ready for match play to begin. Would you do me the honor of partnering with me, Lady Hadley?"

Her eyes flicked to Sebastian and he nodded.

"Yes, my lord. I would be happy to be your partner." She smiled sweetly at Sebastian. "And thank you, Your Grace, for explaining the process of how to strike the ball. Any future success I have will be attributed to your tutoring skills."

He went and stood to the side with Andrew, who held Robby in his arms. The baby gurgled happily as Andrew looked on with pride.

"You enjoy being a father," he said.

"More than anything in the world." Then his friend grinned. "Well, almost anything. Being with Phoebe is my favorite thing in the world but holding my son is a very close second."

They chatted idly about various men they had known in the war and matters regarding their estates as play went on. Sebastian saw Hadley had taken to the game with ease after his brief lesson with her. He could still smell the faint scent of vanilla that seemed to linger on him and idly wondered what it would be like to have her in his bed, only wearing the sweet scent and nothing else.

"She would make for a wonderful duchess," Andrew commented.

"Who? I have met several eligible women here."

Andrew frowned. "You are deliberately being obtuse, Sebastian. It's not like you to pretend. You know I refer to Lady Hadley."

"She is lovely," he agreed. "A little obstinate, however. I think I need a more malleable woman to become my duchess."

Andrew shook his head, his face stern. "I never took you for a fool, Sebastian." He strode off, returning his son to Phoebe's arms and then going inside the house.

Sebastian watched as Hadley and Hayward won the round. Arabella joined him.

"Lady Hadley is quite remarkable."

He said nothing, feeling it safer.

She slipped her arm through his. "I have always been an observer, Sebastian. I spent many hours in the company of my father's students. I can tell you are interested in her."

"She is interesting," he admitted. "But so are many other guests you have invited. I have enjoyed spending time with Lady Pamela and Lady Veronica, for instance."

"They are nice young ladies but they don't have Lady Hadley's intelligence or unusual beauty. And you don't watch them a tenth of the time that you spend gazing upon Lady Hadley."

He looked down at her. "You are like a dog with a bone, did you know that, Arabella? Just because you have found love with Jon doesn't mean I will be able to do the same," he said, his temper rising.

"I never supposed love would come my way, Sebastian," she said softly. "I almost refused it when it came along. Please. Open your heart to the possibility of it."

She leaned up and pressed a kiss to his cheek. "You are as a brother to my husband. I would see you as happy as Jon is."

With that, she slipped away. Sebastian found he had tired of being around others and decided to retreat to the library. He would bury himself in a good book and enjoy a bit of solitude.

Most of all, he would do his damnedest not to think about Hadley Hampton.

HADLEY HANDED HER mallet to a footman and then thanked Lord Hayward for being her partner.

"The pleasure was all mine, my lady."

He captured her hand and brought it to his lips, kissing it as he gazed provocatively at her. She pulled it away.

"I think I will go and join my friends," she told him and made her way to where Phoebe sat with Robby in her lap, talking with Samantha and Elise. As Hadley arrived, Arabella joined the group and also took a seat.

"Ah, fresh off your victory," Elise said as Hadley sat.

"I had an excellent instructor," she said and then looked at Robby longingly.

"Would you like to hold him?" Phoebe asked.

Hadley nodded. "Very much so."

Her new friend handed the baby over and she cradled him in her arms. A strong yearning filled her suddenly, crashing into her like a tidal wave. She had always delivered babies on the estate and then left them with their mothers, never giving them a second thought. In this moment, she realized that she was meant to be a mother. Robby cooed and then shrieked loudly, startling her.

"He does that," Phoebe said. "I think he enjoys testing out his lungs now that he has discovered them."

She glanced at the women seated there, knowing she had already made good friends. They had quickly bonded and all four duchesses had begged her to address them by their Christian names when they were together. Hadley was amazed at how quickly she felt comfortable with the four women, and Elizabeth, too. She had longed for friends for so many years and now seemingly had an abundance of them.

Robby yawned and then closed his eyes. Hadley bent and brushed her lips to his head.

"Shall I have his nanny retrieve him?" Phoebe asked.

"Let me hold him a bit longer," she begged, not quite ready to give up the warm, sweet bundle.

"George and I cannot wait for our child to arrive," Samantha declared.

"How are you feeling?" Elise asked.

"Very well after an initial bout of nausea," Samantha revealed. "I have much more energy recently. I know that will fade as I grow larger, however."

"But it is worth it," Elise said, her eyes following her daughter as Claire chased after a butterfly. Her hand went to her belly. "I am with child again."

Everyone sat up, eager expressions on their faces.

"I haven't told Weston yet. I wanted to wait until I was sure. I am now and so I will tell him tonight. The baby should come next March."

"My brother is already so happy being a father to Claire," Samantha said. "He will be over the moon with this news."

"I may also be with child," Arabella said quietly, gaining everyone's attention. "My breasts have been tender. My courses were to come this week and they haven't. I will give it another week to be sure and then I will tell Jon once all our guests have left."

"Jon will make for an excellent father," Phoebe declared. "He has constantly wanted to hold Robby and play with him. Not many men do so."

"You look like a mother yourself, Hadley," Arabella commented. "Have any of my guests caught your attention?"

She started and the baby frowned, protesting with a wail. His nurse came running over and Phoebe asked her to set Robby down for a nap. Nothing was said until the nurse left. Hadley sensed her cheeks burning as four pairs of eyes focused on her.

"I am getting to know a few eligible gentlemen," she began.

"Lord Dean?" asked Phoebe. "So blond and lean. He's quite shy, though very smart. And you did win at charades with him last night."

"What about Lord Banfield?" asked Elise. "The earl is very nice-looking with his curly brown hair and sturdy frame. He seems a reliable sort and has paid you special attention, I believe."

"I saw you enjoying yourself with Lord Stanhope earlier this afternoon," Samantha said helpfully. "He seems to laugh at everything and is quite amusing."

"They are all very nice," she said primly. "I also spent time talking with Lord Hayward while we were partners but I know he is not for me. He is a terrible flirt. I think he was looking down my gown the entire time we played lawn croquet."

"I think Elizabeth might be interested in Hayward," Samantha said. "She is certainly strong enough to tame the earl's wayward ways. And as they say, a reformed rake makes the best of husbands." She grinned. "I know so for a fact."

"You haven't mentioned the obvious choice," Arabella stated. All eyes turned to her. "I think a match with Sebastian would be ideal."

Hadley's face flamed at the suggestion. "No, that wouldn't be a good idea at all," she protested quickly.

"Why not?" her hostess demanded. "Sebastian is a patriot. A war hero who gave all for his country."

"That's the problem," she said quietly. "I think he gave so much that he has nothing left to give anyone else."

"He's barely been home," Phoebe pointed out. "I know from Andrew that there is a period of adjustment from busy life on the front lines to a more sedate life in the country." She took Hadley's hand. "I think Sebastian is a fine man from what I have seen and what Andrew has shared with me. You should give him a chance. If that is what *you* want. Your heart will tell you."

Tears sprang to her eyes and Hadley blinked them back. "My mind tells me it is foolish to wish for a match with him—but my heart calls out for him," she admitted.

"Have you kissed him?" Elise asked.

"Oh, yes, you must kiss him," Samantha encouraged. "It is the best way to decide if you are meant for one another."

Her gaze dropped to her lap. "I have never kissed anyone. I have no idea how to go about doing so."

Phoebe squeezed her hand. "It's rather simple, Hadley. Just touch your lips to his and let nature follow its own course."

She lifted her head. "But where? How?"

Arabella stood. "I can easily solve that. I believe I need a stroll through the gardens." She glanced around. "I see Jon just stopped Sebastian and is conversing with him now. You will accompany us."

"I am confused," she said.

Arabella gave her a knowing glance. "We will go to the gazebo. Then I will make sure we are far enough ahead of you and out of sight. One kiss will help you determine if Sebastian is your destiny. Come along, Hadley."

She rose and her hostess came to her. Arabella linked arms and led her away from their friends and straight to Sebastian and Jon.

"There's my darling," Jon said, his eyes lighting up as he caught sight of his wife, causing wistfulness to run through Hadley.

"I promised Hadley I would show her the gardens," Arabella said casually. "What condition are your gardens in at Hardwell Hall?" she asked Sebastian.

"I have not toured them," he said. "I have barely seen the inside of the house, much less my estate."

"Then come with us. You might see something you'd like to include in yours that we have in ours." Arabella released Hadley's arm and took her husband's. "Shall we, my darling?"

She led her husband away. Hadley swallowed and looked at Sebastian.

"Are you familiar with the Hardwell gardens, my lady?" he asked.

"Very much so."

He offered his arm to her. "Then you will be an excellent guide."

She tucked her hand into the crook of his arm and they followed

Jon and Arabella. Sebastian's arm felt hard with muscle. She imagined his entire body was the same, based on his broad shoulders and the way his thighs looked in the tight buckskin breeches he wore. A shiver ran through her.

"Are you chilled?" he inquired politely.

"No."

They reached the gardens and entered. Arabella pointed out several varieties of flowers as they continued along the path. Hadley confirmed the ones that were already in the gardens at Hardwell Hall. They passed over a bridge, the gurgling of the stream below unheard because the blood pounded so fiercely in her ears. Each breath caused her to inhale the clean, masculine scent of Sebastian, tinged with the sandalwood soap he used. Her insides were as muddled as her brain.

Would she be able to summon the courage to kiss him?

They reached the gazebo and Jon pointed out aspects about the structure, none of which she heard. Arabella had them all take a seat and Hadley shared a bench with Sebastian, who seemed to take up most of it on his own. Then Arabella stood.

"I forgot that I need to speak to Cook. Come, Jon, escort me back to the house. It cannot wait."

Sebastian started to rise and the duchess added, "No, please, stay and enjoy the peace and serenity. I know being around so many guests can be trying at times. We will see you later."

As Arabella led her husband away, Hadley knew she had been given this opportunity. If she kissed Sebastian and he withdrew, she would know he was a lost cause. If he didn't, though, this place might be the one they started building a future together.

She turned and looked up at him, wondering how her lips were supposed to reach his. They wouldn't unless she stood. She summoned every ounce of strength and courage she had, willing herself to push to her feet.

Before she moved, though, Sebastian lowered his head and pressed his lips to hers.

Chapter Eleven

SEBASTIAN HAD RESISTED the urge to kiss Hadley long enough. They were alone. No one would see. She wouldn't be compromised by a single kiss, forced to wed him. More importantly, he could satisfy his curiosity—and hopefully quell the need for a kiss.

Her kiss . . .

He touched his lips to hers, knowing it would be her first time and wanting it to be gentle. Her lips were as soft as a pillow and pliant beneath his. Need shot through him. His hands moved to cup her face, wanting the feel of her skin. His thumbs stroked her satin cheeks as he pressed his mouth more firmly against hers. Her hands fluttered to his chest, the palms flat, heat searing through him at the touch. He needed more. Much more.

His lips slanted over hers, the kiss becoming harder. More possessive. It still wasn't enough. He gently caught her full, bottom lip with his teeth and softly bit into it. She whimpered, the sound shooting rockets through his blood. His hands slid down the long column of her neck and landed on her shoulders, gripping them. Her fingers tightened, clutching his clothing. The scent of vanilla surrounded them, wafting from her skin.

Slowly, he dragged his tongue along the seam of her mouth, back and forth, until she understood his demand and opened to him. Greedily, he plunged his tongue into her mouth, capturing its sweetness. She mewled like a small kitten, her fingers kneading against him. He deepened the kiss, exploring her leisurely. Fully. Completely.

Then she playfully responded, her tongue gliding along his. Sebastian groaned. He yanked her to her feet and his arms encircled her, pressing the length of their bodies together. Her breasts felt full and he longed for a taste of them. He told himself no. Restraint was key. This was her first kiss. He wouldn't maul her like some scoundrel.

Still, he broke the kiss. She protested but then sighed as he trailed kisses along her jaw. Hadley shivered and satisfaction ran through him. He moved to her ear, kissing the shell and then capturing her lobe and nipping it gently. She moaned, her fingers pushing into his hair. He moved to her throat and found her pulse beating wildly, licking the point to the rhythm of its beat. His hands roamed her back and slid to her buttocks, capturing and kneading them as his mouth returned to hers. Greedily, he drank from the sweet nectar within, the blood rushing to his ears.

Hadley moaned again, pushing herself against him. That was when Sebastian knew he must stop. The one, innocent kiss he had wanted to steal from her had turned him into a raging inferno. His cock stirred and he wanted nothing more than to plunge it deep inside her.

He couldn't. He was damaged goods. She was bright sunshine to the darkness in his soul. She wasn't the cure for the emptiness that raged within him. He would only drag her into the black void within him and she would become lost, swallowed whole, disappearing without a trace.

Sebastian broke the kiss and took a moment to drink in her loveliness. The cornflower blue eyes, slightly dazed. The lips swollen and even rosier than usual. She was everything he wanted and the last thing he should take. He would use her up and make her miserable.

Reluctantly, he released her and said, "I apologize. I never meant to do that. To let things go so far."

Anger filled her eyes. "You are apologizing for kissing me?"

"Yes. It was wrong."

"How can you say that, Sebastian? Everything about it was right."

He agreed—but could never tell her that. If he did, it would give her hope.

"One kiss does not bind you to me," he said, bringing his arms behind his back and locking his fingers because he didn't know how long he could fight the urge to take her in his arms again. "No one saw it. Nothing has changed."

"Everything has changed," she said bluntly. "I know you felt what I did. We are meant to be together, Sebastian."

"No. That can never be." He sighed. "I am broken, Hadley. Things that happened to me during the war have made me an empty shell."

"You are wrong," she said stubbornly. "I know you, Sebastian. We may not have shared but a few conversations together but I know the man you are from your letters. You are good and kind. Loyal to a fault." She frowned. "I never would have taken you for a coward, though."

He winced.

"You know there is something special between us."

Firming his resolve, he said, "Be that as it may, I will not ruin your life. I cannot offer marriage to you, Hadley. I would make you fiercely unhappy and I won't see myself do that to you. You need a man who will be a partner to you. One who will love you. I have no love inside me. I have nothing to give."

Her eyes grew stormy. "But you *will* wed?"

Sebastian nodded glumly. "I must. I will need an heir. I will keep a polite distance from my wife. She will give me an heir and then we will do as many of the *ton* do. Go our separate ways."

Hadley's hands balled into fists. "You *are* right. I deserve someone much better than you. A man who will be my best friend. A lover who will introduce me to mysteries beyond my comprehension. I need a husband who will cherish me and our children. Who won't be afraid to show affection to me in front of those children. A man who is strong and confident in himself and will play an active role in his children's lives, not one who will slink away and lose himself in women and drink."

She stepped to him and it took all his willpower not to release his hands and hold her to him now—and always. She touched her palm to his cheek.

"I hope one day you will heal, Sebastian. That you will recover your soul and spirit and find love."

Hadley softly brushed her lips against his and then pulled away. Without another word, she turned and left the gazebo, her head held high. Sebastian watched her, knowing his only hope for salvation receded with each step she took.

When she was gone from his sight, he collapsed onto the bench. The only time he had ever cried was when his mother died.

Until now.

He buried his face in his hands and wept for what might have been.

HADLEY WAS RELIEVED she didn't start shaking until after she was out of Sebastian's sight. As she wound her way through the gardens, her heart ached, causing a physical pain to throb inside her. Her throat grew thick with unshed tears. She finally stopped and sat on a bench to collect herself before she exited the gardens and came into contact with any of the other houseguests.

Sebastian was wounded far deeper than she had ever believed. She knew the war had harmed him emotionally from what had poured forth from him in his letters but this went beyond that. Something had occurred—possibly in the time when his letters had stopped—changing him in ways she could only guess. He believed himself ruined in some manner, not worthy of finding happiness and pursuing a life of fulfillment.

He'd claimed he would wed and keep his wife and family at a safe distance. That was not the Sebastian she had come to know over the years. For the first half of the years in which he had been gone, his attitude had been positive in each piece of correspondence. Thoughtful. Strong. As the war had continued, though, she could read between the lines how it weighed upon him until finally he wrote of his fears and angst. Still, some event had happened in which he changed fundamentally from the man he had been to the one who wished to lock himself away from the world. Oh, she didn't think he would become a recluse. He would always be diligent in his duties, caring for his tenants and properties. He would see his friends and pretend to the world that nothing was wrong. But it was as if he had died inside and nothing could create a spark of life within him again.

Hadley knew he was not indifferent to her. No man could kiss like that and not feel anything. The thing was that Sebastian didn't want to feel anything. He believed he didn't deserve to feel anything. The question was whether or not she would fight for him.

For them.

Already, he had torn her heart in two by pushing her away and, metaphorically speaking, her heart lay broken and bleeding. Did she have the strength—and courage—to charge forth, regardless of the consequences? She could walk away now and forget him. Try to forge a new life without him in it. Find a man to like, if not love, and learn to be happy. Or she could risk everything, including permanent heartbreak, and attempt to rescue Sebastian from the quicksand in which he sank deeper each day until his essence disappeared for good.

Resolve filled her. She loved him, flaws and all. Hadley knew whether he admitted it or not, he cared for her. More importantly, she loved him. Her love would be the healing balm to pour onto his soul. It was a risk worth taking. If anyone needed saving, it was Sebastian Cooper. She would be like the captain of a ship and go down fighting if she must. She prayed she wouldn't fail. She must succeed.

For both of them.

Drawing on reserves of strength she never realized she had, Hadley stood and returned to the house. The butler told her tea would be served in the drawing room in a quarter-hour. She went to her bedchamber and splashed cold water upon her face. She wouldn't change her gown as every other female would simply because she had a limited amount of them. Instead, she composed herself and thought of a battle plan. She would need help, though.

And now she had friends to see her through the coming trials.

Going downstairs, she saw Arabella instructing two maids where to roll the teacarts. Her friend saw her and smiled, coming toward Hadley to greet her.

"Did you accomplish the mission and kiss our reluctant duke?" she asked quietly.

"I did. He also rejected me outright."

"What?" Arabella gasped. "Surely, no, Hadley."

"Indeed, he was quite clear regarding his lack of intention toward me."

"Despite the fact he kissed you."

"Repeatedly," she confirmed. "And it was divine."

Arabella frowned. "I am confused."

"So was I. I need your help, Arabella. And the others, too."

The duchess nodded sagely. "Tea is come and go this afternoon. I will gather the troops and we will meet to plan our battle strategy. Go to my winter parlor. We'll join you shortly."

Hadley did as requested and, within ten minutes, Arabella brought Phoebe, Samantha, and Elise with her. She closed the door and each duchess seated herself.

"We have a crisis," Arabella proclaimed.

"Does it involve Sebastian and Hadley?" Samantha asked.

"Yes," Hadley confirmed. "We kissed in the gazebo."

"Oh, you were very brave to do so, Hadley," Elise said. "I don't know if I would have had the courage to initiate a kiss with Weston."

"I didn't," she admitted. "I was going to. Arabella and Jon left us alone in the gazebo. I mustered my courage and before I could kiss Sebastian, he kissed me."

"That is wonderful," Phoebe proclaimed and then hesitated. "Unless you didn't like his kiss, that is."

"Oh, I adored it. It felt as if the earth moved beneath me. I yearned for more than his kiss. What, I am not quite sure. I only know I was restless and unfulfilled, despite enjoying his every touch." Hadley drew in a deep breath and expelled it. "Sebastian apologized for kissing me. He said no one saw us together in an embrace and that I was under no obligation to him."

The four duchesses frowned. "Go on," urged Arabella.

"He believes the war damaged him irreparably and that if we wed, he would make me miserable. Yet at the same time, he admitted he needed an heir and would need to make plans to wed another woman. He will be polite and keep his distance from his duchess and they will live separate lives."

"No, that won't do at all," Elise said fervently.

"I agree," Phoebe added. "I know war is hard on a man's soul. Andrew still has nightmares every now and then. What Sebastian needs is a loving woman to soothe him and bring him back to life. You are that woman, Hadley."

"I agree," she said. "But since Sebastian does not, I plan to fight for him. He's already broken my heart. Either I will fail in my efforts and my heart will become permanently trampled upon—or I will succeed in helping him to heal and build a life with him."

"What do you need from us?" Samantha asked. "You know we will help in any way we can. Men are stubborn, though."

"I need your advice. A plan on how I should proceed," she declared. "A way to banish the ghost of Bonaparte that hovers over

Sebastian."

"Do you think he was as moved by the kiss as you were?" Elise asked.

She nodded enthusiastically. "Yes. It wasn't a single kiss. It was many. They began gentle and grew bolder and possessive. By the end, I felt branded by him. I could see he was shaken by the experience, as much as I was."

"It's good knowing he has feelings for you," Arabella said.

"I will do whatever I must," Hadley declared. "I love him, despite him pushing me away. I understand he wishes to protect me from whatever darkness lies inside him."

"Love is a powerful motivator," Phoebe said. "Sebastian may love you, as well, and sees himself as a hero, denying himself of you even as he shields you from whatever he suffered during the war." She paused. "Hadley, Sebastian may be too broken to love a woman. Are you willing to accept that?"

"Yes," she said firmly. "I will have love enough for the two of us. I will not let him slink off into the shadows. I want to bring him into the light." Her eyes filled with tears. "Please, help show me a way to rescue him."

"Since he was obviously moved by kissing you, you will need to make yourself as alluring as possible. Tempt him back to you," Samantha suggested.

"He may need more than that," Elise said. "He may need a firm push. I do not suggest you lead other gentlemen astray but I do believe if you make Sebastian jealous, it will bring him to heel more quickly."

"I agree," Phoebe said. "Be happy and engaged with the other male guests. Let him suffer a bit, seeing you happy in the company of others."

"What if that doesn't work?" Hadley pressed.

"Then we will reconvene and alter your strategy," Arabella stated. "Until then, we will make sure that each of our husbands sings your praises to Sebastian at every opportunity. I know Jon already adores you and has told me he believes you would be good for Sebastian."

The other three wives echoed Arabella's sentiments.

"Very well," she said. "I will commence doing all within my power to stir Sebastian's jealousy."

"Of all the others, you and I are of the same height." Phoebe smiled triumphantly. "And I have just the dress to begin Operation Rescue."

Chapter Twelve

HADLEY FOLLOWED PHOEBE to her bedchamber. As they entered, she saw Phoebe's husband sitting in a chair by the window, an open book on his lap and his infant son in his arms.

"Hello, my darling. Lady Hadley," he greeted. "We have been reading Shakespeare's sonnets."

Robby screeched piercingly and then a huge grin crossed his face.

Phoebe went and lifted her son into her arms and kissed his forehead. "Is Papa teaching you to be a romantic?" she cooed to the child. Turning to Hadley, she said, "He is, you know. A romantic." She smiled fondly at Windham and handed the baby back to him.

"You have a look in your eyes, Wife. You are up to something," the duke noted.

The duchess smiled. "We are. Operation Rescue."

"Hmm. It sounds military in nature to me. Who needs to be rescued, my love?"

"The Duke of Hardwick," Phoebe replied. "He's meant for Lady Hadley here and is too obstinate to realize it."

Windham nodded. "I have pointed that very thing out to him myself, my dear." His gaze turned to Hadley. "Sebastian has feelings for you, my lady. The war changes men, though. It colors the way they view the world. I think my friend was more affected by his experience than most."

"That is my observation also, Your Grace," she said. "Hardwick told me, in so many words, that he doesn't deserve happiness. He kissed me—and then let me know we had no future."

The duke chuckled. "Couldn't keep his hands off you. That's a good thing, my lady." He reached for his wife's hand and threaded his fingers through hers. "I assume Operation Rescue is meant to make Sebastian see the wisdom in offering for you."

"I hope so." Hadley sighed. "I don't know how to save him, Your Grace. My head tells me he is a broken man but my heart wants to help him heal."

A thoughtful expression crossed the duke's face. "War is devastating to a man's soul, my lady. In countless ways. Officers, in particular, carry a heavy burden because of the love they feel for their men. When letters are written to loved ones at home confirming a soldier's death, details and feelings must be suppressed. Duty lies above all else."

He kissed his son's head. "Everything about the war stays with you, long after you have left the battlefield. The sounds of the cannons firing until you feel you might grow deaf. The smell of gunpowder and blood permeating the air. The ground littered with bodies—some still and dead, while others who are maimed or fatally wounded cry out for help or their loved ones. You dread falling asleep because you dream of these things. You awaken from the nightmares in a cold sweat, your heart beating so violently you think you will die. You second-guess yourself after a battle because you wished you could have done more to save the men you lost.

"And you must write countless letters to the families of the soldiers under your command who were lost. Over and over, you describe a man's bravery and his quick yet heroic death, when many times that soldier suffered beyond imagination."

His Grace's smile tore at Hadley's heart. "These are some of the things that haunt Sebastian."

She swallowed, recalling the many letters she had read to the old duke from his son and how not one had mentioned any of this.

"How does a man recover from these life-altering experiences?" she asked. "What could I do to help Hardwick to heal?"

Windham gazed up at her. "You watch carefully. You try to help ease his transition into civilian life. You listen without judgment, refraining from commenting and inserting your opinions. You help him to once more enjoy the small things in life that can bring pleasure." He paused. "And you love him, pure and simple. You let that love flow into him. Love will bring the emotional strength he needs to recover. It will help give him a foundation to help rebuild his broken life."

His Grace smiled at her. "I will do my part and rally the troops to make sure we support your endeavor. What is your first step?"

"Lady Hadley is going to look ravishing at dinner tonight," the duchess said, trying to lighten the somber mood. "In one of my gowns."

Windham nodded. "The royal blue you were to wear this evening?"

"That is the one I was thinking of," Phoebe confirmed.

He closed the volume of poetry and set it aside and then rose, his son still in his arms. "Robby and I will leave you to your work. Good luck, Lady Hadley." The duke winked at her and left the room. A cat jumped into the now unoccupied chair and began bathing.

Her friend rang for her maid and then went to the tabby and stroked him.

"This is Caesar," she told Hadley. "He is an integral part of our family and goes wherever we do." Phoebe laughed. "When the trunks come out to be packed, so does Caesar's traveling basket."

"I have never had a pet," Hadley said. She bent and stroked the cat's silky fur.

"He even sleeps with Andrew and me," admitted Phoebe. "I had to leave him behind once—before Andrew and I were married—and

Andrew brought Caesar a long way so we could be reunited."

"Is that when you knew he was the one for you?" she asked.

Phoebe sighed. "I don't remember a time when my heart didn't tell me that Andrew was for me."

"I have felt that way about Sebastian for years," she said, still petting the cat's fur.

"What?" her friend asked, her confusion obvious.

"Although I only met Sebastian when he returned from the Continent, many years ago I saw him riding away the day he left and I arrived at Hardwell Hall," she explained. "Sebastian wrote home once a month and I would read his letters aloud to the duke over and over until the next one came. Over the years, I drew a clear picture in my mind of the man Sebastian was."

"What a romantic way to fall in love with someone, through letters," Phoebe exclaimed.

"The trouble has been that while I believe I know Sebastian extremely well, he knew nothing at all about me."

"He is attracted to you, Hadley. He wouldn't have kissed you otherwise."

"I know. It's almost, though, as if he wishes to save me from whatever gloom lies within him by pushing me away. He would rather wed a stranger and keep her off to the side than give us a chance at lasting happiness."

Phoebe's maid entered, carrying a beautiful dress in her arms.

"That one will be for Lady Hadley," she told the servant. "Fetch me the gold for this evening."

"Yes, Your Grace." The maid placed the gown across the bed and bobbed a quick curtsey before leaving.

They went to the bed and Hadley saw this must be the gown the duke had referred to. "Oh, my. It's so lovely," she said, fingering the silk.

"It will look even lovelier on you. Come, let me help you into it."

The maid returned with a second gown for her mistress and they both worked on placing Hadley in the borrowed gown. The blue silk shimmered. The only thing she doubted was the scooped neckline.

"You don't think . . . that it is too much?" she asked hesitantly.

"Not at all," Phoebe assured her. "You have a lovely bosom. It is meant to be displayed. The bodice and cut of the gown show enough for a man to be tempted. You will attract more than a few men's eyes tonight. I expect that will include Sebastian."

"You do look beautiful, my lady," the maid seconded.

Hadley smoothed the skirts, feeling the folds of blue were like water streaming about her.

"I do like it," she confided. "I feel quite pretty in it."

"I have two more gowns that you will need to try on. It's a good thing my breasts are larger now that I have birthed Robby else you wouldn't have fit into my gowns before that."

Phoebe told her maid which two dresses to take to Hadley's bedchamber and said if Hadley needed any adjustments made to them, she would loan her maid to make them.

"I will return to my room now and have Millie work on my hair," she said.

"Something simple and elegant, Hadley," Phoebe suggested. "A low chignon would be nice."

"I agree."

Hadley returned to her guest chamber and found Millie waiting for her.

"My stars! You look wonderful, Lady Hadley. That color of blue is striking on you."

"You think so, Millie?"

Her maid nodded emphatically. "I know so. You will have all them lords eating from the palm of your hand. If you are wanting a husband, tonight might be the night you find yourself one."

She didn't want any husband. She wanted Sebastian. Would he be able to cast aside his demons and doubts in order to chase after happiness? She prayed he would, for both of their sakes.

"The Duchess of Windham suggested a low chignon for tonight."

Millie nodded. "Her Grace is right. You have got nice cheekbones, my lady. You need to show them off. No stuffy hairstyle or curls to take away from the beauty of your face and that of the gown."

She took a seat at the dressing table and Millie unpinned Hadley's hair and brushed it until it shone. Then the maid smoothed and twisted and twirled and repinned it so the knot of hair brushed low on Hadley's nape.

Millie stepped back, admiring her work. "You look right nice, my lady."

"Thank you. I will see you later tonight."

"Enjoy yourself, my lady. You deserve a little fun." The servant's eyes twinkled. "Maybe you will even get a kiss."

Hadley stared at herself in the mirror. The royal blue went well with her coloring and her auburn hair. She should wear this color more often. She stood and found herself growing nervous. Glancing to the mirror once more, she knew she looked her best. Now, to either attract Sebastian's attention—or make him jealous by speaking to other male guests.

Operation Rescue had begun.

BARDHAM FINISHED TYING Sebastian's cravat. The valet braced the stump of his right arm against Sebastian and whipped the cravat around using his left fingers, deftly tying it and fluffing the cravat into place. Sebastian looked in the mirror and couldn't help but admire the elaborate knot.

"You are a wonder, Bardham," he proclaimed. "I couldn't do without you during the war and I certainly cannot now."

"Thank you, Your Grace. I am glad to be needed. What you want, though, is more than me."

"What do you mean?"

"You are a fine-looking gentleman, Your Grace. You have a title and a great estate. A fortune at your disposal. What you need is a wife."

His mouth hardened at the suggestion. "You have a candidate in mind?"

"Several lovely ladies are present at Blackstone Manor," Bardham said. "His Grace's sister, Lady Elizabeth, is certainly one of the most eligible women here. Lovely and a bit lively."

Sebastian knew Elizabeth would make for a perfect duchess but, somehow, he only saw her as a little sister. Elizabeth would also never settle for the type of marriage he had in mind. Jon had told him his sister wanted to find love. She would have to do so with someone other than a tired soldier.

"That Lady Callamina seems to be sweet," Bardham continued.

Sebastian had been thinking the same. The blond was a bit shy and very pretty. Gentle and well-bred. If he had to choose from those in attendance at the house party, she would be his choice. Her parents, Viscount and Viscountess Plimpton, were quite overbearing and when they were around, they never let their daughter get in a word edgewise. Lady Callamina would probably enjoy escaping from under their thumbs and having her own household to run.

"Then there's Lady Hadley."

"No," he said firmly.

"No?" questioned Bardham, his brows arching. "Why, she is the cream of the crop, Your Grace. I merely saved mentioning her for last because she seems the obvious choice for you."

"Not to me," he said brusquely. "And I don't like how everyone is forcing her upon me."

Bardham studied him a long moment. "Have your friends suggested a match between you and Lady Hadley?"

"They have," he admitted, seeing in his mind how well Hadley fit in with the wives of his closest friends.

"You have known Their Graces for quite some time, Your Grace. Perhaps they can see what you don't see."

"I see everything perfectly clear," he stated. "Lady Hadley is not going to be my duchess."

His valet sighed, his frustration obvious. "I am sorry to hear that. Everyone at Hardwell Hall thinks quite highly of her ladyship. From what I gather, she made the former duke act more humanely toward servants and tenants alike. She's bright, too, and has kept the estate running like clockwork for several years."

"It is *my* job to run the estate," he ground out. "Not a woman's."

"Oh, so that's how it is."

His eyes narrowed at Bardham's judgmental tone. "What do you mean?"

Bardham shrugged. "Nothing, Your Grace. I will see you later this evening."

As his valet crossed the room, Sebastian demanded, "Where are you going? You haven't been dismissed, you know."

The former batman turned. "You are already dressed. You are about to leave for dinner downstairs. You have no further need of me—or my opinions." With that, Bardham exited the room, shutting the door just a bit too firmly.

Sebastian swore loudly. "I could fire you, you know," he called out to the empty room.

Of course, he never would. Who knew if Bardham could find another job, with his missing limb and poor attitude? In the event Sebastian did try to fire his valet, he supposed the man would simply leave with Hadley. He had sung her praises often enough.

He perched on the bed. What was he going to do? Everyone thought Hadley would make for the perfect duchess, with her beauty and grace and knowledge of his affairs. He couldn't do that to her, though. He felt as if he were drowning every minute of the day. If she was his lifeline, he would clutch at her and she would be dragged down into the abyss with him.

It wouldn't be fair to wed her. Get children off her. Then push her aside and never truly let her in. Hadley was too warm. Too caring. She would fight to find and exorcise his demons. He couldn't allow that. Everyone thought him a hero—only Sebastian knew he wasn't. He was a traitor. A man who had betrayed every principle he had thought he stood for. Hadley deserved a good man. Not a hollow shell. He would tell his friends that they simply didn't suit and strongly consider offering for Lady Callamina.

Determined to stay the course, Sebastian left his guest room and ventured downstairs. Arabella had set up a brief time for the guests to come together and partake in a glass of wine before they went in to dinner. He would seek out Lady Callamina and pay her special attention to see if she might be interested in becoming his duchess.

Only when he entered the room, his eyes swept it until he found Hadley.

Christ on a cross!

She stood conversing with Lord Dean and Lord Banfield. As usual, Banfield must have uttered something witty because Hadley and Lord Dean burst out laughing. Sebastian swallowed, trying to get hold of himself. He wanted to drag his eyes from her—and couldn't.

Hadley wore a gown of bright blue, which hugged her every curve. The scooped neckline exposed a good amount of creamy flesh, her breasts rounded globes that his hands itched to cup. His mouth watered, thinking of lowering the gown and exposing those breasts. Sucking on them. Tasting her flesh as his tongue traced their curves. Already, his cock hardened just thinking of it.

What would it be like to actually *do* it?

Weston and George joined him, a drink in their hands. Sebastian turned and snatched a goblet from the tray the nearest footman held and downed the contents in a single swallow. He replaced it and took another and drained it, as well.

"Slow down, my friend," Weston said.

"I am thirsty," he said curtly, setting the empty container back on the tray. He started to reach again but George stepped between him and the footman and murmured something. Immediately, the servant moved away from the trio.

"What have you been doing to work up such a thirst?" George inquired casually. He glanced across the room and back at Sebastian. "Looking at Lady Hadley, perhaps?"

He swore under his breath.

"I don't know why you are so resistant to the idea," Weston said. "The lady is quite remarkable. Certainly the most beautiful of the eligible women here. More importantly, she is already fast friends with all our wives."

"Who? Lady Hadley?" Jon asked, joining them.

"Quit saying her name," Sebastian hissed.

Jon grew contemplative. "Was it Shakespeare who mentioned protesting too much? I am certain it was."

"Yes," Weston said. "In *Hamlet*."

"How do you remember that?" George asked. "All his plays run together for me."

"Enough," Sebastian said quietly, reining in his temper. "You are all good friends to me. Very good friends. But I am the one who will choose my own wife. Lady Hadley is not under consideration."

"Who is?" Weston asked.

"Possibly Lady Callamina."

"The chit is sweet but to have Plimpton as your father-in-law?" Jon shuddered.

"Perhaps I feel like playing the hero and rescuing her from such an overbearing father."

He heard Hadley laugh again and immediately turned in her direction. Lord Hayward, that damned bastard, was smiling at her like a besotted fool.

Arabella called out to her guests, "Shall we all go into dinner?"

Sebastian watched as Hayward said something to Hadley, bending close, his lips practically touching her ear. She nodded and took his arm. Fury spread like wildfire through Sebastian.

"For a man not interested in the lady, you certainly are . . . engrossed in the company she is keeping," Jon noted.

"Sod off," he said and walked away from his friends.

He went straight to Lady Callamina, who stood with her parents and two other young ladies whose names he couldn't recall.

Smiling, he asked, "My lady, might I lead you into dinner?"

Lady Callamina looked stricken at the attention. Her mother nudged her with an elbow and hissed, "Go on. He's a *duke*."

She gave him a tentative smile and Sebastian offered his arm. She placed her hand atop it and he guided her from the drawing to the dining room. Name cards had been placed at each seat and he led her to her chair.

"Thank you, Your Grace," she said breathily.

"Perhaps we can talk more later this evening," he told her.

He left and continued down the table until he passed the back of Hadley. The blue dress in contrast to her hair was a stunning combination. He glanced down and saw Lord Stanhope would be seated on her left. Continuing along the table and still not finding his name, he turned and started down the other side, finding his name two seats from his hostess. Sebastian took his place as the rest of the guests began finding their seats.

Hadley was four chairs down from him on the opposite side. Close enough for him to easily observe her and yet far enough away to have no way to converse with her. Good. He didn't want to talk to her.

He also didn't want her talking to anyone else.

This was madness. It was foolish to want her and even more foolish not to want anyone else to want her. He knew she was interested in finding a husband at this house party.

Sebastian just didn't want to have to watch her do so.

Dinner seemed interminable. Lady Veronica chatted with him but after receiving only grunts as answers from him, turned to the companion on her other side. Sebastian spent the next two hours observing Hadley without seeming to do so. Arabella led the ladies from the room after the end of the meal so that the men were left to their port and cigars. He wanted neither. His head ached. His cock throbbed.

He wanted to kiss Hadley again. Desperately.

Finally, the men finished and Jon rose, saying, "Shall we join the ladies?"

With that, he filed from the room along with the others, returning to the drawing room. Immediately, Hadley was surrounded by suitors. Irritation filled him.

Arabella clapped her hands to get everyone's attention. "Tonight, we are going to have a treasure hunt. We will draw for partners and you will be given your first clue. It will lead you to another and another until the final clue, which will allow the finders access to the treasure, is finally discovered."

"What is the prize?" called out Lady Veronica. "I could certainly use a new piece of jewelry."

Everyone laughed and Jon said, "I believe it is a crystal rose bowl."

"It is," his wife confirmed, holding up the bowl for all to see. "In it are slips of paper with the names of every gentleman present written on them. The ladies will draw for their partners."

Arabella carried the bowl to Elise, who stood nearest to her.

"Draw, Your Grace," Arabella prompted, "and reveal the name of your partner."

Elise dipped her hand in and pulled out a piece of paper. She unfolded it. "Viscount Dean," she announced.

"We might as well concede now," George quipped. "Dean's brighter by himself than the rest of us put together. Give him the bowl, Your Grace. He's going to earn it sooner rather than later."

The shy viscount turned beet red at the attention. Elise walked to him and said, "I am happy to partner with you, my lord. As long as you allow me to take home the rose bowl when we win the contest."

The group laughed and Arabella stepped to Lady Pamela. She drew and several others did, as well. Then Arabella reached Hadley. Sebastian's heart was in his throat.

"The Duke of Hardwick," she said, her gaze meeting his.

Sebastian smiled and crossed to her. "We are the team to beat," he told the rest. "Lord Dean and the Duchess of Treadwell don't stand a chance."

CHAPTER THIRTEEN

HADLEY'S HEART HAMMERED in her chest. Arabella had told her no matter whose name she drew, Hadley should announce Sebastian as her partner. It had been Samantha's idea. She said not even to put Sebastian's name on a slip to assure no other woman would draw his name.

Carefully, Hadley turned and bumped into Arabella, as planned. Playing her part, Arabella tilted the rose bowl, spilling a few of the slips of paper on the floor. Hadley knelt and scooped them up, replacing them in the bowl, along with the one she had drawn, which had revealed the Duke of Colebourne's name. Now, the correct number of names were back in the bowl and the drawing proceeded until everyone had selected her partner.

"Once you solve your clue and go to the location it directs you, only one clue will be found at that spot," Arabella informed her guests. "You will need to read the new clue and leave it behind for others to discover."

"What if someone takes it so no one else may find it?" called out a guest.

"Cheating will not be tolerated," Arabella said emphatically. "You will answer to my husband if you do. I doubt any of you wish to be soundly thrashed by my duke. I will expect the ladies to keep their partners in line. We shall reconvene here in one hour's time. The couple who discovers the last clue—and it will be marked as thus—

may bring it to the drawing room in order to show proof of their victory." She paused. "You may claim your first clue from any footman you see. They are scattered throughout this floor."

A lone footman stood in the drawing room, off to the side. Sebastian wheeled and practically pounced on the man. The servant handed over the folded page in his hand. Sebastian returned to her as other couples quickly left in search of a footman and the clue he held. Arabella winked at her and then allowed Jon to lead her away.

Sebastian opened the sheet and read the clue aloud. "Toast and jam, perhaps? Or maybe even ham? If you come here, you will be near."

"The breakfast room," Hadley said. "The clue will be where the buffet has been placed each morning."

Quickly, they exited the drawing room and hurried downstairs. The room was well-lit and Hadley knew they were on the correct path. Sebastian's longer legs had him reaching the sideboard first and he lifted the silver tray that sat upon it. Underneath lay another page. He read the next clue written upon it and they thought a bit before rushing to their new destination. They went from a sun parlor to the kitchens, as Hadley claimed the next hint and read it to him.

"A dagger—then death. The stars were not aligned."

Sebastian frowned. "They are becoming harder to solve."

She laughed. "Oh, this is an easy one. Follow me."

Leading him to the library, they entered just as Lord Dean and Elise were leaving. Elise waved gaily at them, while the viscount averted his eyes and shuffled past them.

"We could always follow them and swoop in to claim the final clue," she teased. "Lord Dean is rather brilliant."

"I will not accept a tainted victory," he said, his jaw tightening at the notion of her praising the shy viscount.

"You have proved yourself on the battlefield, Sebastian. You will do even greater things as a duke," she told him. "Even if we don't win the rose bowl."

"Why are we here?" he asked gruffly.

Hadley went to the shelves and began skimming them, seeing if Jon had arranged the volumes in any certain order. She found a grouping of Shakespeare's collected works and ran her fingers along the spines until she found what she was looking for and pulled the tome out.

"Shakespeare?" he asked.

"Yes. In *Romeo and Juliet*, she awakens from her deathlike coma to find Romeo and Paris dead inside the crypt where her body had been placed. Juliet had sent word to Romeo to assure him she had merely taken a potion that mimicked death but he did not receive the message. He drank poison after killing Paris. Juliet cannot stand the thought of life without her Romeo. She takes his dagger and kills herself. The friar who gave her the potion called her and Romeo two star-cross'd lovers."

"I am not fond of reading, especially Shakespeare," he said. "This tale illustrates why. What is the point of having two innocents die? Men have seen enough of that in war."

She took his hand and he flinched. "I know you saw things you can never unsee, Sebastian. The war is over, though. Can you try to leave those horrors in the past and look to the future instead?"

He gazed at her grimly. Doubt filled her. She might never break through the walls he had erected between him and the world. She released his hand, worried that Operation Rescue would all be for naught.

Opening the book, she flipped through the pages until she found a slip of paper tucked between them. Her eyes fell to the page and saw it was the scene where Juliet stabs herself with her lover's dagger. Hadley had read the tragedy several times, always finding herself in tears as the lovers missed seeing one another by minutes. She felt the same now, that somehow she and Sebastian kept missing the opportunity to come together. She refused to think she would fail despite the uneasiness that filled her. Somehow, she had to convince this man that they were meant to be together.

Without showing him the clue, she pretended to read it and then returned it to the book and closed it. Placing it on the shelf again, she said, "I know where the next clue can be found. The stables."

Hadley hadn't even bothered to read the clue. She did need to get Sebastian away from the house and other guests, though. Once she had him alone, she hoped she could change the course they were on.

"What did it say?" he asked as she took his arm and led him from the library.

Having only had herself to play with, Hadley had been very inventive as a child. A lie came to her and she said, "It referred to one of the uncredited tasks of Heracles. Cleaning the Augean stables. Heracles was supposed to perform ten labors as penance for slaying his sons and his wife, Megara."

Horror crossed Sebastian's face. "Good God, why would he do such a thing?"

"It wasn't his fault. He was driven mad by Queen Hera," she explained. "To atone for his sins, Heracles had to complete the ten tasks his cousin, King Eurystheus, set for him. The king refused to credit him with the slaying of the Hydra because Heracles' nephew aided him in that endeavor. The king also denied recognizing Heracles' actions in cleaning the Augean stables since he accepted payment for that task. Since no nine-headed hydras are walking about Blackstone Manor, I assume the clue will lie somewhere in His Grace's stables."

She hated lying to him but she didn't feel she had a choice.

As the left the library and headed down the corridor, he said, "You look very nice tonight."

Hadley's heart skipped a beat hearing him praise her gown. "Thank you. I clumsily tripped and tore the hem of my gown as I left my chamber for dinner. Fortunately, the Duke and Duchess of

Windham were passing by and she had changed her mind and donned a second gown for this evening. Her first choice was still pressed and ready to go. Since we are of a similar size, she offered to loan this one to me so that I would not be tardy to dinner while Millie repaired my hem."

The words poured quickly from her and she wondered if he knew she fibbed.

Instead, he said, "You should see if she will allow you to purchase it from her. While the duchess is a beautiful woman, you look far better in the gown than she would have."

Hadley heard something in his voice. Longing?

"Thank you for the compliment, Sebastian." She deliberately continued to use his first name since he had urged her to do so. Calling him *Your Grace* would put distance between them that she was trying to erase.

They cut through the kitchens and left through the rear of the house. Only a few lanterns burned.

"It's rather dark," he noted. "I would think they would have the path better lit if they expect us to find our way to the stables."

Then he took her hand, his fingers threading through hers. Warmth filled her.

"Watch your step," he advised and slowed his stride to match hers as they continued toward the stables.

"This might be the final clue, I suppose," he added. "Arabella wouldn't make it easy on the winners, I suppose. The path being in partial darkness might discourage others, who think they had interpreted the clue incorrectly."

Now, Hadley truly felt guilty. She hoped he wouldn't be angry with her once they reached the stables and found no clue at all. Her heart was already beating fast enough because of their linked fingers touching one another. She yearned for his kiss and hoped the privacy of the stables would allow her to press her lips to his once more, hoping to convince him by her actions since her words had left too much undone between them.

They arrived and a lone groomsman sat in front of the stables as a guard. He nodded politely to them but as a well-trained servant, he didn't ask why they were there.

Stepping inside, a lantern burned low. Sebastian lifted it from where it hung and held it high as he led her down the row of stalls. Reluctantly, Hadley broke away from him and entered an empty stall. He followed her inside. She reached for the lantern he held and pulled it from his hand, setting it on the ground. Wordlessly, she looked up at him.

"The clue didn't lead us here," she confessed. "I did."

SEBASTIAN HAD THOUGHT fate had intervened and given him one more time to be close to Hadley. He promised himself he wouldn't touch her yet he had taken her hand in his, lacing their fingers together. They fit together as a hand in its glove and he had wavered between wanting to solve each clue quickly to impress her versus deliberately misinterpreting them in order to prolong their time together. She was bright, though, and had come up with the solution to several of them, urging them on toward victory.

Until now.

He hadn't read the last slip of paper which she had found in the volume of Shakespeare's tragedies. He had thought it ironic that the clue had led them to Romeo and Juliet, a play he had never read yet knew enough about from conversations, one in which the hero so fiercely loved the heroine that when he thought her dead, he hadn't wanted to continue living without her. Sebastian understood Romeo's feelings because he didn't know if he could go on living without Hadley.

She deserved so much more in life than a damaged man who had betrayed his country. One whom the world thought was a valiant, fearless officer. Only he and a handful of others, including the Duke of Wellington, knew the difference. All Sebastian's brave acts had led to one incident of bitter betrayal. He had spent the remainder of the war risking everything, trying to atone, as Heracles had, for his monumental mistake.

Yet here they were, not another person in sight, only the faint sound of swishing tails and chuffing horses nearby in the dark. He understood she wanted him for he had that same need regarding her. He wouldn't take her maidenhood but Sebastian planned to make a memory with Hadley. Here. Now. One which would give her pleasure and him something to cling to for the rest of his life.

CHAPTER FOURTEEN

SEBASTIAN ENVELOPED HADLEY in his arms, bringing her close as his mouth crashed into hers. He wished he could be patient and gentle but desire for this perfect woman filled him. His kiss was hard. Greedy. He wanted to brand her as his, unfair as it was. Her arms entwined about his neck and she pressed her breasts into his chest. He could feel the hard peaks of her nipples through the silk of her gown and knew he would soon taste them.

Urging her mouth open, he plundered her rich sweetness, tasting the peppermint she must have sucked on after dinner. The scent of hay and the vanilla on her satin skin wafted up, surrounding them. He dominated her with his tongue, plunging deeper, trying to drink every bit of her up to quench the hunger for her within him. She began fighting back, trying to gain control, and their tongues waged a sweet, hot war. Lovely sounds came from her, urging him on.

His hands caressed her back, the silk gown molded to her, and they slid lower, cupping her buttocks and holding her against him. She was warm and all woman, the object of his desire, which he would give in to for a few stolen moments of bliss. He tore his mouth from hers and she protested until his lips found the slender column of her throat and kissed it. He licked where her pulse pounded, tasting both salty and sweet on her skin.

His tongue traveled lower, down her collarbone, until he reached the upper curve of her beautiful breast. He ran his tongue along its curve and she shivered. He released her buttocks and his fingers found the top of the gown. Slowly, he pulled the gown and the chemise underneath it from her shoulders until both sat at her waist. The dim light from the lantern allowed him to drink in her physical beauty.

"You are perfection," he murmured before his mouth took her breast.

He licked around the nipple and then across it, teasing it with his lips and tongue, then blowing softly on it. Hadley whimpered and shivered in his arms. He scraped his teeth across it and her back bowed, her head falling back as she cried out softly. Sebastian worshipped the breast and then moved to the other, not wanting to leave it neglected. She moaned, her fingers tightening on him, her nails digging into his flesh.

It wasn't enough. He was the first who touched her this way. She needed more. He needed to give her more.

Sweeping her into his arms, he crossed the stall and dropped to his knees, lowering her onto the bed of hay. He kissed her again, long and deep, his hands cupping her breasts. As he kissed her, he reached down and found her ankle, encased in a silk stocking. His fingers encircled it, rubbing it, then gliding up her leg. Past her knee. To her inner thigh. Then he reached her core and stroked the seam of her sex. Her breathing grew shallow and rapid.

"This is for you," he murmured, not sure if she even heard him.

Sebastian parted the folds and caressed her, causing Hadley to cry out. Gradually, he pushed a finger inside her and continued fondling her. Her hips began to rise and she panted as she squirmed beneath his touch. He continued the motion, sensing she was on the brink of discovery.

"Let go," he urged.

Then he found the sweet bud and pressed hard against it in a circular motion. She bucked under him as her heated body gave over to the orgasm. His mouth silenced her cries as his fingers continued to pleasure her. She arched and writhed and then her body shuddered violently. He felt her go limp and slipped his hands from under her gown. She stilled and he kissed her for what would be the final time. Slow. Deep. His heart breaking at having to let this woman go.

He forced himself to break the kiss and pulled her clothing back into place. Looking down at her, Sebastian wished he could wake up to this wonderful woman each morning. Instead, he would find himself in a cold bed, his unnamed wife asleep in her own chamber.

Hadley looked up at him in awe. "I never knew something such as that existed," she said, wonder in her voice.

Pushing himself to his feet, he caught her hands and pulled her up, catching her waist when her legs seemed shaky.

"You are still a virgin, Hadley," he said quietly. "I would not take that from you. Or the man you pledge yourself to."

Her brow knit in concentration, as if she were trying to make sense of his words. Understanding dawned in her eyes.

"You don't want me. You never did," she said dully, pushing hard against his chest, trying to get away from him.

Sebastian refused to let her go and said, "I will always want you. I will go to my grave wanting you." His chest tightened as he spoke. "But I have been scarred by the war. I cannot have you, Hadley. I will not ruin your life and bind you to me when so much is wrong inside of me."

Her gaze grew fierce. "Shouldn't I have a choice in the matter?" she demanded.

"No." He released her waist and captured her hands in his. Bringing them to his lips, he pressed a fervent kiss upon her knuckles. "You need to choose happiness. I could never give you that."

"I love you, Sebastian," she said.

Her words were like a kick in the gut—because he knew in this moment that he loved her, too.

And always would.

"You cannot save me, Hadley, no matter what you think. Love isn't enough to—"

"It is!" she insisted. "Even if you think you have no love in your heart. That you could never love me. I have enough love for both of us, Sebastian. Let me prove it to you."

She jerked her hands from his and grabbed his face, pulling it swiftly to her and slamming her lips against his in desperation. He took her by the shoulders and pushed her away.

"No. You are to find a man who can return your love. I will never be that man, Hadley. Find someone worthy of you."

Her eyes narrowed and she shrugged away. "You will change your mind," she said, her mouth setting stubbornly.

"I won't," he promised. "Go and live your life, Hadley. Make it a great one."

With that, he left the stall and found his way to the front of the stables—leaving behind his heart—with the woman he would always love.

HADLEY DROPPED TO her knees and wept.

It was over. Whatever Sebastian had seen or done during the war had warped him, causing scars so deep that she would never be able to repair him. He had refused her. Her love. Instinct told her that the only person who could make him whole again was Sebastian himself. It might take years before he came around. Years in which she would be miserable. One of her greatest strengths, though, was her resiliency. She would have to accept that being with Sebastian was no longer a possibility. She would move on with her life.

But not with any man. Not just yet.

Instead, Hadley promised herself that she would devote time to herself. Discover who she was without a mountain of responsibility pressing down upon her. Learn what she enjoyed and pursue those enjoyments. In the future, she would seek a husband. She enjoyed being around people too much, especially now that she had begun to make friends. After holding sweet Robby in her arms, she was determined that, one day, she would become a mother. Regret filled her, knowing she would never have Sebastian's baby. Still, she would bide her time and allow her own heart to heal. Only then would she seek to find a man she could share her life with. Raise a family. Grow old together.

Brushing away her tears, she stood and retrieved the lantern. She returned it to where it had previously hung on the wall and left the stables, not glancing back at the servant on duty. Hadley entered the house through the back door. The kitchen was quiet. By now, all the treasure-seeking couples would have returned to the drawing room. The winning couple would have claimed their prize. With it being a rose bowl, she assumed the gentleman would award the prize to his partner.

Hadley slipped up the back staircase and went to her room. Millie sat in a chair, fast asleep. She shook the maid and asked for her help in undressing.

"See that the dress is pressed and returned to the Duchess of Windham," she instructed once she donned her night rail and then climbed into bed.

Sleep wouldn't come, though. She lay there for a long time, playing the scene in the stables over and over in her head. Reliving every kiss. Every touch. Knowing these memories would be the ones she would keep locked in her heart.

Hadley wondered if Sebastian would do the same.

THE NEXT MORNING, she rang for Millie and dressed for breakfast. The maid selected a pale lavender gown for Hadley to wear.

"How would you like your hair to be styled, my lady?" Millie asked.

She had liked the chignon from the evening before because it wasn't fussy and requested that Millie dress her hair in the same manner.

When she finished, the maid stepped back. "This is a perfect look for you, my lady."

"I think so, too, Millie. I believe this will become my signature style. It takes little time to arrange and I like my appearance now."

She ventured downstairs to the breakfast room. For a moment, she recalled coming here only last night, Sebastian as her partner as they searched for clues. Samantha waved her over once she had placed a few items on her plate, hoping she would be able to eat something.

Taking a seat, Samantha frowned at her. "You didn't get much to eat, Hadley. Aren't you hungry?" she asked, concern on her face.

"You must tell us how last evening went," Elise said. "After Lord Dean and I ran into you when we left the library, I never saw you again."

"No one saw you," Arabella said. "I hope that is a good thing."

Phoebe slipped into the open seat beside her. "Have I missed anything?" she asked, hope on her face.

"No," Hadley assured her. "I must thank you for loaning me your dress."

"You looked spectacular in it, "Arabella proclaimed. "I don't think there was a single gentleman who did not notice you in that gown." She paused. "How did our scheme go? You returned the slip of paper to me seamlessly. No one suspected we had rigged the selection process."

The back of her neck tingled and she glanced over her shoulder. As she suspected, Sebastian had just entered the room. Quickly, she turned back.

"May we speak of this later? When others are not present?"

Four pairs of eyes searched the room and returned to her. "Of course," Elise said.

"Who won the rose bowl?" Hadley asked, trying to take the focus from her.

Samantha chuckled. "Well, it certainly wasn't Elizabeth and Lord Hayward. Lord Banfield and I came across them in the kitchen. Both wore a guilty expression." Samantha glanced across the room. "Elizabeth is wearing a rather high-necked gown for this warm weather."

"The better to hide evidence of last night's crimes?" Phoebe teased.

"Do you think Hayward is interested in Elizabeth?" Sam asked, leaning forward. "He possesses the most terrible reputation. Worse than Weston had as the Duke of Disrepute until he married Elise." She smiled at her sister-in-law. "Now, Polite Society talks of how the pretty widow tamed the disgraceful rake and turned him into the Duke of Grace."

"I noticed Hayward watching Elizabeth a few times this past Season," Arabella confessed. "I brought up his name twice and Elizabeth was overly dismissive of him. I thought sparks might be there. It is why I invited him to the house party. If there is something between them, I wanted to give it a chance to blossom."

They continued gossiping throughout breakfast and then Jon addressed the men in the room.

"If you are interested in the fox hunt, we are gathering at the stables now."

A group of gentlemen rose. Hadley noticed Sebastian was among them.

"Don't forget that we will picnic by the lake at two this afternoon," Arabella reminded them. "Be sure you have caught all the foxes you can and have bathed and dressed in time for our picnic. Ladies, there will be bridge in the drawing room soon or you have time to write your letters this morning."

Everyone drifted from the breakfast room after that, with only Hadley and her friends remaining. Arabella signaled the butler and told him the footman could clear the room of dishes in half an hour. Once the servants left, she looked expectantly at Hadley.

She swallowed, composing herself. "I told myself I wouldn't cry but I can't guarantee that won't happen," she began.

Phoebe slipped her hand around Hadley's. "It didn't go well."

"It was not the outcome I had hoped for."

She told them of how Sebastian had complimented her gown and how they had quickly solved several of the clues.

"I knew I needed to get him away from the other guests and so I quickly hatched a plan to do so."

After she explained her idea of a clue hinting about cleaning the Augean stables, the other four praised her brilliance.

"You certainly think fast on your feet, Hadley," Elise praised. "I suppose it is because you have had all those decisions to make regarding the estate and arguments between tenants that needed to be settled."

"What happened when you reached the stables?" Samantha asked.

Hadley wasn't a lady who would kiss and tell all so she merely said, "We kissed at length in the stables."

"Were his kisses as delicious as before?" Arabella pressed. "Enough to make you dizzy and swoon?"

"Yes. Decidedly so," she admitted. "It wasn't enough, though."

"Why not?" Samantha demanded. "I have known Sebastian longer than the rest of you. I never would have taken him for a fool."

"He's not," she said quietly. "He's deeply hurt, though. He told me . . ." She paused. "He told me he would go to his grave wanting me."

"See—I knew it!" Arabella said.

Phoebe squeezed Hadley's fingers. "What else did he say?"

She closed her eyes. "That he had been scarred by the war. He wanted me to choose happiness, something he said he could never give me." A tear coursed down her cheek. "That's when I told him I loved him."

The four duchesses gasped.

"I shouldn't have said anything of my feelings. I thought my love for him would be enough to save him. He refused it. And me. He begged me to find a man worthy of me and then he left."

The tears came freely now. Her friends comforted her as best they could. She dabbed her eyes with her napkin.

"I don't know what he suffered. Whether he saw or did something that changed fundamentally who he was. He believes he is behaving nobly by suffering alone." Hadley shook her head sadly. "I came to understand that I cannot heal Sebastian. Only he can make himself whole again."

She blew out a long breath. "I will go about living my life. Exploring things that are interesting to me. Seeing who I am apart from the heavy burden I carried for the previous Duke of Hardwick."

"You must come stay with us a while," Phoebe urged. "Andrew and Robby would enjoy that."

She smiled as her eyes brimmed with tears again, touched by her friend's offer. "I would like that, Phoebe. Very much."

"You can't have Hadley all to yourself," Elise protested. "You must also come visit Weston and me."

"And I would like you to be present when I give birth to my and George's babe," Samantha said. "I know you have delivered many of them. I cannot think of another woman I would want by my side during that time."

Hadley laughed. "It seems that I will be quite busy traveling between several houses." She paused. "Eventually, I would like to go to London. I have never been to town before and there are things there I wish to see there."

"Will you take part in next Season?" Arabella asked.

She nodded. "I think I should. Until then, I will be a free woman, indulging myself by deepening my friendships and taking up a few hobbies. As long as it doesn't involve sewing."

They all laughed.

"We should join the others," Arabella said.

As they rose, Arabella held Hadley back and said, "Whenever you wish to go to London, you must stay at our townhouse. If I am with child, as I suspect is the case, I will give birth in April. I doubt Jon and I will return to town for that. We are enjoying our time at Blackstone Manor too much. I want you to feel free to treat the place as your own. Go before the Season and enjoy what cultural arts London has to offer. Stay the entire time and experience all the social events."

"Thank you, Arabella. It is most kind of you."

"I feel I have made you very unhappy, trying to help you win Sebastian over and seeing your efforts fail. I want to make it up to you in whatever way I can."

"I am blessed to have a friend such as you. And the others."

Arabella embraced her. "I want you to be happy, Hadley. If not with Sebastian, then I hope you will find a good match in the near future."

"You invited several nice gentlemen to your house party. I will be here another week. I will make the most of it, getting to know as many men as I can."

They linked arms and made their way upstairs to the drawing room. While her heart still felt heavy, Hadley knew she shared her burden with her friends and they would help see her through this difficult time.

Chapter Fifteen

SEBASTIAN HAD SUFFERED through four days of pretending that Hadley didn't exist as every unmarried man at the house party fought for her attention. She was friendly to all, enthusiastic and charming. He heard several of the women extend invitations to her to visit them at their country estates. He had seen her being rowed in a rowboat. Escorted through the gardens. Taken riding and walking. Partnered at cards and parlor games. He bore it all stoically, turning his attention to the other ladies present.

His idea had been to offer for Lady Callamina at the end of the house party but his heart wasn't in it. He thought it better to leave Blackstone Manor and lick his wounds at Hardwell Hall until next Season. If Lady Callamina was still unattached at that time, he would strongly consider making her his duchess. If she were betrothed by that point, he would have plenty of women to choose from. After all, he was a duke—and they didn't grow on trees.

All he had to do was get through tonight and tomorrow. Then he could return home. Of course, he would have to ride in the carriage those ten miles with Hadley. He remembered she was to go over the status of his various estates with him once they returned from the house party. After that, he assumed she would leave with all due haste because of the strained relationship between them.

They hadn't spoken a single word to one another since their time in the stables. Sebastian had lain awake every night, burning for her kiss. Longing to delve into her sweet recesses. Each morning, he rose with only a few hours of sleep, feeling more distant from his friends as he watched how happy they were with their duchesses. While he was thrilled the four men had found beautiful, charming, intelligent women to share their lives with, he felt they had moved on in a direction he would never travel.

He took the last sip of port as those gathered around the table rose to go to the drawing room and mingle again with the ladies. Jon fell into step with him.

"You seem glum," his friend noted. "Have we not provided adequate entertainment for you?"

He didn't want his friend to think himself a poor host. "You and Arabella have done an admirable job shepherding thirty guests through a week of activities with the greatest of ease. I am merely restless and ready to return home. I was gone for so many years. I am ready to settle down and plant roots beneath my feet."

Jon nodded but remained silent. Sebastian was grateful his friend didn't press him about finding a wife. In fact, none of his friends had done so after the treasure hunt. He supposed Hadley had told her friends of his rejection and the women had relayed that information to their husbands.

In the salon, baccarat tables had been set up and guests drifted to them to begin play. A few gathered around the pianoforte and began singing as different women played a tune or two and then traded places. Everywhere in the room he heard conversation and laughter as he stood off to the side for a good hour.

Sebastian had never felt more out of place.

He caught sight of Hadley singing, her eyes bright. She wore a gown of purplish-blue, the same shade as her cornflower blue eyes. He didn't think she had ever looked lovelier.

Except when she had been lying on the hay, her gown down to her waist, her magnificent breasts displayed as he touched her.

Quietly, Sebastian slipped from the room. No one would miss him. In truth, he would relish a bit of solitude. He went to the gardens and took one of the lighted lanterns that hung from a post at the entrance. Winding his way through them, he drank in the scent of the blossoms, hanging heavily in the air of the dark night. He came to the gazebo where he had once sat with Hadley. Where he had kissed her for the first time. Rage poured through him and he wished he could punch through a wall. If only he had been a better man. The soldier he was supposed to be. Then he would have gladly wed Hadley, knowing how happy they could be together. He imagined little girls with her burnished auburn hair, knowing he would have spoiled them outrageously, just as he would have their mother.

He cursed aloud and dropped his head into his hands. He wished he had died during those days of torture. It would have been better than living now.

Quickly, he hurried back to the house and entered the library. He had the room to himself—and the numerous decanters of spirits grouped together on a table. Sebastian never drank to excess. He wasn't a man who particularly cared for the taste of alcohol and only drank it upon occasion. He knew, though, that it could dull his pain. Make him forget. If only for a little while.

Locating a bottle of brandy, he poured the amber liquid into a snifter. Not a quarter or half. All the way to the brim. Taking the glass and the bottle, he retreated to the nearby settee and proceeded to get thoroughly soused. Sebastian drank several glasses in quick succession before giving up the snifter and swigging straight from the bottle. He moved from the brandy to a smooth, smoky whiskey. The two tastes clashed in his mouth until he drank enough of the whiskey not to notice—or care.

He thought drinking would cause him to forget Hadley's face. Her curvaceous body. Instead, though everything about him swam, her visage remained clear. He grew hot and stood to remove his coat and then waistcoat, stumbling and hitting the ground as it came off. The room swayed perilously and he thought it safer to remain on the carpeted floor, leaning his back against the settee. He found it hard to breathe and clawed at the perfectly knotted cravat Bardham had tied, finally dragging it from his throat.

Reaching up, he stretched his arm as far as he could and slapped at another bottle. It fell from where it stood and hit the thick carpet without breaking. He opened it and drank some more, growing more morose with each sip. Still hot, he wondered if drinking too much might cause a fever. He tore at his cuffs and somehow managed to roll the sleeves of his shirt to his elbows.

And still all he could think of was Hadley.

He picked up the bottle again and drained it, tossing it aside. His head ached. Dizziness consumed him. He thought he might be sick. Sebastian slumped and then felt the carpet against his cheek. If only he could sleep. Escape.

Closing his eyes, darkness rushed up to meet him.

HADLEY WAS AWARE when Sebastian left the room. She had seen him enter the salon with the other gentlemen because she had been keeping an eye out for him. Her body was attuned to his presence and she could tell when he was nearby without ever seeing him. At least, it had been that way for the past several days. Days in which they had never spoken to one another. Days in which she longed to comfort him.

She didn't believe he had shared what was wrong with him with any of his friends though he had spent a majority of his time with them. She could only hope that, sooner or later, he would feel the need to talk. To unburden himself from whatever he carried deep inside him. Hadley wanted him to tell his friends what troubled him. If he did, it might be the first step to recovering and returning to the man he once was.

The only good thing was that Sebastian hadn't interacted much with any of the other ladies present. She had feared he would leave their encounter and deliberately betroth himself to another woman to keep Hadley from pestering him. Fortunately, he hadn't. It didn't mean that one day in the future—near or far—that he wouldn't seek a bride. She fully expected him to because he had pointed out to her that he did need an heir. It wouldn't be fair, though, to wed another when he still suffered so much. She might not be the woman for him but she wanted him to be happy, along with whomever he chose as his bride.

After singing, she joined one of the baccarat tables and had a run of luck. The game was new to her. The old duke had taught her chess and backgammon and they had spent many evenings engaged in play. She had been introduced to both baccarat and bridge at the house party and preferred bridge because it reminded her more of chess with its plotting and strategies. It was a challenging game and she knew it would take several years for her to master it.

The clock chimed nine and people began saying their goodnights. Country hours were different from those in London, or so she had been told. Since she had spent her entire life in the country, it didn't bother her to retire so early but she knew everyone else present had, except for Phoebe and Andrew, come from the London Season and were having to adjust to different hours.

She walked upstairs with Elizabeth, whom she had gotten to know better over the past few days. Hadley had noticed Lord Hayward eyeing Elizabeth and wouldn't be surprised if the two might rendezvous once the house settled down for the night.

"I was telling Lady Callamina about *Tom Jones*," Elizabeth said. "That girl needs to have her eyes opened some. Her parents are much too protective of her."

"Who is Mr. Jones?" she asked. "He's not a guest here or I would recall meeting him."

Elizabeth laughed. "It's not a he. It's a book. A bit naughty, I might add."

"And you recommended it to Lady Callamina? I would think that would be more to Lady Veronica's taste. What is it about?" she asked, her curiosity getting the better of her, especially thinking of the naughty things Sebastian had done to her in the stables.

"Tom is a bastard orphan whose nasty uncle sends him away to London. It's full of adventure. Duels. Imprisonment. Love affairs. I found it quite funny and very entertaining."

Hadley said, "I have only read a few novels. Perhaps I will try this one."

"There is a copy in the library downstairs," Elizabeth confided, leaning closer. "Hidden behind a longwinded treatise by Warren on the second bookcase, the third shelf. I put it there myself, knowing no one would find it because no one will ever read such a dry bit of politics."

"I will look for it tomorrow."

"Feel free to take it with you. I will reclaim it the next time I see you."

They reached her bedchamber and Elizabeth told her goodnight. Hadley entered and allowed Millie to disrobe her and prepare her for bed.

"Be sure you return this dress to the Duchess of Windham."

She had borrowed another of Phoebe's gowns and had asked for the name of her modiste because she liked the design so much. Once she arrived in London, Hadley would seek out the woman, using Phoebe's name as a reference since the dressmaker rarely took on new clients.

"Yes, my lady. Will there be anything else?"

"No. I will see you tomorrow morning, Millie. Thank you."

Restlessness filled her. She didn't seem a bit sleepy. She thought about going downstairs to retrieve *Tom Jones* and read a chapter or two but didn't want to ring for her maid and don her gown again to do so. Instead, she climbed into bed, where she tossed and turned for a good hour. Deciding the house had quietened down by now and she had little chance of running into anyone, Hadley rose and shrugged into her dressing gown, belting it and taking a candle to light her way downstairs.

The corridor was silent as she moved along it. She wondered if she passed Sebastian's room and if he slept. She pinched herself. This had to stop. Sebastian was a beautiful dream which she had longed for, one that would never become a reality. Thankfully, she had the memory of his kisses to treasure.

She descended the stairs, the thick carpet absorbing any sound she made. She arrived at the library and opened the door. One light still burned low. She crossed the room and held the candle high as she skimmed the shelf until she found Mr. Warren's work. Pulling the book out, she tucked it under her arm and then moved her fingers until she found the hidden novel. Hadley replaced the Warren book and started across the room again.

Then she heard a groan and froze. Her eyes darted about, seeing no one. She waited several moments and then decided she was merely hearing things. Before she could take another step, though, the sound came again. And then weeping.

Alarmed, she stepped gingerly, holding the candle up as she searched. A moan caused her to pause and she glanced to the floor. A long, dark shape lay on the ground.

It was a man.

Fearful that he had tripped and hurt himself, she hurried toward him and knelt. She gasped when she saw it was Sebastian.

He was asleep and obviously very drunk from the strong smell of spirits rising from him. She glanced around and saw three empty bottles and assumed he had consumed all their contents. He began moaning again, thrashing about in his sleep. Hadley placed a hand upon his shoulder, hoping to soothe him. Immediately, she felt the heat of his body and realized he had stripped off his coat and waistcoat. They lay nearby. His cravat was also gone and his shirtsleeves messily pushed up his arms. She stared a long moment at the forearms, something she had never seen on a man. Something beautiful.

And horrible.

She held the flame closer and saw his arms riddled with scars. Some stood out white against his skin. Others puckered angrily. Some looked as though they had been burned into him. Her stomach roiled angrily at the sight.

These weren't war wounds.

They came from being tortured.

Hadley placed her hand on his shoulder again and moved the light closer to his face. Sebastian looked as if he were in dreadful pain and she wondered if he was dreaming of what had been done to him. She now saw that his cravat also hid multiple scars. Without thinking, she touched her hand to his throat and petted him as she had Caesar, Phoebe's tabby. His skin wasn't smooth. She took the hem of his shirt and lifted it—and almost gagged.

His chest was riddled with scars, the same as his arms, only longer and deeper. He had been badly abused. Instinctively, she knew this was why his letters had halted for a period of time. Sebastian had been taken by the enemy. It crushed her to think of what he had suffered at their hands.

Yet he had never written of it. She knew it was something he must be ashamed of, something he had locked deeply within him. Anger poured through her, rage pointed at a nameless, faceless enemy who had marred him physically and damaged him emotionally. This must be why he didn't want her as his wife. He didn't want her to see the physical punishment he had endured.

Hadley set the candle down and brushed back the hair from his forehead. He continued muttering incoherently. She supposed his nightmares to be frequent, another thing he probably wanted to hide from her. She lifted his head and moved nearer, placing it in her lap. She continued stroking his hair, wanting to wash away his pain.

He seemed to wake, blinking several times, his words slurring now from the drink.

"Hush," she told him. "Go back to sleep."

"I am sorry," he said as tears began streaming down his cheeks. "I tried to hold out. I fought so long. So long."

"I know you did," she said, gently smoothing his hair over and over.

"It got so bad. I wanted it to end. I wanted to die. I would have done or said anything for it to be over."

He hiccupped and moaned. "I thought I was a patriot. Loyal to my king and country. They broke me. I am broken still."

"You are healing, Sebastian," she said softly. "The war is over."

"It will never be over," he said vehemently. "I told them what they wanted to know. I told them everything. I betrayed England. I betrayed myself." His voice broke and his sobs grew louder.

Hadley couldn't believe her ears. Shock filled her. This was Sebastian, a colonel in the king's army. A leader among men. The man she had idolized ever since she was a girl. He had been captured—and broken. What he had revealed to the enemy might have cost countless number of lives. No wonder he had such self-loathing. And even though pity filled her, seeing his marred body, she found her soul crushed by his intoxicated confession. She couldn't reconcile the vision of the hero she had worshipped, one whom she had placed upon a pedestal, and this drunken, weak man before her who had feet of clay.

Though she hurt for him and what he had been put through, something inside her shifted. It was more than bitter disappointment filling her. It was as if Sebastian had betrayed her, as well, pulverizing her heart. He had also deceived the world, allowing everyone to think he was a paragon of the perfect officer. She couldn't understand why Wellington had continued to keep Sebastian as a valued part of his staff after he committed treason against his fellow men and country.

Tears streamed down her cheeks. She, too, was now shattered beyond repair. Sebastian had destroyed her belief in not only him—but herself. She had badly misjudged who he was, which made her question everything about herself. She had wanted to marry this man but that could never come to pass because she could never live with the lie that would always be between them. She had trusted him—and now that trust had been smashed into a thousand pieces.

Hadley slipped from under him. His eyes were closed again and he was asleep once more. She quickly left the library, her entire body trembling at the awful discovery. Now that she knew his terrible secret, she didn't think she could ever be around him without bursting into tears. She felt shame at how his touch had affected her. It would be imperative to distance herself from him. Though she could keep a straight face during gameplay, she had no confidence in being able to do so now that she knew the ugly truth.

The one thing she would do is keep his secret. It was not hers to divulge. She would make sure a permanent break occurred between them. If he questioned her, let him think it was about the scars that disfigured his flesh. That she was shallow enough not to want him for that reason. It no longer mattered what he thought of her and it would be an excuse to part from him.

Returning to her room, Hadley thought until dawn and decided what she would need to do.

Chapter Sixteen

Hadley rose and washed her face. She had remained dry-eyed through the night. She was done crying tears over the Duke of Hardwick and grateful that he'd had enough sense to push her away. She couldn't imagine what would have become of their marriage had she actually wed him. It was one thing for her to learn his awful secret and remove herself from his presence. It would have been another thing entirely had she wed the man and then learned of his treason. She would have had to remain by his side, pretending to all of Polite Society that he was a war hero. She would rather never have children than have their father be a traitor and a liar.

She rang for Millie, pacing until the maid arrived.

"Got the dress returned to the duchess' maid, my lady. What would you like to wear today?"

"Anything. You choose."

Millie brought a gown of pastel blue. Hadley nodded her approval and the maid dressed her. She went and sat at the dressing table while Millie took up her brush.

"I need you to do something for me today," she began.

"What, my lady?"

"I am going to return to Hardwell Hall for the day and pack up my things."

The servant looked stricken. "You are leaving?"

She didn't want to get into the particulars with her maid and said,

"Now that His Grace has returned, there's no further need for me to stay. He will assume all of his duties, ones which I had handled when the previous duke was unable to do so himself. I am of age and no longer need a guardian. In fact, it is quite improper for me to be living in His Grace's home without a chaperone."

Millie's nose scrunched up. "Gentry has some funny rules."

"Nevertheless, I will be leaving Hardwell Hall and will need to have all my belongings gathered up today."

"So, you won't be returning with His Grace after the house party?"

"I will not," she said firmly. "I know you have served as a parlor maid and assisted me at times. I don't wish to ask you to choose—"

"I choose *you,* my lady," Millie interrupted. "I didn't really like the old duke. I don't know this one. My loyalty is to you. That is, if you will have me. I know I am not a true lady's maid." She cast down her eyes, her mouth trembling.

Hadley turned. "Millie, I would be most happy if you choose to come with me."

The girl brightened. "Truly?"

"Yes. I cannot guarantee where we will live, though."

"Oh, it don't matter a bit to me, my lady. I will follow wherever you go."

"We will leave shortly after breakfast and be at Hardwell Hall several hours before returning to Blackstone Manor. Tell no one where we are going. Do you understand? This is very important."

Millie looked perplexed by her mistress' request but said, "Of course, my lady. Whatever you wish."

"Good. I will summon you shortly."

Hadley went downstairs for breakfast, earlier than usual, but she hoped to catch Arabella alone. The only people present at this hour were Elizabeth and Lord Hayward, who sat off by themselves, their conversation intense, and Arabella, who sat with her husband and Phoebe.

Going to them, she said to Arabella, "I have a favor to ask of you."

Sympathy filled her friend's eyes. "Whatever you need, Hadley."

"I must go to Hardwell Hall today. Could you provide transportation for me and my maid?"

Jon studied her a moment and then said, "Of course. Our carriage is at your disposal. Might I ask why you wish to go there today when the house party ends tomorrow and you will be returning then?"

"I won't go back to Hardwell Hall after today," she stated. "His Grace needs the allegiance of his retainers. My presence would only result in divided loyalties. Besides, it isn't proper for me to be under his roof, an unmarried woman with no chaperone."

"Where will you go?" Phoebe inquired.

"I haven't decided yet."

"Well, I have. I had invited you to come visit the three of us. You may ride back to Windowmere with us tomorrow."

Gratitude filled Hadley. "I am very thankful for your invitation, Phoebe. Would you do me a favor and not reveal to anyone, other than your husband, that those are my plans?"

"Is this about Sebastian?" Jon asked.

Hadley nodded, afraid to trust her voice for a moment.

"I know things went badly between you," he continued. "Arabella told me."

She had sworn to herself that she would never be the one to divulge what lay deep in Sebastian's past. It was his secret to share with his friends, whether he chose to do so or not. Because of that, she chose her words carefully.

"In the end, I believe things worked out as they should have. I can see now why His Grace and I would never suit. I am eager to get away and start my own life. I am certain he feels the same."

"Are you packing your belongings then?" Arabella asked.

"Yes. My maid, Millie, has expressed a desire to go with me. I hope it is all right if I bring her along tomorrow, Phoebe."

"Both you and Millie are welcome to stay at Windowmere for as long as you wish though I know Samantha has expressed a desire for you to attend her birth."

"I am happy to be with her when the child comes. I have delivered a good number of babies over the years on the estate."

"You may return to Blackstone Manor whenever you wish," Jon encouraged. "Arabella and Elizabeth would be happy for your company."

She smiled. "I will keep that in mind, Your Grace. Thank you. I also plan to visit Elise at some point."

"Don't forget that you will have full access to our London townhouse," Arabella reminded.

"Since we will be staying at Blackstone Manor indefinitely," her husband added, gazing fondly at his wife.

Hadley knew from his comment that Arabella must have shared with her husband that she believed herself increasing.

"Then it is settled. I will go and collect my things and make sure everything is in order for His Grace when he returns tomorrow. I will be back in time for dinner and the dancing tonight," she promised.

"Eat something," Jon urged, "and then come to the stables. I will make sure the carriage is ready to depart by the time you are ready to leave."

After a quick cup of tea and a few bites of toast, Hadley excused herself, wanting to avoid Sebastian. She wondered if he had spent the entire night on the carpet in the library and then decided it was none of her concern. She would do her duty and see that his home would be ready for his arrival tomorrow.

She rang for Millie and the two went to the stables. Blackmore introduced her to his coachman and instructed him to take the pair to Hardwell Hall. Hadley closed her eyes in the coach and the motion lulled her to sleep, which she badly needed. Millie shook her once they arrived and she told the girl to pack her own belongings first before seeing to Hadley's.

"I don't have much, my lady," Millie revealed.

She laughed. "I don't either. I took all the new gowns which Mrs. Porter made up for me to the house party. All I have here are the few threadbare ones and my usual wardrobe of shirts and breeches."

"Don't go wearing those again, my lady," Millie cautioned. "You look ever so pretty in a gown."

"Lay out my clothing and shoes. I will decide what I will take and what will remain behind."

"Yes, my lady."

Radmore greeted them as they entered, along with Mrs. Sewell.

"You have returned early, Lady Hadley," the butler said. "You weren't expected until tomorrow."

"I will no longer be residing at Hardwell Hall, Radmore," she shared. "Millie has instructions to pack my things. Once she had done so, we will go back to the house party and see it to its end. Millie is also coming with me, Mrs. Sewell, so you will need to hire a new parlor maid."

Both servants looked stunned by her declaration and Hadley added, "This is for the best. His Grace needs to be fully in charge now. I will go to the study and make certain everything is left where he can review it." She was thinking of the reports she had composed during the days Sebastian had traveled to London. "Once he reads through what I have written, it should be self-explanatory."

"Where will you go, my lady?" asked the housekeeper.

"London," she said. It was her eventual destination and she didn't want Sebastian knowing she would be in Devon with the Windhams. Not that she thought he would come after her, but she believed what she did from this point on was her own business and not his.

"You will be missed," Radmore said, his eyes full of sorrow. "I know there is no time for you to ride the estate and say goodbye to all the tenants but would you mind if I gathered the servants and allowed

a farewell when you depart?"

"That would be lovely," she told him. "Give me two hours' time and then I will let them see me off."

Hadley went directly to the study. Everything was already in excellent order because she kept meticulous, neat records. She did lay out the various reports she had prepared and wrote a few notes to Sebastian, telling him where to look for certain items and improvements she had made to the system Mr. Vickers, the former steward, used in the ledgers. Once that had been accomplished, she ventured upstairs, where Millie had set out the clothing that remained in the wardrobe.

"There's very little here, my lady," the maid apologized.

"I agree. The gowns are too worn for me or anyone else to ever use them. Give them to Mrs. Seward to be used as rags. I will keep a pair of breeches and one each of my shirts and short coats, along with my boots. The rest can be distributed among the servants here. There are a few young grooms that are small and might actually fit or grow into the remainder of my wardrobe."

She had no mementos from her childhood. No books she wanted to take with her. No jewelry. No personal items of any kind. It saddened her to think how little she had. Oh, she did have access to funds. She would need to write her solicitor in London and make him aware of the situation, that she now ventured out on her own. She decided she would travel and spend time with her new friends until the new year. Only then would she make her way to London and see what the great city held in store for her.

Millie packed the few clothes and pair of boots Hadley wanted in a small valise and placed it on the floor next to one of similar size.

"You have everything you need?" she asked the girl. "Remember, we won't be coming back."

"I do, my lady." Millie smiled. "I am ready for our great adventure."

"Then let us go say our goodbyes."

The pair went downstairs and Hadley saw all the servants lined the foyer. As she descended the stairs, they began applauding. Tears sprang to her eyes as she went down the line, hugging every one of them, memories of the past decade flooding her.

Finally, she reached Mrs. Sewell. "You were a fine mistress, my lady," the housekeeper said. "Even though you were so young when you first came to us. I wish you every bit of the best."

"Thank you, Mrs. Sewell. You taught me a great deal. One day when I have a house of my own to manage, I will incorporate everything you taught me into running the place."

Radmore escorted her to the carriage and said, "It was the best day I'd seen at Hardwell Hall when you arrived, Lady Hadley. And each progressive day only grew better under your leadership. You will be missed."

She kissed the butler's cheek. "Thank you for everything, Radmore. Take care of His Grace," she added, despite her ambivalent feelings toward the duke.

The coachman helped her into the carriage and Millie followed. As the vehicle pulled away, Hadley closed the door on the years she had spent at Hardwell Hall.

Chapter Seventeen

SEBASTIAN HEARD A voice coming from a long way off.

"Go away," he mumbled and tried to swallow. His mouth felt as if he had been eating sand. He desperately needed something to drink but the thought of acting on that impulse overwhelmed him.

"Sit up, Your Grace," the voice said firmly and he was pulled to a sitting position.

He tried to open his eyes and found them practically glued shut, matted together. His head throbbed painfully. Every muscle in his body ached. Nausea enveloped him. He felt as weak as a newborn kitten.

A warm rag was placed against his eyes. "This will help you open them in a moment. Hold it in place."

He obeyed the voice, realizing it was his valet.

"Where am I?" he asked, pressing the rag to his eyes as a blinding shot of pain zipped along his forehead, causing him to gasp.

"Best drink this," Bardham advised. "It is a Highland Fling."

The valet took Sebastian's free hand and wrapped it around a mug, helping guide it to his lips.

"Drink it all," cautioned Bardham. "The quicker, the better."

He parted his parched lips and greedily guzzled the concoction, which tasted awful. Grimacing, he continued swallowing it merely because it was liquid and he hoped it would moisten his dry tongue and throat.

Once he drained the nasty brew, he shoved it away and pulled the rag from his eyes, prying them open with force. His head pounded fiercely and the nausea continued to ripple through him as his heart beat rapidly.

Glancing about, he asked, "Is the room spinning?"

"Not the last time I checked," his valet remarked, taking the wet cloth and rubbing it over Sebastian's face as if he were a child incapable of doing so.

"Where am I?" he asked again since it was too much effort to look about a room that kept moving.

"The Duke of Blackmore's library."

He frowned. "Why am I here?" he demanded, wincing at the sound of his voice.

"I suppose because you drank yourself into a stupor and passed out, Your Grace."

"What time is it?"

"Almost noon."

He put his hands to his pounding head. "I was here all night?"

"I assume so," confirmed Bardham. "You never rang for me. You are still wearing last night's clothing. I searched the house and found you here half an hour ago when I discovered you hadn't slept in your bed."

"And you are just now awakening me?" he asked, his irritation obvious.

"I have sent for a bath. I also had to perfect my special concoction."

"That foul liquid you poured down my gullet?"

"The Highland Fling is a well-known Scottish remedy for a hangover."

"You are not a Scotsman," Sebastian growled, rubbing his temples, seeking relief.

"But I grew up within a hair's breadth of the border, Your Grace."

"What was in it?"

"I stirred corn flour into buttermilk and heated it in a pan. Seasoned it with a bit of salt and pepper to make it more palatable."

"It was rot."

Bardham glared at him. "Do you want my help or not, Colonel?"

"Yes," Sebastian said meekly, beginning to realize the position he was in.

"Then we'll get you up first. That will be an accomplishment in itself," predicted the valet.

"I don't want anyone to see me like this," he said, thinking immediately of Hadley.

"Her Grace has gathered all of the guests and they have gone outside now for luncheon on the terrace."

"Good," he mumbled, grateful that no one would see him in such a dismal state.

Somehow, Bardham got Sebastian on his feet. He realized he wasn't wearing some of his clothes but had no memory of undressing. The valet gathered the missing items of clothing and gently led Sebastian to his room, passing only one maid. She lowered her eyes and scurried down the stairs past them.

By the time they arrived in his assigned chamber, the hot water had been sent up and was still steaming. Bardham stripped the rest of Sebastian's wrinkled clothes from him and helped lower him into the large tub. The water felt good, immediately easing his aching muscles.

"Wash. You stink of spirits and sweat," Bardham said and left.

Sebastian braced his neck against the tub and simply soaked for several minutes. His heartbeat lessened somewhat though the raging headache remained. Finally, he lowered himself completely, dipping his head under the water and rising again. He washed his hair and lathered his ruined body, each movement painful, though the room no longer swam. As he bathed, he tried to remember anything about last night that he could. He had gone to the salon. The gardens. Then the library. Yes, the library. He had deliberately drunk as much as he could because he wanted to forget his troubles.

An image of Hadley swam before his eyes. He could almost feel her touch.

Had she come across him in his drunken state?

He had no recollection of it. Just an eerie feeling that somehow she had been with him. He prayed that it was his imagination. He had already hurt her so much. He would hate for her to have seen him this way.

Bardham returned and helped Sebastian to stand, pouring fresh water to rinse him. The water sluiced down his body. He glanced briefly and always seemed startled by the scars, a permanent part of him. Thankfully, Bardham never mentioned them.

He stepped from the tub and wrapped a bath sheet about his waist.

"You need to be shaved."

"I can do it," he said stubbornly, grasping for some kind of control.

The valet's brows rose. "Can you, Your Grace? Your hands are shaking."

Holding one out, he saw how it trembled.

"I will do it," Bardham said gently.

After the shave, the valet dressed him and led him to a chair by the window. A tray sat there and Sebastian smelled strong coffee.

"Coffee with plenty of sugar in it. Dry toast. Keep that down and we'll see if you get anything else," Bardham pronounced.

Sebastian took his time eating and drinking the meal. The throbbing in his head had lessened to a dull ache. His body still hurt but he knew he would live.

"What have I missed today?"

"This morning, several guests went riding after breakfast. They came back in time to change and freshen up for luncheon. I believe Her Grace plans for archery this afternoon."

"I will skip it."

"You will do no such thing," chided the valet. "That would be rude to your hostess."

"When did you become such an expert on manners in Polite Society?" he grumbled.

"You don't have to participate. Just sit and watch."

"Then tea, I suppose," he guessed.

"Yes. Followed by a light dinner and dancing with a midnight buffet. Several musicians have already arrived and the Blackmores have invited guests from the nearby village to the country ball to close out the house party."

He remembered now. The thought of dancing made the room swim again.

"We will be leaving first thing in the morning after breakfast," he told Bardham. "Be sure Lady Hadley's maid knows and has her packed and ready."

"Very well, Your Grace. Any more to eat?"

The thought of ingesting more food caused his belly to turn over. "No."

Sebastian made his way carefully downstairs and outdoors. The day was overcast and he gave thanks for it since what light there was burned his eyes. He found Andrew at a table and sat next to him. They remained in companionable silence as two dozen other guests participated in an archery contest. He appreciated that his friend didn't comment on his appearance.

Once the contest ended, tea was brought out to the terrace. Others joined them and he managed to get down half a sandwich and a sand tart, along with four cups of tea. His immense thirst didn't seem to be quenched no matter how much he drank. Sebastian swore never to touch a drop of whiskey again.

He did surreptitiously watch Hadley as tea progressed. He hadn't seen her during the archery contest but he couldn't stop looking at her now. She sat with Elizabeth, Lord Hayward, and Lord Stanhope. She never glanced in his direction.

After tea ended, he managed to stand and thank Arabella.

"You have two hours until dinner, Sebastian. Might I suggest you lie down and rest during that time?"

He supposed it was her polite way of telling him that he looked like hell.

"An excellent idea," he agreed, mustering a smile.

"Not everyone will attend dinner. I can always have a tray sent up to your room if you would prefer to dine alone."

He nodded. "Please do so, Arabella. Thank you."

Sebastian returned to his room, where Bardham sat reading a book.

"Wake me when the meal tray comes. Not a second before," he said as he collapsed onto the bed, falling into a dreamless sleep.

SEBASTIAN STILL FELT a bit shaky but he had eaten the dinner sent up to him. Dancing might be difficult to navigate, however.

Bardham removed the tray. "I need to shave you again, Your Grace."

"You did that earlier," he complained.

"I did but I already see new whiskers upon your chin. Tonight is the culmination of the house party and the duke and duchess have invited both their tenants and townsfolk to this country ball. The least you can do is turn out looking your best. His Grace is a good friend to you and you do not want to embarrass him."

He thought of what Jon—or Arabella—might have thought if they had stumbled upon him passed out in the library and was grateful they hadn't discovered him in such a sorry state. He owed Bardham for locating him and smuggling him upstairs.

"Very well. I am at your disposal."

After shaving Sebastian, his valet dressed him in his evening clothes, taking extra care to perfect his cravat.

"You look marvelous, Your Grace," Bardham said. "Do you plan to offer for a wife this evening?"

"No," he said succinctly and left it at that.

"Very good, Your Grace. I hope you enjoy a pleasant evening with your friends."

"Have you spoken to Lady Hadley's maid?" he asked, wanting to be sure that issue had been resolved.

"I have. Millie is quite aware of your urgency to return to Hardwell Hall and will convey that to her mistress. I will see you when the ball is over."

"Bardham?" Sebastian called out as the valet reached the door. "Thank you. For everything."

His servant smiled. "Of course, Your Grace. It is a pleasure to serve you."

He was truly grateful the former batman had come calling after the war. It was nice to have a familiar face around him. He did remember some of the servants at Hardwell Hall from his childhood, such as Radmore and Mrs. Sewell, but so many new faces had come to work at the estate during the years he had been absent. He looked forward to meeting his tenants and getting to know more about his estate. The thought caused him to wonder how long Hadley would remain at Hardwell Hall. He didn't think she would stay more than a week or two. Just enough to see that he could manage on his own.

Sebastian hated letting her go. Part of him believed she was the tonic he needed to rid himself from the dark shadows of his past. The saner part of him agreed it was best to let her move on. That he was a lost cause and would only cause her heartache and grief. Still, he longed for a dance with her this evening though he doubted she would grant it to him.

He had put it off long enough and decided to go downstairs. He followed the music wafting up the staircase he descended and soon entered a large ballroom. Being a country ball, the guests included the well-dressed houseguests who danced alongside and even partnered with staff members at Blackstone Manor and Jon's tenants. Citizens from the nearby village were also in attendance. Despite the swelling number in the ballroom, he easily found Hadley. She wore a gown of deep magenta and looked as regal as any queen ever had. He watched her dancing down a line with one of the footmen, joy on her face as she whirled about.

"Ready to make for home?"

Sebastian turned and found George at his elbow. "Yes. Though the idea of home seems almost foreign."

"You were away a good number of years," his friend noted. "Give it time. I am sure you will settle in nicely within a few weeks."

"Are you ready to be a father?" he asked.

"The thought terrifies me," George admitted. "And then I look at Sam. How radiant and serene she is. I feel my love for her flowing through my veins. Then a calm descends upon me, knowing how much we want this child and how lucky we are to have found one another after so many years apart."

Weston and Jon joined them and they talked at length about everything and nothing in particular. Eventually, each of his friends drifted away to find their wives and Sebastian searched until he found Hadley again. She stood next to a man that Jon had pointed out as the local doctor who had been to see Arabella. Jon had revealed to them earlier that his wife was expecting a child come the spring.

He moved nearer to them, knowing he wouldn't ask Hadley to dance but just wanting to walk past her and inhale the familiar vanilla scent that clung to her.

Suddenly, a servant brushed past him. "Doctor, can you come quick? One of the scullery maids burned her hand badly and Cook asked me to find you."

"Certainly." The man looked at Hadley. "My apologies, my lady, for missing our dance."

"Please, go. See to the maid," she urged.

The doctor turned and spotted Sebastian. "Oh, Your Grace. Might you partner with Lady Hadley? I must abandon her to see to a patient." He quickly exited, leaving Sebastian gawking at Hadley.

He tried to recover his composure as the music began and he asked, "Would you care to dance?"

Without waiting for her reply, he took her in his arms and launched into the waltz. She averted her eyes, looking over his shoulder, feeling stiff and unwieldy in his arms. None of the grace she had exhibited on the dance floor was apparent now.

"Hadley?"

Her eyes cut to him. "I'd rather you address me as Lady Hadley, Your Grace. Actually, I prefer you not to address me at all."

As her mouth tightened, his insides went cold. She gazed at him with revulsion.

She knew . . .

He hadn't dreamed of her soft hands touching him. She had been there last night—and had seen his scars.

Sebastian had to realize that she was, for all her intelligence, a very sheltered woman. She had never been exposed to that kind of horror before. It was only natural for her to be uncomfortable in his presence now, knowing what lay beneath his finely-tailored clothes.

Dully, he said, "I don't remember but I can guess that you found me last night. I must apologize for my state of drunkenness."

She remained silent, once more gazing over his shoulder, as if she couldn't stand to look at him.

His heart hurt but he had to let her know that he understood her feelings. "I disappointed you. I also know you . . . you saw what . . . was done to me. I understand I physically repulse you."

Hadley's gaze whipped back to him. "You are certainly right about that, Your Grace. I find I can no longer be in your presence. I find it awkward and distressing. You are repugnant to me."

It was like she had bayoneted him in his gut. His feet stopped moving. His mouth gaped. A secret part of him had dreamed that he would one day reveal his disfigurement to her and that she would be able to look past the damaged flesh. His arms fell from her.

"I wish never to speak to nor see you again, Your Grace."

With that, Hadley left the dance floor and walked out of his life.

Chapter Eighteen

SEBASTIAN SAT IN the chair next to the window, his eyes grainy from lack of sleep. A knock sounded on the door.

"Come," he called and watched as his valet entered the bedchamber.

"You did not ring for me, Your Grace. I was worried and came to check on you. Breakfast is almost over and most of the guests are beginning to depart."

"I wasn't hungry. I need to dress now." Wearily, he stood.

Bardham helped him into fresh clothes without trying to make conversation. He supposed word had spread even to the servants' hall of Lady Hadley abandoning the Duke of Hardwick in the middle of a dance and storming off the ballroom floor.

He had felt the intense, questioning stares and quickly exited the ballroom himself, not wanting to see or speak to anyone. Retreating to his room, he had barred the door and remained in his evening clothes all night, moving restlessly about the chamber, sleep impossible.

Once his cravat had been tied, he said, "Have my trunk brought downstairs and the carriages brought around." He paused. "And notify Lady Hadley's maid that we will depart soon."

Sebastian left the room and went downstairs. The foyer was a flurry of activity, servants scurrying about. He saw Elizabeth deep in conversation with Lord Hayward and decided not to interrupt them in order to tell her goodbye. Venturing outside, he saw carriages lining the drive, trunks being loaded onto them. He went to Jon and Arabella.

"Thank you for having me," he said. "I apologize for not being an ideal guest."

Jon placed a hand on Sebastian's shoulder. "You are just home from the war. It will take time to adjust to society. I know you are eager to return to Hardwell Hall."

Arabella leaned up and kissed his cheek. "We aren't that far away, Sebastian. We are here when you need us."

He noticed she said when—and not if.

"Thank you," he said humbly, admiration for her swelling within him. He was happy his old friend had found such an amazing woman to be his duchess.

"Sebastian!" Andrew called.

He turned and saw Andrew carrying Robby in his arms, Phoebe beside him. Sebastian approached them and heard Robby babbling contentedly, drool running down his chin. Impulsively, he bent and kissed the baby's head.

"I am glad you made it back in time to attend the house party," Andrew said. "It's good to have you back in England for good."

"I am happy to have finally met your wife," he said. Looking to the duchess, he added, "You have made my friend the happiest of men by giving him a son."

Phoebe gazed at him thoughtfully. "I am pleased to have made your acquaintance as well. Know that Windowmere is open to you at any time. We hope you will visit us soon."

"It may be a while before that occurs," he shared. "I need to see to my country seat first and then travel to my other holdings and look them over. I do appreciate the invitation, however, and hope I can take you up on it in the future."

He offered his hand and Andrew took it. "Safe travels to you and your family."

The Windhams made their way to the first carriage in line. A nurse leaned out from it and took Robby and then Andrew handed Phoebe into the carriage. He turned and waved goodbye and then entered the vehicle himself. Moments later, it took off, soon followed by a second carriage carrying their servants.

"Sebastian, good, we didn't miss you," Weston said, coming up and pounding him heartily on the back.

He saw Elise, George, and Samantha followed Weston and he told each of them farewell, congratulating Elise on the babe she carried and wishing Samantha the best as she awaited the birth of her child.

"You have married well," he told his two friends. "Former rogues who are now settled as doting husbands."

"And fathers-to-be," George added, a huge grin on his face. "Don't be a stranger, Sebastian. Come to see us. Our estates are so close that visiting one of us is like a trip to see both of us. In fact, we rode to Blackstone Manor together."

"Our carriages are next to depart," Weston said. "This is goodbye."

Sebastian watched the two couples leave and looked about to see if Hadley had made an appearance yet. Frowning, he saw she hadn't. Bardham came hurrying toward him.

"Why isn't Lady Hadley here?" he demanded, trying to keep his voice down and his emotions in check.

"She has already departed, Your Grace," the valet informed him. "We may leave whenever you wish."

Disappointment filled him. Though he had known the short journey home would be awkward, it surprised him that Hadley had inconvenienced their hosts by asking for separate transportation to Hardwell Hall. It also let him know just how much she loathed him, not wanting to spend any time alone together.

"Very well." He strode toward his carriage and nodded to the driver before climbing inside. Within seconds, the vehicle started up.

He allowed his mind to go blank during the ride. During his time in captivity, he had done the same thing as he had been beaten and tortured. Mentally, he fled to another place of quiet and total whiteness. No thoughts. No looking forward or backward. Just a place of existence. He remained there until he sensed the motion of the wheels come to a stop and disembarked once the coach came to a complete halt.

Radmore met him. "It is very good to have you home, Your Grace."

Sebastian's stomach grumbled noisily in reply.

"I will have Cook prepare something for you at once," the butler said, chuckling.

"Have it brought to my study," he instructed. "And have Lady Hadley meet me there. We are to go over estate matters together. See that we are not interrupted."

Sebastian strode off, wondering how to prepare himself to see her again. Perhaps they would forego any personal conversation and move strictly to discussing the estate and its upcoming autumn harvest. That would be best. She would impart her knowledge. He would ask questions to clarify matters. Then she would be free to leave and never return.

He opened the door to the study and saw neat stacks of papers atop the desk, so unlike the days of the former duke when Hardwick left things haphazardly. It seemed everywhere he looked, he would find Hadley's hand in things. Moving to the window, he saw that a chessboard sat on the table between the two chairs and recalled her telling him of Hardwick teaching her how to play, well enough to not only master the game but for the pupil to claim victory over her teacher.

He gazed out the window, steeling himself for her arrival. Some minutes passed, tension filling his body as his head began to pound at the temples. He had led men into battle, cannons firing and bullets whizzing past, yet he had never felt as apprehensive as he did at this moment. She thought the very worst of him and nothing he could do or say would ever change her mind.

A light rap sounded on the door and he turned as Radmore pushed it open, a tray in his hands. He set it on the table behind the desk.

"Tea and sandwiches, Your Grace. It was all Cook had time to prepare with short notice. She will prepare a more substantial meal—"

"Did you summon Lady Hadley as ordered? She should have arrived by now."

Radmore shook his head. "I am afraid Lady Hadley isn't here, Your Grace."

"Not here? She left the house party before me this morning. Has she already come and gone again?" he demanded.

The butler cleared his throat. "Lady Hadley no longer resides at Hardwell Hall. She left with her things and told the staff goodbye yesterday." He paused, sadness blanketing him. "She will not be returning."

Stunned, he merely shook his head back and forth, not comprehending what the butler had just revealed.

"Lady Hadley wishes for everyone to give you their full attention and respect, Your Grace. She thought it best to leave before you even arrived. However, she did spend a great deal of time preparing the reports on your desk. She told me they are self-explanatory and should guide you through the coming weeks."

"I see." He felt adrift. "That will be all," he said dismissively, wanting to be alone.

Radmore hesitated and then nodded, leaving without a word.

Sebastian went and sat behind the desk. The sheaf of papers directly in front of him was labeled Hardwell Hall. He began with that stack, reading slowly through voluminous notes written by Hadley. It contained a wealth of information. The name and position of every servant and their years of service. Work that had been completed on the house during his absence, including the cost of the repairs and who had completed each project. A list of bills to be paid monthly. Names of every tenant on the property and those of his family. Twice, Hadley had made a notation of a babe that was expected and when the wife might deliver the child.

He delved deeper and read about various crops produced during his time away. Which ones had seen the largest profit. The fields in which they had been rotated to and from. He found pages regarding livestock and the pastures they frequented. The number and types of horses in his stables. Sebastian had never seen such thorough work in his life.

As his tea grew cold and the food remained untouched, he moved his attention to the various piles. Each pertained to a different estate in his holdings and were just as thorough as the ones he had perused. A wealth of knowledge was contained in all of these reports. He couldn't imagine how long they had taken to research and prepare. It must have been all Hadley had done while he had been away in London.

Her notes directed him to various ledgers on the shelves behind him and he began pulling those from the shelves and flipping through their pages. Ignoring the knocks at the door, Sebastian spent all day and most of the evening going through what had been left for him. He heard the chiming of a clock in the distance and counted to ten. Weary, he emerged from the office, his head full of numbers and names, all swimming about.

Sebastian wished he could at least write to Hadley and thank her for such a treasure trove of detailed information. The trouble was, he hadn't a clue where she had gone.

HADLEY WOKE IN her bed at Treadwell Manor and stretched. Cleo, who had been snuggled against her side, stood and did the same. The cat moved up to her mistress' face and rubbed her cheek against

Hadley's. She stroked the smooth fur, grateful for her companion.

She had fallen in love with Caesar during her time at Windowmere. The tabby must have sensed her sadness because he began following Hadley about, sitting in her lap anytime she sat and even choosing to sleep with her over Phoebe and Andrew. Because of this, Phoebe had insisted Hadley accompany her to the stables, where a mama cat had given birth to a litter of kittens that spring. The head groom had given away all of the kittens save for one, a tiger-striped female, who remained with her mother to help keep the stables free of mice.

Hadley fell in love with the kitten, who was five months old, and had named her Cleo for Cleopatra. Cleo and Caesar had become close companions during Hadley's three months at Windowmere. When she left for Colebourne Hall, Cleo came with her. The cat became her shadow and constant companion and the very pregnant Samantha had told George that when spring came, he needed to find her a kitten, as well. George had teased that a baby should be enough but Samantha insisted. Knowing how George doted on his wife, Hadley knew Samantha would get her wish.

She had delivered Samantha's daughter, Sophie, the first week of December and stayed through Christmas with the Colebournes before returning to Blackstone Manor, where she spent the entire month of January with Jon and Arabella. She felt safe doing so only after learning that Sebastian would be away from Hardwell Hall as he toured his various properties. He had spent Christmas with Jon and Arabella and then departed for the north of England, where he had a property near York.

Her time at Blackstone Manor passed quickly. Arabella was in good spirits and had reached the point of her pregnancy where she still had abundant energy. Hadley knew from experience that once she left, Arabella would begin slowing down and going through a nesting period before she gave birth.

She petted a purring Cleo again and told the cat, "We should get up. I need to dress and take you to the kitchens for your breakfast. Then it will be time to pack."

Hadley had journeyed to London after visiting the Blackmores and spent many hours at Madame Toufours' dress shop. The modiste had taken Hadley's measurements and then they had looked at countless bolts of fabric and discussed various designs for her wardrobe for the upcoming Season. She would be returning to London tomorrow since Elise had given birth ten days ago and all seemed well with both her and her newborn son. After time spent with her three good friends the past six months, Hadley was ready to return to London for more fittings and to begin discovering more about the city that she already loved from her short sojourn there.

She rang for Millie and the maid appeared, her usual cheerful self.

"Good morning, my lady. And a good morning to you, Miss Cleo."

At the start, Millie had been leery of the cat. She had never been around one and was afraid it would bite or scratch her. Cleo had a sweet nature, however, and soon Millie doted on the cat as much as Hadley did.

As Millie assisted her, Hadley said, "You will need to do our packing today. We will leave for London first thing in the morning."

The maid's eyes lit up. "I can't wait to go back, my lady. London's very exciting."

She bit back a smile, knowing that Millie found London exciting because of a certain footman at the Blackmores' townhouse, where they had stayed for the two weeks in February during their first trip to the city. They would return again and remain at the townhouse during the entire Season since Arabella was less than a month away from giving birth at this point. Hadley had begged for Arabella to let her come and deliver her child but her friend insisted that it was more important for Hadley to go to London and participate in the Season. She understood why. All her friends were so happy and in love with their husbands. Naturally, they wanted the same for her.

Would this Season—her first—actually lead to marriage?

It had weighed on her mind ever since the end of the house party back in August. Her yearning to be a mother had only grown stronger in that time, especially seeing Samantha and Elise with their newborn babes. Hadley had also met several interesting gentlemen during her extended stays at Windowmere, Colebourne Hall, and Treadwell Manor and knew all of these eligible bachelors would be in town for the upcoming Season. She supposed her friends' husbands had invited the gentlemen at their wives' urging. It did help, though, because now she would go into the Season actually knowing others. Hadley had dreaded attending social events not knowing a soul. She did also have acquaintances from the house party, such as Lady Pamela and Lady Callamina, and looked forward to connecting with them again.

The hardest thing would be encountering Sebastian at the various events. She could still see the look of anguish upon his face as she had abandoned him on the dance floor during the house party. Despite her vow to keep her thoughts away from her memories of him, Hadley had found herself remembering small things about him. She pushed aside her regrets, knowing to dwell on them would only bring on more heartache. She had her future to look to and not her past.

Leaving Millie to begin the packing, Hadley carried Cleo to the kitchen. One of the scullery maids took the cat.

"I will be sure Cleo gets her breakfast and is let outdoors, my lady, then bring her back inside when she's done her business."

"Thank you."

Hadley left for the breakfast room, where Weston sat poring over a newspaper.

"Ah, good morning, Hadley."

She thought how handsome Weston was and how he and his sister favored one another so much. Samantha's daughter had the same coloring as her mother and uncle and their raven hair. She wondered if

Weston and Elise's new boy would favor his mother or father. The baby had been born without a hair on his head, so it would take time to see if he received Elise's rich, brown hair or Weston's dark locks. As most babies, he had blue eyes now but Hadley had learned most babies' eye color changed after several months. Whether they turned aquamarine as Weston's or became violet as Elise's, he was still a beautiful boy.

"Good morning, Weston."

A footman seated her and another brought her a cup of tea and a plate with toast points, ham, and eggs. She liberally spread the jam on her toast and bit into it.

"Today is your last with us, isn't it?" he asked.

"Yes, and I must thank you for allowing me to stay so long."

"We've enjoyed your company and Elise wouldn't have had it any other way. She was determined for you to deliver her baby, just as you did for Sam."

"I only wish I could be there when Arabella gives birth."

"Don't fret over that, Hadley. You have spent plenty of time in the country. It is time for you to be back in town. I am sure you have all those womanly things to see to in order to prepare for the upcoming Season. Hats. Reticules. Gowns."

She laughed. "Madame Toufours' shop will be one of the first places I call once I return to London."

Weston grew serious. "I am sorry Elise and I won't be there this Season to support you."

"Oh, I didn't expect you to be there, Weston. Elise certainly doesn't need to travel since she has just given birth. The country air will be better for her and the baby."

"At least you will have Andrew and Phoebe there with you. Sam told me yesterday that she and George plan to go for the first couple of months. Once the weather grows warmer, though, Sam promised to return to Devon."

"See? I won't be alone at all."

He studied her intently. "You do know Sebastian plans to be in London for the Season. I received a letter from him yesterday."

Hadley clutched her hands tightly, glad they were in her lap and hidden from his sight. "Yes, I assumed he would be in London. He left me with the impression that he would be seeking a wife on the Marriage Mart."

"It will be impossible to avoid him," Weston pointed out. "I do think he will behave in a gentlemanly manner toward you, though. At his core, Sebastian is a good man."

The constant war that raged within her continued upon hearing the duke's remark. While Hadley resented Sebastian for betraying his countrymen, a part of her couldn't help but feel pity for what had been done to him. Worse, deep within her, she still found herself terribly attracted to him. No, not just attracted. Fool that she was, she still loved the man, despite everything. She would need to mask those feelings when they encountered one another, as they inevitably would at the various social events.

"I am sure we will be distantly polite to one another, Weston. Please, don't worry on my behalf. I plan to enjoy myself completely."

He gave her a worried look. "That is what I am afraid of." Sighing, he added, "My gut still tells me the two of you belong together. I won't asked what happened between you but all I can beg is for you to give Sebastian a chance—if he asks for one. If he doesn't, then I hope you find a man worthy of you, Hadley."

She doubted Sebastian would ever beg her for anything. Frankly, she doubted they would ever converse again, other than a civil greeting before they moved on.

Still, she wanted to ease her host's mind. "I would always be willing to listen to whatever Hardwick had to say to me."

"Good morning," Elise sang out, breezing into the room and kissing her husband's cheek. She seated herself across from Hadley. "I thought I would join you this morning instead of lazing about in bed while I have my chocolate. Have I missed anything?"

"Nothing, my darling," Weston said, taking her fingers and lacing them through his as a footman brought the duchess her breakfast. "It is good to see you. Hadley and I were just talking about her traveling to London."

Elise smiled. "Though I have thoroughly enjoyed your company, I know you are eager to take in the sights and begin the Season. You will want to see the British Museum in Bloomsbury, of course. And you must go to Gunter's in Mayfair. Their ices are divine, especially on a hot day."

"I have never had an ice," she said. "I look forward to trying one."

As they talked of places in London, Hadley couldn't help but wonder when Sebastian might arrive.

And who would be the woman he would take as his wife.

Chapter Nineteen

London

HADLEY SIPPED HER tea as she went through the morning post. She found a letter from Arabella and eagerly opened it.

My dearest Hadley –

I am officially the size of a large carriage now. Or at least it feels as if I am. Jon tells me daily how beautiful I am but I find it hard to believe any man could be attracted to someone as broad as a mountainside. Still, he is my husband and I will choose to believe him. Sometimes, we simply sit together, holding hands, waiting for the baby to kick. Jon will place his palm against my belly and then he lights up once he feels a kick. He will stroke my belly and then kneel, talking to it, telling the little one inside how much we love it and can't wait for its arrival.

Jon says it doesn't matter if it is a boy or girl. I always thought men didn't care much for female children and were only interested in their wives providing them with heirs. If that is the rule, then Jon is the exception. In fact, he has whispered to me as we lie in bed that he hopes this first babe is a girl, one that favors me. At this point, I only want our child to be born healthy and happy—and soon. I find I cannot let two hours pass without having to relieve myself. Sometimes, only one! It is also much harder to breathe these days. I try to inhale deeply and it seems there is nowhere for the air to go.

Oh, forgive me for complaining so! I am tired these days and frus-

trated because I want our baby to come. I long to hold it in my arms and see the physical manifestation of mine and Jon's love in the flesh. The doctor says it should be a week or so until that happens. He has warned me that once the process begins, first babies seem to take their time coming and I should be prepared for a long day and night.

How are you? Are you enjoying London? Thank you for writing to me of Elise and her precious newborn son. I am glad you were there to deliver her babe. I received a brief note from her telling me you never left her side and how grateful she was that you and Weston helped her remain calm. I only hope I will be able to do the same once my babe decides to make his—or her—appearance in the world.

Write to me of the Season, my darling friend, and of all the parties and balls. Tell me of the beautiful gowns you wear and the latest gossip. Especially tell me if you find a special someone. It is my most fervent prayer that you will find a good man to love and that he will love you, in return.

Ah, nature calls again so I will end this. Do write, Hadley. I miss you and love you.

Arabella

P.S. My water has broken! Only a twinge of pain so far. Jon has sent for the midwife and doctor. The next time you hear from me, Hadley, I will be a mother! I will have a footman post this now.

Hadley wished that she could have been by Arabella's side when she delivered her child but her friend had expressly forbidden it, wanting Hadley to concentrate on the Season at hand. All her friends had written to their friends about Hadley and invitations had begun to pour in. With the Season starting in less than a week, her calendar was already very full. She also had a wardrobe worthy of being seen in, much better than the gowns she had worn at her first house party. Phoebe's modiste had been happy to accept her as a client, thanks to the personal recommendation she had received. Hadley felt like a butterfly emerging from its cocoon and looked forward to wearing her new gowns and meeting all kinds of wonderful people.

She finished going through the post and took it to Arabella's parlor, placing it upon the escritoire. She would pen her replies later to both the invitations she had received and also write to Arabella. She had already sent letters to Samantha and Phoebe this week and would write Elise in the next few days. Perhaps she would wait for tomorrow's post to see if Jon sent news of the babe's birth before she wrote to Arabella. Now, though, she was ready for her morning walk to Hyde Park. Millie had insisted upon coming along as her chaperone but she did allow Hadley time to herself once they arrived. She had discovered a bench near the Serpentine and liked to sit upon it and watch the ducks swimming by.

Millie appeared. "Ready to walk, my lady?" She had Hadley's spencer and reticule in hand.

"Yes, thank you, Millie. I do enjoy my daily outing to the park."

The maid helped her slip into the spencer and they set out, embarking upon their usual route to the park, which was only a few minutes' walk from the Blackmore townhouse. The early morning air was cool and crisp. This had become her favorite time of day because few people were at the park at this early hour.

They reached her favorite bench and she sat.

"I will see you in an hour, my lady," Millie said.

"Yes, that will be fine. And then we will need to go to Madame Toufours' shop for a final fitting."

"Very well, my lady," Mille said.

Hadley let her thoughts drift and then became aware of someone nearby. It was a slim gentleman, elegantly dressed, whom she had seen in the park two or three times in the last week. He looked familiar to her but she didn't know where she would have made his acquaintance.

He came toward her and asked, "Might I share this bench with you, my lady?"

"Of course," she replied.

Up close, it immediately hit her who the mystery man was.

Wellington.

She had seen sketches of the commander in the newspapers often enough during the war years. His wavy hair was quite distinctive. In person, though, his blue eyes shone brightly, intense and curious. She decided not to address him. Wellington probably came to the park at this time for the solitude, as she did, and she didn't want to distress him.

They sat in companionable silence for some minutes, watching the ducks swim along the Serpentine.

Finally, he spoke. "I like to come here in the early mornings. Hyde Park is one of my favorite places. Sitting here, I bask in the peace and serenity, knowing England is safe. This park is my refuge." He paused, those bright, blue eyes penetrating her. "I believe you have recognized me, my lady."

"I did, Your Grace. I followed the war carefully for many years."

"I suppose you thought I would be taller. Larger than life." He chuckled. "Most all I meet do. I am three inches under six feet—but well above Bonaparte's height."

"I don't think your height has anything to do with your brilliance," she observed. "You are an astute strategist. It was your mind—and the men you commanded—that brought Bonaparte down."

"Thank you for the compliment. Did you have family or friends fighting on the Continent?" he inquired.

She clasped her hands tightly in her lap. "I did know someone," she said quietly.

"Oh, I do hope he made it back."

Hadley swallowed. "He did. In fact, he was on your staff."

The duke's brows rose. "Who might this soldier be?" he asked eagerly.

"Colonel Cooper," Hadley said, referring to Sebastian by the name and rank that Wellington would be familiar with.

A smile broke out on the duke's handsome features. "Marbury is quite the hero. One of the most honorable men of my acquaintance. The newspapers had it right when they nicknamed him the Duke of Honor upon his return. I wish I'd had a dozen more like him."

His words took her by surprise. "How can you say that?" she demanded. "After what he did?"

Wellington studied her carefully. "What is it you think he did, my lady?"

Hadley felt the anger heating her cheeks. "He betrayed England to our enemy," she declared.

His gaze penetrated her. "Is that what Marbury told you?"

She grew uncomfortable, recalling how she had come to form her ill opinion of Sebastian.

"He was deep in his cups when he spoke of it, Your Grace. I had known something was amiss when he came home." She hesitated. "You see, the colonel's father was my guardian. I came to know Marbury through the letters he wrote to his father. We would read them aloud dozens of times. When the colonel arrived at Hardwell Hall, though, he was different."

Sadness blanketed Wellington. "Marbury suffered a great deal."

She felt her face flame, thinking of Sebastian's marred flesh. "Yes, I have seen the scars on his arms and neck. I assume from what he said that he was taken captive and tortured. But he revealed he had given up precious information to the enemy. He cost the lives of who knows how many Englishmen? I find it incomprehensible that you would speak so highly of him after his betrayal."

Wellington shook his head. "You haven't the full story, my lady," he said sternly.

Something shifted inside her. "Please," she whispered. "Tell me."

The duke gazed out over the river and began to speak. "Marbury was one of my most talented officers. Bright. Eager. Ruthless when it came to strategizing. He cared a great deal for his men and they worshipped him in return. I always weighed carefully whatever opinion he shared with me because I knew he spoke with both caution and experience.

"Occasionally, I would send him ahead as a scout or with important dispatches to be delivered. He became an expert in avoiding the enemy. We found ourselves at a stalemate at one point, however. Marbury requested to see me in private and pitched an idea that I found dreadful—and yet quite enticing because of the impasse we found ourselves up against."

Dread filled Hadley. "Go on," she urged.

"His plan was that he would go behind enemy lines and allow himself to be captured. He would, after three days in captivity, pretend he had broken and feed false information to those who had abducted him."

She gasped. "No!"

"Oh, yes. Normally, I wouldn't consider such an absurd scheme, knowing he wouldn't be merely held—but tortured. I was desperate, though, and Marbury so idealistic and loyal and faithful to me and our cause. He begged to be sent and I finally acquiesced to his demand. I had three men follow him at a distance, tracking his movements and keeping the house where he was taken under observation. Once they saw riders leave, they would know Marbury had fed the false information to his captors. They were to allow the messengers to leave so they could spread the false intelligence before my men attempted to rescue him."

"You knew they would kill him once they got the information they needed from him," she accused.

"I did. I only hoped those men would be able to save him in time."

Wellington pulled his gaze from the water and directed it to Hadley. "He had been brutalized. He had finally broken after what he thought were the three days. Days in which he bought me time to move thousands of troops, who set a trap for Joseph Bonaparte's men.

Marbury lasted eight days under their cruel hands. He lost track of time in the haze of pain and suffering. My men found him more dead than alive and brought him back. My doctor proclaimed it was a miracle that Marbury didn't die on the way. Then the fool actually felt guilty about being broken. It sounds as if he still does. So you see, my lady, the colonel didn't betray his country. He saved many lives. Too many for me to begin to measure."

The duke rubbed his fingers along his jaw. "It took time for his body to heal. Of course, I welcomed him back to my staff and never considered sending him behind enemy lines again. In time, he seemed to become himself again, as brilliant and purposeful as ever. I suppose in his heart, though, he feels he let down not only me—but his king and country. That's ridiculous, of course. Marbury is a man of honor. A man of valor and integrity."

Tears streamed down her face. "I misjudged him badly."

"Do you love him?" the duke asked.

She nodded. "I do."

"Does he love you?"

Hadley shrugged. "I don't see how he could. The things I said to him were so hurtful. So hateful. We parted on the worst of terms."

"When did you last see him?"

"August."

"He is coming to London for the upcoming Season," Wellington revealed. "We still correspond. He wrote to me of needing to take a wife. Are you unattached, my lady?"

"I am," she told Wellington, a sliver of hope beginning to bloom within her.

"I am not one to meddle—and my own marriage is not to be used by anyone as an example—but my advice to you is seek him out. Ask for his forgiveness. If you truly love him, you should fight for him. He is still in the grips of his enemies' hands. End their hold upon him. He deserves a bit of happiness."

Boldly, Hadley reached out and took the duke's hands and kissed them, her tears flowing freely now. "Thank you, Your Grace. I will do so." She released his hands. "Forgive me for being too familiar."

He smiled. "It will take strength and every bit of courage you possess to break through the barrier Hardwick has erected around him."

Hadley stood. "I am a most determined woman, Your Grace. I would rather risk all and fail miserably."

Wellington rose. "You would have made an excellent soldier, Lady Hadley. I must go now but I wish you much luck."

The duke left, his hands held behind his back, his posture straight and true. It was only when he was too far away to hear her call out that she realized something.

Hadley had never told him her name.

Chapter Twenty

SEBASTIAN WENT TO the breakfast room, a place he had avoided in the years after his mother's death. He had arrived in London late the evening before, with Bardham and Radmore in tow. He figured Mrs. Sewell could manage the running of Hardwell Hall on her own and much preferred the trusted butler to be with him in London. It had proved to be a smart move on his part when Mrs. Waters, the housekeeper, had greeted them last night and informed Sebastian that the previous butler had grown ill with some lung disease and had left two weeks ago for his sister's home in Essex, presumably to die there under her care.

He entered the light, sunny room that was free of the former duke's presence. That had been the reason Sebastian had refused to come down in the mornings. When Hardwick learned that Cook sent a tray up to him, the duke had put a stop to the practice. Sebastian had decided to skip the meal, choosing to go hungry rather than suffer Hardwick's presence.

The footman seated him. Another brought him the strong coffee he enjoyed, while a third placed a heaping plate in front of him. Digging in with gusto, he savored the meal as he turned the pages of the newspaper.

Until a sobriquet caught his eye.

Sources reveal that the Duke of Honor, otherwise known as His Grace the Duke of Hardwick, will soon arrive in London with an eye to peruse the Marriage Mart. Honor's closest friends from university—the Dukes of Renown, Charm, Disrepute, and Arrogance—have all done the unheard of thing and made love matches. Will Honor follow suit and lose his heart to a young woman making her come-out? Anxious mamas are eager to pounce upon His Grace and hope that he bestows his attention upon their eligible daughters.

Disgust filled him. He hated the idiotic nickname. Honor. He didn't deserve any respect or fame for his war service. Countless other soldiers and officers had proven themselves more worthy than he. The fact that the *ton* already knew of his decision to take a bride bothered him, as did the thought of dozens of mamas foisting their girls upon him, all in search of a title.

When all he wanted was Hadley.

He cursed inside his head. He had striven to avoid thinking of her but had been reminded almost daily of her as he had toured his various holdings. She had been in constant contact over several years with both estate managers and housekeepers and her hand was evident in all he saw. Thinking of her now shouldn't hurt so much yet Sebastian felt as raw and bleeding as he had the night she had walked away from him last August.

Radmore entered the room carrying a silver tray piled high with correspondence.

"The morning post, Your Grace. Mrs. Waters says she has placed previous correspondence upon your desk."

"What is all of this?" he demanded, still upset by the newspaper item and the fact he couldn't seem to get Hadley out of his mind.

"Why, I assume they are invitations, Your Grace," the butler told him. "The Season does start next week."

He doubted he knew even a tenth of the people who had issued all these invitations yet due to his rank in Polite Society, he would be invited to almost every event held. The beginnings of a headache throbbed at his temples at the thought of responding to the slew of invitations and then actually having to attend the events.

"Very well, Radmore," he said, resignation in his voice. "Place them with the others."

Sebastian finished his breakfast, the newspaper pushed aside. He dreaded searching for a wife yet he owed it to the dukedom to do so and provide an heir. If he didn't, a distant cousin whom he had gone to school with would succeed him as Hardwick. The cousin had been a bully and a boor and was undeserving of being a Cooper, much less becoming a duke.

Radmore appeared at his elbow again, this time a lone page visible on the silver tray.

"Your Grace, a message from the Duke of Wellington. The messenger is waiting for a reply."

He smiled despite his sour mood. He had struck up a correspondence after the war with Wellington during the time Sebastian was stationed on Elba Island. It had continued once he returned to England. He enjoyed hearing from his former commander, missing the almost daily contact he'd had with the man during the war days.

Opening it, he saw where the duke requested that Sebastian accompany him to Tattersall's this afternoon at one o'clock to gain his opinion on a set of horses he was considering for purchase. If agreeable, his carriage would call for Sebastian.

He looked to Radmore. "Tell the messenger I am eager to see His Grace and will be ready at the appointed time."

"Very good, Your Grace," the butler said and left the breakfast room.

Sebastian ventured to his study. A mountain of previous posts awaited him. He seated himself behind the desk and opened each one, composing terse replies of acceptance to every invitation. When finished, he pushed them aside. He realized that he needed a secretary to handle matters such as this and keep a calendar for him.

A knock sounded and he bid the person to enter. Radmore and

Bardham both appeared and he hoped no trouble was to be had from the look upon their faces.

The butler began. "Your Grace, Mrs. Waters recommends that we hire at least one more parlor maid and another scullery maid, especially since you will be entertaining."

He had only thought about going to events—not holding any himself. Yet he supposed he would need to give at least a few dinner parties. Possibly even a ball to announce his betrothal.

"I will leave that to you, Radmore. Hire two or twenty. It doesn't matter to me. What does is the fact that I need a secretary in London. You may interview for any openings you deem necessary but I would like to personally see any applicants for that position."

"Of course, Your Grace. I will begin the search immediately." Radmore left and Bardham took a step forward.

"We need you to change your waistcoat and coat, Your Grace. You also need a cravat with a more intricate knot tied."

"Whatever for?" he asked irritably.

"For your meeting with the Duke of Wellington. That's what for," Bardham snapped.

"You realize I am a duke," Sebastian said, a warning edged in his tone.

"I most certainly do and as your valet, I cannot have you meet Wellington looking like that. You know how concerned with his attire the duke is. You don't want him judging you in a poor light because of your clothing."

"What on earth is wrong with what I am wearing?"

"It's not fancy enough," Bardham insisted. "In fact, you need to see your London tailor as soon as possible. As it is, you only have two sets of evening clothes."

"What of it?"

"It won't be enough once the Season begins. You will also need a variety of—"

"All right," Sebastian interrupted. "You have made your point. I don't need to go in person, however. You do that for me, Bardham. They have my measurements from several months ago and can use those. Tell them to prepare for me whatever I will need for the upcoming Season."

"I will leave as soon as you are properly attired, Your Grace. Come along. The duke's carriage will be here shortly."

Sebastian saw nothing wrong with what he wore but he did recall what a clotheshorse Wellington was. Even at the height of the war, the slim commander had eschewed being seen in a uniform and preferred wearing the stylish garb of a civilian. He followed his valet upstairs and allowed Bardham to select a more elegant waistcoat and coat and sat patiently while the valet created an elaborate knot with his cravat.

Bardham stepped back and admired his work. "I know you don't like being fussed over but I will say that you look splendid, Your Grace. You will rival Wellington himself. I am off now to your tailor. Enjoy looking over the horseflesh at Tattersall's."

As Sebastian returned downstairs, he thought he also might make a purchase today for himself. He had been using the ducal carriage over the last few months as he went from estate to estate that he owned. Now that he would be settled in London for several months, he would need to get some exercise. Riding was his preferred choice and so he would look for a mount today.

In the foyer, Radmore met him. "His Grace's carriage has arrived."

"Thank you," he told the butler and went outside.

A footman greeted him and then said, "His Grace was detained on urgent business and will be unable to accompany you today, Your Grace. He asked that if you wish to go to Tattersall's that we take you and then bring you back to his residence."

Knowing how much in demand Wellington was, Sebastian understood. "Very well. I have business of my own at Tattersall's and I had better go today than wait for when they are open again next week."

"Of course, Your Grace."

The carriage traveled from Mayfair to near Hyde Park Corner, where he was met by none other than Richard Tattersall, the eldest of Edmund Tattersall's three sons, and the one who had taken over the business a few years ago upon his father's death.

"Welcome, Your Grace," Tattersall said, looking about.

"If you are looking for Wellington, he was delayed," Sebastian told the owner. "However, I am in need of a horse myself."

Smiling, Tattersall said, "Tell me your requirements, Your Grace, and I am sure I can match them with several choices of horseflesh."

An hour later, Sebastian had bought a black beauty of seventeen hands, with sleek lines and a feisty temperament.

"I hope you are pleased with your decision, Your Grace," Tattersall said. "I will see the horse delivered to your townhouse immediately."

"Thank you. I must leave now to visit with the Duke of Wellington but look for us both next week. Perhaps you can talk me into new carriage horses, Mr. Tattersall."

The man beamed. "I look forward to doing so, Your Grace."

The carriage took him back to Mayfair and he was met by the butler, who told him Wellington should arrive within the half-hour. Taking Sebastian to the library, the servant asked if he cared for a whiskey. Sebastian waved away the notion. He had only partaken in the rare glass of wine and avoided strong spirits totally since he had left Blackstone Manor. He didn't trust himself to keep from drowning his sorrows and so refrained from hard liquor.

He walked the room, perusing the shelves and then settling down with an atlas he discovered. He traced the various campaigns he had been involved with on the Continent, wondering what those places had become now that peace reigned. Perhaps one day, he might visit them again and blot out the terrible memories of war.

"Colonel Cooper!"

Turning, Sebastian saw the Duke of Wellington sail into the room, a broad smile on his handsome face. As Bardham predicted, the duke cut a fine figure in what Sebastian assumed was the latest in fashion. He now was glad his valet had insisted he change clothes.

He set aside the atlas and rose, thrusting out his hand, which Wellington ignored. The duke drew him into a bear hug instead. Pulling away, his host beamed at him.

"I am sorry. You are Hardwick now. I must adjust my thinking," Wellington apologized.

Sebastian laughed. "You may call me anything you wish, Your Grace. It is very good to see you in the flesh after all this time."

"Indeed. Shall we have a seat? Do you need anything?"

"No, thank you," he said, taking the same chair he had been sitting in as Wellington sat to his right. "Your staff has been most kind."

"I am sorry I was unable to accompany you to Tattersall's."

"It was not a problem, Your Grace. I wound up making a purchase of my own." Sebastian described his new mount and added, "Mr. Tattersall expects both of us next week when they open again."

"Then we better go. I wouldn't want to disappoint the man." Wellington sighed. "I am not supposed to disappoint anyone these days."

He thought the remark odd. "How so?"

The duke shook his head. "They think I should enter politics again."

Sebastian recalled how after Bonaparte was defeated and sent to Elba, the newly-named duke had been appointed Ambassador to France. Following that assignment, Wellington had taken Lord Castlereagh's place as first plenipotentiary to the Congress of Vienna, only leaving the position to take command of the Waterloo Campaign when Bonaparte escaped and marched toward Paris again.

"Is politics something you are interested in, Your Grace?"

The duke shrugged. "Now that peace has come to both Europe

and North America, I have to find something to do with my time. I suppose a career in the military is as good as anything to prepare myself for the world of politics within England. Enough about me, Hardwick. How did you find your properties during your travels?"

He had written to Wellington of his plan to visit all the country estates that now belonged to him.

"It went rather well. All are being run by competent, efficient stewards. The crop yields are good. Livestock is being emphasized on a few of the estates over farming."

"I met Lady Hadley, you know," Wellington said abruptly.

Sebastian felt as if all the air had been sucked from the room. He struggled a moment to regain his composure and finally said, "Is that so?"

Wellington nodded in understanding. "You mentioned her in our correspondence. How she had seen to the running of your father's estates while you were away. You seemed to greatly admire her."

"She is a very capable woman," he managed to get out.

Sympathy shone in the duke's eyes. "I see you have feelings for her. Strong ones by the look on your face which you are so desperately trying to hide."

He said nothing.

"She was under the false impression that you had deliberately given our enemies information they sought. She believed you to be a traitor of the worst sort and not the true patriot that you are."

Sebastian felt his face heat with embarrassment. He hadn't known exactly what he had said to Hadley when in his cups. Then he realized it was not only his scars which had disgusted her. It was the fact he had revealed how weak he had been when confronted by the enemy. He must have spoken of the one thing he had vowed never to tell another soul once he returned to England, the darkest time when he hadn't lived up to be the man he wanted to be. She must truly have despised him—yet she had kept silent in that regard.

"You say you need a wife, Hardwick. Lady Hadley would make for an excellent duchess. Swallow whatever false pride you have and go to her. Make known the truth," Wellington told him. "Your truth."

"I don't think she would believe me," he said, discouragement filling him.

His former commander gazed at him with fondness. "I may have helped clear up some of the misunderstanding and I expect you to stop dwelling on your past, Sebastian. Yes, you were disappointed in yourself even though no one else was. I demand that you let go of the past and look to build a future with Lady Hadley."

The duke looked at him fondly. "You are like a son to me, Sebastian. I would see you happy in marriage, not as I am. Kitty and I lived apart far too long, thanks to my military career. We came together to have our boys but even now, during peace, we spend most of our time apart. Yes, I have been misrepresented by the press for having countless mistresses. I will admit that I have sought out the company of women who interest me. Ones who are attractive and intellectual.

"Yet if I had it to do all over again, I would find one woman to love and be faithful to her."

If the duke had shared the truth with Hadley, then she might not hate him after all. He rose unsteadily. "You truly think I have a chance with her, Your Grace?"

Wellington nodded, a smile playing about his lips. "I would say better than a chance."

"Thank you for sharing this with me. I will do my best to win over Lady Hadley."

The duke stood. "I would expect nothing less of you, my boy. Good luck to you."

With his heart lighter than it had been in months, Sebastian took his leave and returned home.

CHAPTER TWENTY-ONE

HADLEY ARRIVED AT Phoebe and Andrew's townhouse as Samantha and George pulled up in their carriage. They greeted one another and proceeded inside where the butler led them to the drawing room.

Phoebe came and kissed Hadley's cheek. "My, I do love you in that color."

The peach satin was new, one of the creations Madame Toufours had made up for Hadley. She had done a final fitting on it and a slew of other gowns yesterday after she had left Hyde Park. She had barely paid attention to anything the modiste had said, merely nodding her head in agreement. Madame wasn't one to argue with, at any rate. Hadley had learned that the modiste's word was law and that she was right about everything concerning fashion and what looked good on a woman. She learned to trust Madame's judgment completely and merely told the assistant to deliver everything she had tried on with no adjustments.

She had ventured to the park this morning, hoping to catch sight of Wellington again and press him further about how he had known her name. It had to be through Sebastian, who must have written something about her to his former commander. It gave her hope that even though she had behaved abominably toward him, he still might have an ember of feelings left for her. The question was should she try to stir that spark and nurse it into a flame?

Having waited an hour without catching sight of Wellington, Hadley had returned home. She spent the day restlessly moving from one activity to another, not finishing anything, her thoughts on how to approach Sebastian. She already knew which townhouse was his, having corresponded over the years with the butler in charge of it. Should she write to Sebastian for an appointment? Show up unannounced?

"Is it one of Madame Toufours' creations?" Samantha asked, bringing Hadley's attention back to the present.

"It is," she confirmed. "Madame is the only modiste I have seen in London."

"I cannot wait to see what else she has designed for you," Phoebe said. "I am eager for the Season to start next week, especially since we missed it last year with me staying home in Devon to give birth to Robby."

"I adore dancing," Samantha said. "I am glad to be back in town. Just think—we are now mothers, Phoebe. One day, I will be preparing my daughter to make her own come-out."

"Perhaps our boy or Elise's might be the perfect match for her," Phoebe said with a smile. "Only time will tell."

The butler announced dinner and they went in for a light meal since they were supposed to head to the theatre soon and planned to stop for supper after the performance. The wine had barely been poured when the butler presented a note to Phoebe.

"Oh, it's from Blackstone Manor," the duchess shared as she broke the seal.

"I received a letter from Arabella only yesterday," Hadley said, remembering her friend had gone into labor. "I hope this is good news."

Phoebe opened and scanned it, a joyful smile crossing her face. "It's from Jon. Only a few lines. He wanted us to know that Arabella has given birth to a healthy girl. They haven't named her yet but he says she is an angel. Arabella is also doing well."

"That is delightful news," Samantha said. "So, we have two boys and two girls in our circle." She smiled at Hadley. "You need to find a husband soon so that you don't fall too far behind."

She smiled in return, wanting more than anything to have a child. Sebastian's child.

In that moment, Hadley made a decision. She could beg for Sebastian's forgiveness but he was a former military man. A man of action. Her actions should speak for her. Loudly.

They finished dining and as Andrew called for the carriage, she said, "Would you mind dropping me at home?" Pressing a hand to her temple, she added, "I feel the beginning of a headache coming on. I fear I wouldn't be good company."

"Of course," Andrew told her.

The five went to the carriage and, minutes later, Hadley allowed the footman to hand her down. She stood on the pavement and waved at her friends as the vehicle pulled away and then walked toward the door. Pausing, she made certain the carriage rounded the corner and then she turned. The servants weren't expecting her home for several hours. Though she knew it was not the done thing for a young, unmarried woman to call upon a gentleman, she had to see Sebastian now. She didn't want to write for an appointment. Enough time had already been wasted. Either he would see her or he wouldn't.

She traveled the two blocks to his townhouse and knocked upon the door. When it opened, a surprised Radmore stared back at her in astonishment. Then a huge smile broke out on the butler's face.

"Lady Hadley! What a surprise this is. Do come in."

She stepped into the foyer. "It is good to see you, Radmore. How have you been?"

"Very well, my lady." He paused. "You have been missed at Hardwell Hall. Mrs. Perkins would want you to know that she birthed a healthy boy. Almost a month ago, I believe it was."

"That is good to hear, especially after having already had three little girls." She hesitated and then asked, "How has His Grace been?"

The butler sighed. "His Grace has remained busy viewing his various properties. He is lonely, though. He wears an air of melancholia like a greatcoat." He looked at her eagerly. "Do you wish to see him?"

"I do, Radmore. I am afraid, though, that he won't wish to see me. Things ended quite poorly between us. I am here to apologize to His Grace and ask for his forgiveness."

Radmore nodded sagely. "Then you will need privacy. Come with me, my lady."

The butler led her up the stairs. Hadley thought they might stop at the library or drawing room. Instead, he opened a door and ushered her inside.

"This is His Grace's sitting room. I will bring him to you."

Hadley watched the servant disappear and discovered she was suddenly a bundle of nerves. Her heart thundered at what she was attempting to do. The next few minutes would either prove to be a disaster—or life would change dramatically. Anxiously, she sat, trying to calm her nerves.

Operation Rescue didn't involve only Sebastian anymore. She had become an integral part of it. Because to save Sebastian, she also had to save herself.

SEBASTIAN SAT BEFORE the fire, contemplating what to do. Ever since he had left the Duke of Wellington's residence this afternoon, all his thoughts had centered upon Hadley.

She knew the truth about him now—or at least more than she had. He needed to persuade her that he was the man for her. To do so, he must convince himself that he was worthy of her.

Was he?

Could he put the past behind him? It had haunted him for years. He had never felt good enough. Becoming the new duke only made him feel even less confident. He hadn't had Hardwick's hand in raising him. Guiding him on how to run a large estate and explaining the ways to assume the plethora of responsibilities that fell to being a duke. All he had known was war. He had learned a great deal since his return, being thrust into the role of a duke. Fortunately, it had gone better than he had anticipated, in large part to Hadley's notes. He had merely followed every instruction she had left and become familiar with as much as he could.

He wanted more, though. He wanted her. In his life. By his side. Giving him advice. Bearing his children. Loving him. It might be too much to ask but Sebastian would give it a try. He had sent word to Andrew and George that he had arrived in town, knowing they would also be here for the Season. The two were meeting him tomorrow at White's. Surely, they knew from their wives where Hadley resided. He wanted to call on her before the Season began. He needed to see if he had a chance to charm her. He couldn't let their first meeting take place in a crowded ballroom with hundreds of onlookers. No, they needed privacy. A quiet conversation. And, hopefully, an understanding.

"Your Grace?"

Startled, Sebastian turned and saw Radmore standing before him.

"I am sorry. I was so lost in thought that I did not hear you enter."

"Quite all right, Your Grace. There is something you need to see. If you will follow me."

The butler turned and strode out.

"What the devil?" he muttered, thinking Bardham's insolence had now spread to Radmore. Didn't his servants know that he was in charge of the household and not the other way around?

Sebastian sprang to his feet and hurried after Radmore, who was already down the corridor and headed up the stairs. He took the stairs two at a time in an effort to catch up. By the time he did, Radmore stood in front of Sebastian's rooms, his hand on the doorknob.

"All I ask is that you keep an open mind, Your Grace," he said mysteriously and opened the door.

Sebastian stepped into the room and heard the door close behind him. He froze.

Hadley rose and came toward him.

"Am I dreaming?" he asked aloud.

She took his hands and the warmth that rushed through him told him she was here, in the flesh.

"I came to ask for your forgiveness, Sebastian," she said softly. "I was very cruel to you."

He laced his fingers through hers. "There is nothing to forgive, Hadley."

"There is," she insisted. "I also want you to forgive yourself."

"What?" Her words confused him.

Those cornflower blue eyes gazed at him, stirring something within him that Sebastian didn't dare identify.

"I spoke with Wellington yesterday. He cleared up what I misunderstood. You are a hero, Sebastian. One who did far more than any newspaper reported."

He shook his head stubbornly. "No, you are wrong." He tried to pull away from her grasp.

Her fingers tightened around his. "I am not wrong. You are. You completed your mission, one which was risky and life-threatening. Wellington told me that you ended the stalemate. You gave England the advantage by misleading our enemy. Claim that victory, Sebastian. Own it. You are a part of it."

Could what she said be true?

For so long, all he could focus on was how the enemy had shattered him. He came out of the experience a broken man, physically mutilated and sorely lacking in confidence. He had been so cocky going in to the situation, knowing he was superior to his captors. They had quickly shamed him. Crushed his spirited. Destroyed his equilibrium. When the men Wellington sent finally rescued him, he was a shell of his former self. His body finally healed, though the scars had been left behind as a constant reminder of his lack of value. His mind still heard the taunts of his captors, telling him how worthless he was. He heard the voices so often that he had eventually believed it. That was why he had taken every risk he could in battle afterward, trying to make up for betraying Wellington's trust in him. Even though his commander had praised Sebastian's work on the mission, even seeing him cared for by Wellington's own personal physician, he never had believed in himself again.

Until now.

"I wasn't a traitor, Hadley," he said hoarsely. "They never knew what I told them was false."

She squeezed his fingers. "I know." Her eyes brimmed with tears.

"Had I known . . . had I known while I was soused that I told you of . . . the incident . . ." His voice trailed off as emotion overcame him. He drew in a deep breath and continued, knowing this might be his final chance to set things right with her.

"I would have followed you from that ballroom. I would have made you understand. But . . . I saw the look in your eyes. How distressed you were. I knew my appearance disgusted you and I had to let you go." His gaze met hers. "Though it was the last thing I wished to do."

She winced. "I am so very sorry, Sebastian. I was so shocked and upset by what you had revealed. I revered you. Adored you. And suddenly, you didn't seem to be the man I thought I knew." A tear slid down her cheek. "It wasn't your scars which drove me away. It was the fact I judged you to be lacking in character. I should have known better. I should have taken the time to have a conversation with you and ask you about what you revealed. I didn't. Instead, I fled like a coward."

Hadley shook her head. "It is what has pained me over these long months apart. Can you forgive me—and yourself?"

Something moved inside him. A shift that Sebastian couldn't describe. Then understanding dawned within him.

It was . . . hope. Hope that he could become the man he had once been. No, one who was even better. Because if he read the situation correctly, he would have Hadley by his side. And when his demons became too strong for him to stand up to, she would stand with him.

"Yes," he replied. "I know I did my duty. To Wellington. To the army. To my king and country." Sebastian blinked back tears. "And to you, my love. I didn't even know you existed and yet everything I have ever done, it has been for you."

Her radiant smile was like seeing the sun rise, conquering the night's darkness.

"I need more than your forgiveness, Sebastian."

She freed her hands from his and brought her palms to where they cradled his cheeks. Her gaze met his and he felt lost in her eyes.

"You have my heart, Sebastian. My soul. Now, I want you to claim my body. Make me yours tonight."

He crushed her to him. His mouth crashed down on hers. Greedily, he drank her in, the kiss full of fiery passion. Desire filled him. He needed to make her his. Without breaking the kiss, he swept her from her feet and carried her into the next room where his bed stood. Gently, he laid her onto it, only breaking the kiss to stare at her.

Sebastian knelt by the bed, capturing her hands in his and brushing his lips against her knuckles.

"Are you certain of this, Hadley?"

She smiled. "I am certain that I love you. Words aren't enough, though. I want to show you how much I want you," she proclaimed boldly.

He kissed her and then touched his fingertips to his chest. "This heart beats for you. Only you."

Chapter Twenty-Two

SEBASTIAN'S WORDS TOLD Hadley everything she needed to know.

She pushed up on her elbows and swung her legs from the bed. Taking his face in her hands, she pressed her mouth to his. The kiss started slow, gradually heating up as he parted her lips and leisurely explored her. Her fingers pushed into his thick hair and tightened. She never wanted to let go of this man.

He came to his feet and his arms went around her, bringing her to him. In them, Hadley felt as if she had come home.

They kissed for a long time, until her breasts grew heavy and the place between her legs throbbed almost painfully. Her body heated until it felt as if she had become a furnace and fire licked her veins. His lips left hers, trailing hot kisses along her throat.

"Touch me," she cried.

Sebastian lifted his head and smiled. "Where?" he asked playfully.

"Everywhere."

"Oh, I plan to, Hadley. Even in places you have never dreamed of being touched."

She brushed the back of her fingers against his cheek. "I find I am overdressed for this adventure, Your Grace."

He grinned, his features boyish. "I can help solve that."

Sebastian released her and reached for the hem of her gown. He lifted it up her body and over her head before removing the other layers that stood between them. Her skin now felt on fire as his hands brushed against the curve of her hips as he knelt and removed her shoes and untied her stockings. His fingers slowly rolled them down her legs and brought them over her ankles and feet.

He rose, his eyes drinking her in. Hadley knew she should be embarrassed at standing nude before him but her body cried out for his touch. Slowly, his arms went about her and his body pressed against hers. He was still fully clothed and yet it seemed almost erotic, his wool coat brushing against her bare flesh. Guiding her backward, they reached the bed again, the backs of her knees bumping against it as he eased her onto the mattress and swung her legs up.

His eyes never left hers as he stripped off his coat and waistcoat. Slowly, he untied his cravat and tossed it to the floor. She could see more of his body now. The broad shoulders and wide chest. The breeches that hugged his muscular legs. She wondered if he would remove the rest of his clothing.

Instead, he turned and sat upon the bed and struggled but finally removed his Hessians.

"It's much easier with Bardham helping me," he muttered.

Hadley sat up and wrapped her arms around him from behind. "I will help you next time."

She could feel the hard muscle beneath her fingertips as her hands began to roam over his chest. She pressed soft kisses along his nape, her lips finding bumps in the skin. Signs of what had been done to him.

He growled, prying her hands away and quickly turning, pushing her back onto the pillows and covering her body with his. Long, drugging kisses followed, heating her blood and causing the throbbing at her apex to pound out of control. Sebastian finally broke the kiss and his mouth moved to her breast. Slowly, his tongue circled her nipple as his hand palmed her other breast, tweaking its nipple. A ripple of desire ran through her.

He lifted his head and blew softly, causing a delicious shiver. Then he began sucking on her breasts, causing her to arch her back and cling to him. He laved the nipple and sucked and his teeth dragged across it, bringing forth a deep need that needed fulfilling. She held his head to her, wonder filling her at what her body was experiencing. He turned his attention to her other breast and feasted upon it as his hands caressed her belly and glided along the curve of her hips, back and forth, back and forth.

Then his tongue started on a journey, tantalizing her as he dragged it down her torso. To her belly. Past it. Lower.

"Sebastian?" she questioned, unsure of what he was doing.

Glancing up, she saw his piercing blue eyes had darkened with desire. "Yes?"

"Never mind."

"Good."

His mouth, hot on her skin, continued its path and reached where the throbbing seemed out of control. He kissed her there, shocking her. Pleasing her. His fingers parted the folds of her sex and his tongue thrust inside, caressing her. Hadley gasped, her back bowing. He fastened his fingers to her hips and held her in place as his teeth and tongue did the most wicked things to her body. A fierce longing rose within her, followed by a fluttering sensation that had her spinning out of control as untold pleasure rippled through her. She cried out his name as the waves crashed, driving any cohesive thought from her mind.

Gradually, she came back from the heights of heaven and he kissed his way back up her body until his mouth was once more on hers again and she could taste herself in him.

Hadley broke the kiss. "Can I do that to you?" she asked eagerly, wanting so much to please him.

He cradled her face. "Not now, my sweet. We have other things to accomplish." A shadow crossed his face. "It will hurt this first time but then never again. Do you understand what I am saying?"

She nodded. "My maidenhead. You must breach it for us to become one."

He smiled and kissed her. "I like the sound of that."

"Sebastian," she said quietly. "Would you . . . would you let me see you? All of you, as you have me?"

He looked stricken. "I don't know, Hadley. I am afraid to."

She captured his face in her hands. "I love you. Every part of you."

"It is . . . horrible to look at. I avoid doing so," he admitted. "I am afraid if you see me . . . you won't want me."

She kissed him slowly. "That would never be true. I told you. I love you. Please."

As he rose from the bed, she saw the doubt in his eyes and braced herself. He would be studying her carefully. No matter what she saw, she couldn't react adversely—or she might lose him forever.

He stood a moment and she saw he gathered his courage before he unbuttoned the two buttons of the shirt and then in a quick movement, grabbed its hem and yanked it over his head.

His chest was a map of scars. Some deep. Some still an angry red years later. Others stark white against his skin. He raised his arms, palms flat to the floor, and slowly turned until his back was revealed to her. Hadley bit back the gasp of horror that threatened to erupt. Sebastian's back was a kaleidoscope of thick, deep scars. She couldn't fathom how much his captors had brutalized his flesh.

Still facing away from her, he lowered his hands and spoke in a monotone. "They used a cat o' nine tails on me. A multi-tailed whip of nine knotted thongs. It lacerates the skin. The pain is intense. They tied my wrists above my head and would flog me until I lost consciousness. Sometimes, I lasted for ten lashes. Or twenty. I never made it to thirty."

He lowered his arms and stood stock-still.

Hadley swallowed the raging emotion and came off the bed. She wrapped her arms around him, holding on tightly. Her cheek rested against his devasted flesh. She could feel his entire body trembling.

"They burned me," he said softly. "Sliced me with knives. I prayed for death—but somehow kept clinging to life."

She released her hold on him and turned him until he faced her.

"It already has been a life well lived, Sebastian. You fought bravely for your country. You helped win a war against a despot that tried to bring all of Europe under his iron grasp."

Wrapping her arms about him, she drew him to her and pressed a kiss upon his ruined chest. She continued kissing him everywhere she could as he broke down and wept. He held her to him tightly, kissing her hair.

"Is it too much?" he asked hoarsely.

Hadley lifted her head, meeting his gaze. "You are everything I dreamed of and far, far more. I am not sure I deserve a man as wonderful as you. Your scars are a part of you and your past but they do not define you, Sebastian. Accept them and let me become your future."

"Hadley. Hadley." He shook his head as she rested her cheek against him.

She looked up at him. "I believe you promised me things that must be accomplished."

He looked at her still in disbelief. "You truly want me? Even like this?"

She pressed a kiss to his damaged flesh. "I want you even more than I did before. You have let me in, Sebastian, and I am not going anywhere." She grinned. "Except perhaps that bed over there."

Laughing, he lifted her into his arms and fell onto the bed with her. Then he rose and stripped his breeches from his legs, flinging them across the room. Returning to the bed, he began stroking and caressing her body, his heated kisses driving her into a frenzy. He slipped his hand between her legs and pushed a finger inside her, causing her to whimper and then squirm. He brought her again to those heights of dizzying pleasure and then pushed his cock inside her. In one quick motion, he broke through her maidenhead. She bit back a cry and then waited a moment. The quick sting of pain already subsided and she was aware of how he filled her.

Completed her.

Slowly, his body began to move and she soon joined in the sensual dance until they moved as one, the dance speeding up, driving her over the edge. Suddenly, a wave of pleasure erupted through her, even as Sebastian called out her name, pumping wildly into her and then collapsing against her. He kissed her hard, branding her as his and then rolled so that she sprawled atop him.

He held her close, his arms possessively around her. Hadley's ear rested against his beating heart. She understood the physical miracle of love now and why she would catch her friends and their husbands gazing at one another with deep longing. It was if she had joined an exclusive club and now its secrets were laid bare.

As Sebastian's fingers glided through her hair, he said, "You know you have been quite naughty."

"Have I?" she asked seductively, hoping he would kiss her again.

"After all, you are an unmarried lady who has come to a duke's bed. You are absolutely ruined now."

"Hmm," she mused. "And here I thought you'd ruined other men for me."

He kissed the top of her head. "Good. What kind of wedding you do want? Did you dream of a large one as a little girl?"

"No. I wasn't that kind of girl. Mama died too young for us to talk of things such as that. Then I came to Hardwell Hall and any thought of marriage became buried."

"Do you want a large wedding or a small one?" he persisted.

Hadley placed a hand on his chest and rested her chin atop it, gazing up at his handsome face. "Well, I would have to be betrothed first. No one has asked me." She batted her lashes at him playfully.

Sebastian grinned. "Then may I be the first, my lady, to ask for your hand?" He took it and threaded his fingers through hers. "What say you? Will you have me, Hadley Hampton, for better or worse?"

"I will have you," she said. "Many times."

"Ah, my betrothed is a little minx." He kissed her and then grew serious. "I would like to plan the wedding if you are agreeable."

"You want to plan a wedding. *Our* wedding."

"Yes. After all, you are a woman who has yet to even make your come-out. I am an older man and know more about these things."

Hadley giggled. "I will allow you to do so. Just don't make me wait long, Sebastian. We have been apart far too long as it is."

He kissed her, hard and swift. "I will make sure you are in my bed—our bed—sooner rather than later. For now, though, we need to get you back to . . . I don't know. Where are you staying?"

"At Jon and Arabella's townhouse. They encouraged me to stay there during the Season and I agreed."

"You didn't allow their carriage to remain waiting out front?" he asked worriedly.

She explained about skipping out of the theatre plans and then added, "I walked since it was but two blocks."

"Then we will walk back. Fortunately, the hour is late and there shouldn't be anyone out and about. Just in case, we will go the back way, slinking through the dark like thieves in the night."

He untangled their limbs and climbed from the bed. Hadley couldn't help but admire his tall, muscular frame. It would soon be hers. It was funny how she didn't even notice his scars. She only saw the man she loved.

She watched him dress and then he assisted her into her clothes again before kneeling to locate her hair pins, which had somehow been lost during their heated embraces. She did her best to smooth and twist her hair into its usual chignon.

"Come along," he said, linking their hands together and leading her to the bottom floor and back to the kitchens. A clock in the distance chimed eleven times as they crept from the house and through the yard behind the townhouse.

They kept off the main road until they reached the Blackmore residence and he led her through the shadows to the front door.

"I will see you tomorrow," he promised, kissing her fingers.

"You better intend upon seeing me every day," she retorted. "I will expect it from my betrothed."

"I will send the announcement to the newspapers in the morning."

Hadley grinned. "Just think. I am betrothed to a duke and have yet to make my come-out. It sounds like a fairy tale."

He cradled her cheek. "Some fairy tales do come true. Go inside now," he urged.

She nodded and stepped to the door. Turning around, she saw he had already faded into the shadows and supposed it was a skill from his war years. Opening the door, the footman on duty greeted her.

"How was the theatre, my lady?"

"I found the performance rather invigorating. Goodnight."

Hadley made her way upstairs, almost floating. She loved Sebastian more than she would have ever thought possible. He hadn't said the words to her but his actions spoke loud enough. If the words eventually came, she would be happy. For now, she would bask in the glow of being affianced to Sebastian Cooper, Duke of Hardwick.

CHAPTER TWENTY-THREE

HADLEY WELCOMED PHOEBE and Samantha as they entered the drawing room. She had invited her friends to tea in anticipation of tonight's ball given by Sebastian. It was only the second week of the Season and it had surprised her that he chose to hold one, which he revealed would be in her honor. As promised, he had sent the notice of their betrothal to the newspapers and she had entered London society last week being engaged to a duke. She had been stared at and certainly gossiped about ever since.

It disappointed her that Sebastian had said no more about their wedding, other than telling her that he had purchased a special license and that she better prepare and have an amazing dress to wear. Having no idea what a special license was, Hadley waited and had asked Phoebe about it. Her friend told her it allowed a couple to wed whenever and wherever they chose, with no banns needing to be read.

The women waited for the teacart to be rolled in and the maid to leave before they began discussing tonight's ball.

"Andrew tells me that Sebastian has spared no expense," Phoebe said. "The food will be sumptuous and the flowers and other decorations spectacular."

"George said that Sebastian has hired the best musicians, as well," Samantha confided. "It is already being talked about as the ball of the Season. What are you wearing, Hadley?"

She looked from Samantha to Phoebe and then shrugged. "I haven't decided yet. I was hoping the two of you might come and look through my new wardrobe and suggest what would be appropriate."

"I adore looking at clothes," Samantha said and sighed. "Phoebe and I will help you select the perfect gown to wear. It will probably be hard settling on one because everything Madame Toufours creates is brilliant."

The butler entered bearing a silver tray with a small package on it. A note rested beside it.

"For you, my lady. The messenger said you were to open it at once."

"Thank you."

"What could it be?" Samantha asked. "I am most curious. I think it has to be from Sebastian," she declared.

Hadley opened the note first, already knowing it was from Sebastian, having opened dozens of his letters and recognizing his handwriting.

H –

I hope you have a gown to match these gems and that you will wear them tonight.

S

She looked up. "Sebastian has sent me a gift to wear to tonight's ball."

"Sebastian is very thoughtful fiancé," Phoebe said, her azure eyes misting with tears. "Open the box, Hadley."

With trembling fingers, she set the note aside and lifted the box. She raised the lid and gasped.

"Let me see," Samantha said, leaning over. "Oh, my! They are so beautiful."

Hadley gazed at the stones. "I have never had any jewelry before. What are these?"

Phoebe came close. "They are diamonds."

"Not like any I have ever seen," Samantha protested.

"They are blue diamonds," Phoebe added. "Very rare and very expensive."

"I don't think I can accept such a gift," Hadley said, taken aback by the dazzling beauty of the gems.

"Of course you can and will," Samantha chided. "Sebastian is a duke. He has plenty of money and he wants to spend it on the woman he loves."

She blinked back tears. "He has never told me that," she confided.

Phoebe patted her hand. "Some men find it very difficult to say those words, Hadley. We are of a class where love isn't a consideration in a majority of marriages. Just because Sebastian has never told you he loves you does not mean he doesn't have those feelings for you."

Hadley remembered how he had worshipped her body, his touch almost reverent. They had only been alone once since then because Sebastian said he didn't want to give anyone reason to gossip about her. He had interrupted tea two days ago when Phoebe and Andrew had brought Robby along with them. After visiting a few moments, Sebastian had suggested the other couple take a turn in the gardens with their babe. During the Windhams' absence, Sebastian had kissed Hadley senseless.

But he had never spoken words of love.

"I agree with Phoebe," Samantha said. "It may be hard for Sebastian to express the depths of his feelings for you. His mother died when he was quite young. His father was no father to him at all. Sebastian neither saw a loving marriage nor received any affection from Hardwick. Then he spent almost a decade at war. Give him time, Hadley. The words will come. I am sure they will."

She nodded, her throat thick with unshed tears.

"We need to finish our tea," Phoebe said, "and then decide which gown Hadley should wear tonight with these marvelous earrings and necklace."

"Pish-posh. We can drink tea anytime," Samantha said. "I say we look at Hadley's wardrobe now."

Laughing, the three went upstairs to the bedchamber she had been using during her stay at the Blackmore townhouse. Millie joined in to help with the decision and they narrowed it down to three gowns, then two, and finally settled on a pale, ice-blue satin. The diamonds, with their slight bluish hue looked wonderful against her skin and almost were the same color as the gown itself. Phoebe said the jewelry enhanced her rich, auburn hair and made Hadley's eyes sparkle.

"You will be the envy of every woman tonight," Samantha said. "A ball given in your honor. Your upcoming marriage to a duke. And a spectacular gift of blue diamonds."

Hadley didn't care about anything except marrying Sebastian.

"Let's go back downstairs and fortify you for tonight," Phoebe said. "You need to eat something so you will have the strength to endure all that dancing."

Reluctantly, she removed the necklace and earrings and placed them on her dressing table. The trio returned to the drawing room and Hadley called for a fresh pot of tea while they dined on sandwiches and sweets.

"Would you like Andrew and me to call and transport you to the ball?" Phoebe asked an hour later as Hadley walked her friends downstairs to their waiting carriages.

"That is very thoughtful of you, Phoebe, but it won't be necessary. Sebastian is sending his carriage for me."

First Phoebe and then Samantha embraced her and then they left to return to their own homes to prepare for tonight's festive occasion. Hadley went upstairs and told Millie to call for a bath. She wanted to be clean and perfumed, knowing all eyes would be on her tonight.

Several hours later, she made her way outside to the ducal carriage that awaited her. A footman handed her up and she found a single, long-stemmed white rose lying across the seat. She picked it up and sat, inhaling the bloom's rich fragrance, and then spied the folded note on the seat. Eagerly, she opened it.

H –

I await you with longing.

S

She smiled and held the note to her. Sniffing the rose again, she waited contentedly as the carriage went through the streets of Mayfair and came to a halt. The door opened and Sebastian climbed inside, closing it behind him. He looked breathtakingly handsome in his elegant, dark evening clothes, with his shirt and cravat whiter than snow.

Her eyes misted and she said, "Thank you for the rose and the jewelry. They are my first pieces."

He eyed her appreciatively. "The necklace and earrings look lovely on you."

Leaning close, he softly pressed his lips to hers in a tender kiss and then broke it.

"I couldn't do that in front of all the servants that are still scurrying around, getting ready for our guests," he declared. "Thank you for coming early to see everything before the horde arrives. Remember, if you want anything changed, let me know."

"I am sure everything will be lovely," she assured him.

He opened the door and climbed out, reaching his hand to hers. Even through their gloves, she could feel the heat of his fingers and longed for them to caress her body again.

They entered and went upstairs to the ballroom. Hadley gasped. It was a sea of color, with flowers of every shade. She saw tulips, daffodils, and hyacinths in varying hues.

"It's like being in a garden!" she exclaimed.

"You like it?" he asked, uncertainty creasing his brow.

"I adore it." She smiled and softly said, "I adore you."

Sebastian took her hand and tucked it into the crook of his arm. "I am glad you are pleased."

A pang of disappointment filled her. This would have been the perfect time for him to say something of his feelings for her. She chastised herself for even thinking such a thought, especially after all the trouble her fiancé had gone to for tonight. She didn't know how long it took to arrange a ball but believed his servants had pulled off a minor miracle in the short amount of time he had given them.

He insisted she remain beside him as they received all of his guests. She stopped trying to remember names after a quarter-hour because simply too many people entered. It was nice when Samantha and George arrived with Phoebe and Andrew, giving her a glimpse of familiar faces.

"Wait until you see the ballroom," she told her friends. "Sebastian has outdone himself."

"Will you join us for supper?" Sebastian asked the two couples.

They all beamed at her and George said, "Of course, we'd be delighted to. See you inside."

After a crush of more guests, the last seemed to have arrived and Sebastian escorted her to the ballroom.

"We will dance the first dance together and the supper one, as well," he told her. "They are a scotch reel and the waltz."

He led her onto the dance floor and nodded to the musicians, who had been warming up and now paused, instruments ready to be played at the duke's signal.

"We'll start with a scotch reel," he announced and couples began making their way from the sidelines to the center of the floor, forming their lines.

The music began and Hadley lost herself in it. She had always enjoyed dancing and did so at assemblies held near Hardwell Hall. The last few years, she had attended them infrequently, due to the duke's growing ill health. Arabella had suggested she hire a dance master to sharpen the moves she knew and help her learn the waltz, which had been considered far too racy for a country assembly. She had done as her friend had suggested and now felt comfortable in her movements.

The evening passed quickly. Several ladies complimented her on her new jewelry. She let them know the ensemble had been a gift from her betrothed and they looked suitably impressed.

Hadley saw Sebastian heading her way and figured it was time for the supper dance. Once more, he led her to the center of the room and as the musicians began to play, he swept her into his arms and into the steps of the waltz. It was an intimate dance and she enjoyed having the man she loved so close to her. She could smell the spice of his cologne and feel the heat that radiated from him.

"Are you happy tonight?" he asked, smiling down at her.

"I don't know if I have ever been happier," she replied and then added, "unless it was a time when I visited a certain duke in his bedchamber."

He bit back a smile. "You, my lady, are full of mischief but I have a trick or two up my sleeve," he said mysteriously.

The dance finished and Sebastian took her hand and then shouted, "Might I have your attention?"

The room quieted immediately. It wasn't every day a duke addressed an assemblage and she saw curiosity on the sea of faces surrounding them.

"While it normally would be time to go into supper, I am afraid that must be delayed for a few minutes." He turned and faced her even as he spoke to those gathered in the ballroom. "You see, I invited you all not just to a ball tonight—but to a wedding."

Hadley's heart skipped a beat as Sebastian smiled down at her.

"My betrothed has brought me more happiness than I can say and I love her with all my heart," he proclaimed.

She felt tears spring to her eyes. He had just told her an entire room of guests that he loved her.

"With your patience, we will now be wed and though it isn't a wedding breakfast, we will sup together afterward and celebrate my union with Lady Hadley Hampton."

The room began buzzing and Sebastian gazed at her with love shining in his eyes.

"I hope you don't mind, my love. I wanted to not only tell you but show you just how much I care for you. Everything this evening has been done for you. Because I love you. So very, very much."

He pressed his lips to hers, causing another buzz to circulate through the room. Breaking the kiss, he motioned and a man stepped forward, holding a Bible.

"This is Reverend Causey. He will marry us now."

She saw Samantha and George, along with Phoebe and Andrew, come toward them. From the look on her friends' faces, they had known all along that the wedding would take place tonight. Both women stood to her left and their husbands took their places on Sebastian's right. In a semi-circle, they faced Reverend Causey and were wed in front of a ballroom crowded with guests. As Sebastian pledged his love to her in front of the entire *ton*, Hadley knew this was only the beginning of a love story that would play out across the decades.

The ceremony concluded with a public, tender kiss. Her new husband looked down with her, his blue eyes bright with love.

"Would you like to go in to supper, Your Grace?" he asked.

"No, Your Grace."

Sebastian frowned, confusion filling his face. "But I have planned a feast to celebrate our marriage," he protested.

Hadley placed her palm against his chest. "I would rather celebrate in private, Husband. As only a man and wife can."

A slow smile spread across his face. He turned and called out, "The wedding banquet is through those doors. Champagne and food await. Enjoy yourselves."

Then he swept her into his arms. She entwined her arms about his neck as he carried her from the ballroom, Polite Society agog as they watched the Duke and Duchess of Hardwick leave their own celebration.

To be with one another. And celebrate their union in private.

They reached the bedchamber and Sebastian carried her across its threshold, kicking the door shut with his foot. He carried her through his sitting room and to the bedroom, setting her down gently. His arms enfolded her.

"We have all night, Duchess. What do you have in mind?"

When Hadley told him, Sebastian's eyes darkened with desire. As they kissed, she knew each day—and night—would be better than the one before, all because of this man. Her hero. Her love.

Her life.

EPILOGUE

Hardwell Hall—July 1816

HADLEY WOKE, HER cheek resting against Sebastian's beating hart. She listened to his soft breath and closed her eyes again, relishing the feel of his arms about her as she lay nestled within them.

She would tell him today.

She was relieved to be back at the place that had been home to her for so long. When Samantha and George left after two months of the Season, Hadley had begged Sebastian if they could do the same. She explained that while she had enjoyed getting to know a bit of the city and had fun attending some of the *ton* events, she would rather be back in the country. He had shared that he had never liked London much and had only wanted to stay to allow her to spread her wings in Polite Society. She assured him she would much rather be back at Hardwell Hall and so they had returned. Hadley believed their child had been created their first night back, a night of tenderness and wonder that she would always look back on with fond memories.

Sebastian stirred and she knew the moment he came to because his fingers began combing through her hair and his lips pressed a sweet kiss upon her brow. Soon, her husband was making slow, leisurely love to her, bringing her to those dizzying heights that she had never known existed until she had come to be in his arms.

Afterward, he held her close, nuzzling her neck, stroking her arm.

"Do you have plans today?" he asked.

"Actually, I do. I wish to go see your mother."

His fingers stilled. "What did you say?"

"I used to visit Her Grace's grave every few weeks. I would talk to her about what went on at Hardwell Hall. She seemed as a friend to me."

"You are the one who put the flowers on her grave. A bundle rested atop it when I visited her the day I came home."

Hadley nodded. "Yes, I often brought her flowers. The gardens were so beautiful and the gardener told me how fond she had been of flowers. I thought she would like having some every now and then."

Sebastian kissed her deeply. "She would have loved you, you know. The two of you would have gotten along famously."

She smiled. "I would like to think so."

"When would you like to go? After breakfast? I am starving." He rose from the bed.

The thought of food brought a wave of nausea to her. "I am feeling lazy this morning. I think I will have a tray brought to my room and breakfast in bed if you don't mind."

He bent and kissed her brow. "Not at all. I will dress and go downstairs for the meal, however. Will you be ready to leave in an hour's time?"

"Yes. I will meet you downstairs," she told him and climbed from the bed.

Hadley slipped into her dressing gown and then hurried through his dressing room and hers, emerging into her own bedchamber and rushing to the chamber pot. She vomited and immediately felt better, washing her face with cool water. She rang and Millie appeared.

"Oh, it's like that," the maid said, glancing from Hadley to the chamber pot. "Does His Grace know?"

"Not yet. I am going to tell him this morning."

"Do you think you can eat something, Your Grace?"

"Perhaps weak tea and some dry toast."

"I'll fetch it now," Millie said and left the room, returning a quarter-hour later with a tray.

Hadley drank the tea and kept down half a piece of toast. She was afraid to press her luck and try for more.

"I need to get dressed," she told her maid. "We will be leaving the house shortly."

Millie helped her don her clothes and arranged Hadley's hair. She claimed her shears and went to the gardens, clipping a few flowers and tying a ribbon about them which she'd remembered to bring. Entering the house, she gave Mrs. Sewell her shears.

"Going to see Her Grace?" the housekeeper asked.

She nodded and went to the foyer, where Radmore greeted her.

"His Grace is waiting outside for you, Your Grace," the butler told her.

"Thank you, Radmore."

Hadley went outside and saw Sebastian standing by a cart, a single horse attached to it.

"I thought instead of the carriage that we could enjoy this fine summer morning by using the cart to take us to the village."

He handed her up and joined her, saying, "The flowers are lovely. Some of Mama's favorites."

"I would like to hear more about her. I did not press the duke for stories about his wife," she revealed.

As they drove the short distance, her husband regaled her with a few tales of his mother and their short time together. They reached the church yard and he helped her from the cart. She saw no one in sight and was grateful they would have privacy for her announcements.

Going to the grave, Hadley placed the bundle of flowers atop it and said, "Good morning, Your Grace. It has been a while since we visited."

Sebastian placed a hand atop the stone and with his free hand, threaded his fingers through hers.

"Good morning, Mama. I have brought my wife to you. I hear you are already good friends."

"Now that I have met your son, Your Grace, I must tell you what a remarkable man he is. Sebastian was a wonderful soldier. He has become a marvelous duke. He is an attentive husband and will soon be a loving father."

She paused, turning her face to his to see his reaction. His gaze met hers.

"You mean . . . you are . . ."

"We are," she assured him. "A new little Cooper will arrive most likely by the end of February."

He pulled her into his arms, covering her face with kisses. "Oh, Hadley, you have made me the happiest I have ever been." He paused. "I have something to give you. Something which I believe you will cherish as much as I have."

Curiosity filled her as he reached into his pocket. He opened his palm, revealing a beautiful locket which she had never seen before. Sebastian lifted the chain, holding it up so she could see it better.

"This belonged to my mother," he shared. "I went to her rooms and claimed it the day I left for the army. I carried it with me into battle as a talisman and it has been with me every day since. I always wanted you to have it and was waiting for the right moment to give it to you." He smiled. "I can think of no better time than now."

She touched it. "And I can think of no better present. Thank you, Sebastian. I will treasure it always. Will you place it on me now?"

She turned around and he lifted the locket over her head, fastening the clasp. She brushed her fingers against it, glad to have this link between the woman in the grave and the man who now stood by her side as her husband.

Facing him again, she asked, "Do you wish for a son or daughter?"

"I want a healthy child. Boy or girl, it matters not. I hope this babe will be the first of many." He turned back to the grave. "We will bring the child to meet you, Mama. He or she will hear all about you. You will never be forgotten."

With that, Sebastian kissed Hadley deeply. She felt his love pour from him into her and knew their love story was only beginning.

About the Author

Award-winning and internationally bestselling author Alexa Aston's historical romances use history as a backdrop to place her characters in extraordinary circumstances, where their intense desire for one another grows into the treasured gift of love.

She is the author of Regency and Medieval romance, including: Dukes of Distinction; Soldiers & Soulmates; The St. Clairs; The King's Cousins; and The Knights of Honor.

A native Texan, Alexa lives with her husband in a Dallas suburb, where she eats her fair share of dark chocolate and plots out stories while she walks every morning. She enjoys a good Netflix binge; travel; seafood; and can't get enough of *Survivor* or *The Crown*.

Made in the USA
Middletown, DE
15 October 2021

50362742R00136